'W   ᵉ,'
Th   .ve
chosen. There is nothing else for
me.'

stalked away, ending the conversation. ...nneth stared after him, weighing the jar in her hand.

'Curiosity can get you killed, Cwenneth,' she ...tered. 'Treacherous Norse blood runs in his veins. You have to think about saving your life and escaping. Keep away from him. Stop trying to see good where none exists.'

The trouble was a small part of her heart ...used to believe it.

AUTHOR NOTE

Some characters just decide they want to be written. Lady Cwenneth was one of those characters. She popped into my head and refused to go. Part of the trouble with writing this book was that the primary source documentation is not very good for Northumbria in the ninth century. It is a mixture of legend and fact. Sometimes the facts masquerade as legends, and sometimes it is the other way around.

One of the inspirations for this story was an archaeological dig in Corbridge, where they discovered a woman buried in the Viking rather than the Christian manner. The Vikings did not settle around the Tyne—rather they had the area as a client kingdom. Just how friendly everyone was towards the Vikings remains an unanswered question.

I do hope you enjoy Cwenneth and Thrand's story. In case anyone is wondering, Thrand is the grandson of the hero's stepbrother in TAKEN BY THE VIKING and the sister of the heroine in THE VIKING'S CAPTIVE PRINCESS. This is why he knows how to make the healing balm which Cwenneth uses in the story.

As ever, I love hearing from readers. You can contact me through my website, www.michellestyles.co.uk, my blog, www.michellestyles.blogspot.com, or my publisher. I also have a page on Facebook—Michelle Styles Romance Author—where I regularly post my news. And I do Twitter as @michelleLstyles

SAVED BY THE VIKING WARRIOR

Michelle Styles

Published in Great Britain 2014
by Mills & Boon, an imprint of Harlequin (UK) Limited,
Eton House, 18-24 Paradise Road, Richmond, Surrey, TW9 1SR

© 2014 Michelle Styles

ISBN: 978-0-263-90982-1

Harlequin (UK) Limited's policy is to use papers that are natural,
renewable and recyclable products and made from wood grown in
sustainable forests. The logging and manufacturing processes conform
to the legal environmental regulations of the country of origin.

Printed
by Bl

Born and raised near San Francisco, California, **Michelle Styles** currently lives a few miles south of Hadrian's Wall, with her husband, three children, two dogs, cats, assorted ducks, hens and beehives. An avid reader, she became hooked on historical romance when she discovered Georgette Heyer, Anya Seton and Victoria Holt one rainy lunchtime at school. And, for her, a historical romance still represents the perfect way to escape.

Although Michelle loves reading about history, she also enjoys a more hands-on approach to her research. She has experimented with a variety of old recipes and cookery methods (some more successfully than others), climbed down Roman sewers, and fallen off horses in Iceland—all in the name of discovering more about how people went about their daily lives. When she is not writing, reading or doing research, Michelle tends her rather overgrown garden or does needlework—in particular counted cross-stitch.

Michelle maintains a website, www.michellestyles.co.uk, and a blog: www.michellestyles.blogspot.com. She would be delighted to hear from you.

Previous novels by the same author:

THE GLADIATOR'S HONOUR
A NOBLE CAPTIVE
SOLD AND SEDUCED
THE ROMAN'S VIRGIN MISTRESS
TAKEN BY THE VIKING
A CHRISTMAS WEDDING WAGER
  (part of *Christmas By Candlelight*)
VIKING WARRIOR, UNWILLING WIFE
AN IMPULSIVE DEBUTANTE
A QUESTION OF IMPROPRIETY
IMPOVERISHED MISS, CONVENIENT WIFE
COMPROMISING MISS MILTON*
THE VIKING'S CAPTIVE PRINCESS
BREAKING THE GOVERNESS'S RULES*
TO MARRY A MATCHMAKER
HIS UNSUITABLE VISCOUNTESS
HATTIE WILKINSON MEETS HER MATCH
AN IDEAL HUSBAND?
PAYING THE VIKING'S PRICE
RETURN OF THE VIKING WARRIOR

*linked by character

And in Mills & Boon® Historical *Undone!* eBooks:

THE PERFECT CONCUBINE

For my youngest son, Patrick, who wanted a
Viking story because there was more fighting and who
passed his A levels and now is studying at university.

Sometimes hard work does have its own reward.

Chapter One

Spring 876—near the border between
Viking-controlled Northumbria and
Anglo Saxon-controlled Bernicia

'We've stopped again. How many times can the wheels get clogged with mud? Perhaps we should have waited until the spring rains stopped.' Lady Cwenneth of Lingwold peered through the covered cart's one small window. 'This journey to Acumwick has taken twice as long as it should have with all the stops Hagal the Red's men insist on making. Delay after delay. I want to prevent hostilities rather than be the excuse for them.'

Her new tire woman, Agatha, glanced up. 'Are you that eager for marriage to Hagal the Red? You went on about his unsavoury reputation only a few nights ago. About how your brother threatened you into the marriage.'

Cwenneth pressed her lips together as the cloying scent from the herbs Agatha had spread to help with the stuffiness of the cart tickled her nostrils. In her loneliness, she had confided too much the other night.

'I spoke out of turn, Agatha. It doesn't do to remind me.'

'I was just saying,' the maid muttered, stirring the herbs and releasing more of their overpowering scent. 'Some people…'

Cwenneth concentrated on smoothing the fur collar of her cloak rather than giving a sharp answer back. Squabbling created enemies. She needed friends and allies more than ever now that she was about to live in a foreign land amongst people with a reputation for barbarity and cruelty.

Her marriage to the new Norseman *jaarl* of Acumwick would ensure her brother and the inhabitants of Lingwold would finally achieve peace after years of war. As part of the marriage contract, Hagal the Red agreed to provide protection particularly against Thrand the Destroyer, the berserker who enjoyed killing for the sake of it and exacted more than his fair share of gold from Lingwold.

Hagal's sworn oath to bring Thrand's head to Lingwold had ensured her brother had put his signature on the marriage contract's parchment.

'You look solemn, my lady. Are you that unhappy?'

Cwenneth hastily composed her face into a more cheerful countenance. 'I'm eager to begin my new life. A fresh start away from the unhappiness of the past few years.'

Cwenneth gave the only positive reason she could think of sharing with Agatha. Her brother had given her a stark choice when she had protested at the match—either marriage to Hagal the Red or a convent of his choosing with no dowry, nothing to look forward to except a barren cell and hard physical work for the remainder of her existence.

'It will happen if you please your new lord and master, my lady. It's easy if you know how.' Agatha gave a superior smile and arched her back slightly so her ample breasts jutted out. 'Men are such simple creatures. Easy to please, if you take my meaning.'

Cwenneth glanced down at her own slender curves. Positively boyish and flat in comparison. She had to hope Hagal the Red liked thin women.

'The journey was supposed to last a week.

Thanks to the incessant rain, it has been twice as long.' Cwenneth frowned. Once the rain stopped and the mud dried, the raiding season would begin in earnest. If the marriage wasn't formalised, would Hagal the Red actually provide the promised protection? Would he end the threat of Thrand the Destroyer? 'What if Hagal takes the delay as an insult?'

'I am sure it rained in Viken where they came from. He will understand.' Agatha gave a throaty laugh and stirred the herbs another time. 'They appreciate a woman up north, and Hagal the Red will be all the more impatient for the wait. They say he is very vigorous in bed.'

The dusty dry scent of the herbs invaded Cwenneth's mouth, making her throat feel parched and her head ache.

'I hate travelling in a cart. It makes me feel ill with its swaying and bumps.' Cwenneth firmly changed the subject away from bed sport. She knew the rumours about Agatha's prowess in that area and how her sister-in-law had caught her cavorting with Cwenneth's brother.

She craned her neck, trying to see more, but there was nothing except for bare trees, raising their branches to the sky. 'My brother would have allowed me to walk for a little, but Hagal's man refuses even to discuss it. When I am officially his lady, things will have to change.'

'I'm sure it will,' Agatha said in that overly familiar way she'd recently adopted. Cwenneth gritted her teeth. She needed to assert her authority over the maid. 'Change is in the air. For everyone. You never know, you might not be cursed any longer.'

Cursed—the word pierced her heart. What else could you call a woman who had failed to save her husband and child from a fever? Who had lost her home to a stepson who hated her and blamed her for the death of the woman he had considered his mother?

'Repeating gossip is wrong,' she said far too quickly.

'Your husband died and then your child after that old crone died on your doorstep. What is that if not cursed?'

'It is unlucky and has nothing to do with my forthcoming marriage. We will speak no more of it.'

Cwenneth hated the lingering sense of guilt that swamped her. Her stepson's former nurse had been caught stealing gold from the local church. She had had to request her departure. The priest had threatened to withhold communion from the entire household if she continued to shelter her. The woman had gone muttering curses and predicting vile things including that Cwenneth should lose all she held dear and that her womb would remain barren for ever.

Although she had laughed off the words at the time, dismissing them as the ravings of a confused woman, less than three weeks later, the bad luck started. Aefirth had returned home wounded and died.

Six weeks after that, she had lost her young son and any hope she might be carrying another. She had returned to her childhood home unable to bear her stepson's accusations any longer. The whispers about her being cursed began in earnest. Even now the memory caused cold sweat to run down her back. What else did she have to lose before the curse lost its power?

Agatha kept silent, so Cwenneth adopted an innocent face and added, 'A wonder you want to serve under such a woman as me, then.'

Agatha fiddled with the dry herbs. 'There was no prospect for advancement at Lingwold. That much was made very clear to me. I've no wish to be a beggar woman. I have plans.'

Cwenneth leant forward. No prizes for guessing who had made her that offer—the same person who had delivered the ultimatum about her marriage when she had tried to stall:

her brother. 'I expect my servants to be loyal, Agatha, and not to repeat old gossip. I expect them to speak with a civil tongue as well. Remember that or you will not remain my maid for long.'

Agatha's cheeks flushed at the reprimand. 'I beg your pardon. And I do hope for a bright future for you. Maybe you will find happiness...'

Happiness? Cwenneth hadn't expected to fall in love with the much older Aefirth either, but she had. Their marriage had initially been one of duty and the joining of estates. She clearly remembered the instant she'd known—Aefirth had put his hand on her belly when she had said that she felt their baby stir. The delight in his eyes had taken her breath away, and she had known that she'd love him for ever. He said that she made him young again. All that had gone in the space of a few days. All because of the curse.

The interior of the cart with its overpowering stench of herbs seemed small and more confining than ever once she started to think about all she had lost and would never have again.

'I'm going out to breathe fresh air. You may remain here. I'll be back before you miss me.'

'Surely, you should stay here. The last time you tried to leave the cart, things went badly.'

Cwenneth firmed her mouth. She knew precisely what had happened the last time. Narfi, Hagal's steward with the shifty eyes, had shouted at her, calling her all sorts of filthy names. She had retreated rather than argue like a fishwife. But what was a name compared to a few final breaths of freedom now that the marriage truly loomed? What if they never allowed her out of the hall again? If she never saw the spring flowers in the woods?

'Lend me your cloak. From a distance and if the hood covers my hair, we look about the same,' Cwenneth said. 'No one will see that I lack your curves.'

'Yes but…'

'Hagal's man forbade me, but not you. I will take full responsibility if anyone questions me. You won't be beaten. I won't allow it.' Cwenneth touched her maid's cold hand. 'When we reach Acumwick, I'll speak with Hagal and quietly explain that I dislike rough treatment and being shouted at. If that man, Narfi, can't learn to keep a civil tongue in his head, he'll have to go. Hagal the Red wants this marriage. He will have to respect my wishes.'

Agatha tapped her finger against her mouth, but did not meet Cwenneth's eyes. 'No one has shouted at me. Tell me what you want and I can fetch it.'

Cwenneth frowned. Agatha's bold manner grew the nearer they got to Acumwick.

'I *need* to go out and stretch my legs,' Cwenneth said, adopting a superior attitude and pinning the maid with her gaze. Agatha was the first to look away.

'It is on your head then.' Agatha fumbled with her cloak. 'Don't go blaming me. I did try to warn you. Do what you have to do quickly.'

The exchange of cloaks was quickly accomplished. Agatha stroked the rabbit fur collar of Cwenneth's cloak with an envious hand.

'I appreciate it. I'll return before anyone notices.'

'Just so you are.' The woman gave a great sigh and ceased stroking the cloak.

Cwenneth raised the coarse woollen hood over her golden blonde hair and quickly exited before Agatha found another reason to delay her.

The bright spring sun nearly blinded her after the dark shadows of the cart. Cwenneth stood, lifting her face to the warm sunlight while her eyes adjusted. All the worry and anxiety seemed to roll off her back as she stood breathing in the fresh, sweet-smelling air. The

stuffy woollen-headed feeling from the herbs
vanished and she could think clearly again.

Without pausing to see where anyone else
might be, she walked briskly to a small hollow
where the bluebells nodded. The rich perfume
filled her nostrils, reminding her of the little
wood behind the hall she'd shared with her late
husband. Aefirth had loved bluebells because
her eyes matched their colour. He'd even had
her stitch bluebells on his undergarments, pro-
claiming that they brought him luck.

Always when she thought of Aefirth, her
heart constricted. She had desperately wanted
to save him when he returned home with his
wounded leg, but the infection had taken hold
and he'd died. Old warriors died all the time
from wounds. No matter how many times she
tried to remember that, her mind kept returning to the woman's curse. Aefirth had recov-
ered from worse before. Why had the infection
taken hold that time?

Impulsively, Cwenneth picked a bluebell
and held it in her hand. The scent made her
feel stronger and more in control—what she
needed in the cart rather than evil-smelling
herbs which made her feel tired and stupid.

She picked a large handful of bluebells,

stopped and breathed in their perfume one final time before returning to her duty.

'I'll be brave. I'll be kind to Agatha and make her my ally instead of my enemy, but I will remember my position,' she whispered. 'I will make this marriage to Hagal the Red work because it is for the good of everyone. A new start for me and a chance to leave past mistakes far behind. I'm certain that is the advice Aefirth would have given me.'

A great inhuman scream rent the air before the dull clang of sword against sword resounded.

Cwenneth froze. A raid! And she was too far from the cart's safety. Her men would rally around the cart, thinking they were protecting her. No one would be looking for her out here.

She should have stayed where she was supposed to be. Her brother's men would defend the cart to their last breath. She wished Edward had allowed her a few more men, but he'd bowed to Hagal's wishes and had sent only a token force of six. Agatha would be fine as long as she stayed put in the cart and did not come looking for her.

'Stay put, Agatha,' she whispered. 'Think about yourself. I can look after myself. Honest.'

What to do now? She could hardly stand like

some frozen rabbit in the middle of the blue-bells, waiting to be run through or worse.

Hide! Keep still until you know all is safe. Aefirth's advice about what to do if the Norse-men came calling resounded in her mind. *Find a safe spot and stay put until the fighting has ended.* She was far too fine to wield a sword or a knife. She tightened her grip on the flowers. The same had to hold true for bandits and outlaws.

Cwenneth pressed her back against a tree and slid into the shadows. Hugging the rapidly wilting bluebells to her chest, she tried to concentrate on her happy memories of her husband and their son. Before she had been cursed. She whispered a prayer for the attack to be short and easily repulsed.

An agonised female scream tore the air. Agatha!

Cold sweat trickled down Cwenneth's back. The bandits had breached the cart's defences.

How? Hagal's men were supposed to be hardened warriors. He'd given her brother his solemn oath on that.

The pleas became agonised screams and then silence. Cwenneth bit the back of her knuckle and prayed harder. Agatha had to be alive.

Surely they wouldn't kill a defenceless woman. The outlaws couldn't be that depraved.

The silence became all-encompassing. Before the attack, there had been little sounds in the woods and now there was nothing. Cwenneth twisted off her rings and hid them in the hem of her gown before gathering her skirts about her, sinking farther into the hollow beneath the tree and hoping.

Two Norseman warriors strode into the rapidly darkening glade. She started to stand, but some instinct kept her still. She'd wait and then reveal herself when she knew they had come to save her. They could belong to Thrand the Destroyer's band of outlaws rather than Hagal. He had every reason not to want this marriage. It must have been his men who attacked them because they knew what it would mean. Her heart pounded so loudly she thought they must hear it.

'The maid is dead. One simple task and she failed to do that—keep the pampered Lady Cwenneth in the cart. Refused to say where she'd gone. Claimed she didn't know,' the tall one said. 'Now we have to find the oh so spoilt lady and dispose of her.'

'Good riddance,' Narfi said. 'That woman

was trouble. She knew too much. She asked for too much gold and then got cold feet. Couldn't bring herself to be associated with murder. No spine.'

He put his boot down not three inches from Cwenneth's nose. She pressed her back closer to the hollow and fervently prayed that she would go unnoticed. Her brain reeled from the shock that Agatha was dead! And that she had been willing to betray and murder her!

'We spread the rumour it was Thrand the Destroyer who did this? Clever!'

'No, Thrand Ammundson is in Jorvik, attending the king. Halfdan keeps him close now that he fears death. More is the pity.' Narfi chuckled. 'The Northumbrians fear him more than any. Can't see why. He isn't that good. Sticks in my craw and Hagal's. Ammundson gets gold thrown at his feet without lifting his sword simply because of his legendary prowess on the battlefield. I could take him in a fight with one hand tied behind my back.'

'Why did Hagal want the Lady of Lingwold dead? Did he hold with the curse?'

'Revenge for her husband killing his favourite cousin three years ago. He swore it on the battlefield. Hagal is a man who settles scores. Always.'

A great numbness filled Cwenneth. Not an ambush because of the gold they carried for her dowry or a random act of banditry, but a deliberate act of revenge by Hagal the Red. She was supposed to die today. There was never going to have been a wedding to unite two peoples, but a funeral. The entire marriage contract had been a ghastly trick.

Her stomach revolted, and she started to gag, but Cwenneth forced her mouth to stay shut. Her only hope of survival was in staying completely silent.

Cwenneth tightened her grip about the flowers and tried to breathe steadily. Why hadn't Edward questioned him closer? Or had the opportunity to get rid of the menace that was Thrand Ammundson tempted her brother so much that he never thought to ask?

All the while, her brain kept hammering that it was far too late for such recriminations. She had to remain absolutely still and hope for a miracle.

She had to get back to Lingwold alive and warn her brother. Why go to all this trouble if Hagal had only wanted to murder her? She had to expose Hagal the Red for the monster he was before something much worse happened.

'Gods, I wish that maid had done what she

promised and slit the widow's throat at the sig-
nal. I was looking forward to getting back to
the hall early like. Now we have to trample
through these woods, find her and do it our-
selves.'

The second man sent a stream of spittle
which landed inches from her skirt. Cwenneth
forced all of her muscles to remain still, rather
than recoiling in revulsion.

'She won't survive out here. Soft as muck
that woman. Pampered. Unable to walk far. Everything had to be done for her.'

'You only have that maid's word that the
Lady Cwenneth had no weapons.'

'It doesn't matter if she does. Imagine that
useless creature coming up against any wild
beast! How would she fight? Boring it to death
with her complaints about food or the slowness
of our progress? The woman doesn't know one
end of a sword from another. She wouldn't last
more than a few heartbeats even if she does
have a knife.'

They both laughed and started to search the
undergrowth off to her right. Quietly, Cwenneth searched the ground for something sharp,
something so she could defend herself if they
did find her. She did know how to use a knife.
The pointy bit went into the flesh and she

should go for the throat. Her fingers closed around a sharp rock.

A solitary howl resounded in the clearing. Cwenneth's blood went ice-cold. Wolves. She didn't know which sort were worse—the four-legged variety who lurked in the woods or the two-legged variety standing not ten feet from her who had just slaughtered people for no good reason.

Narfi clapped his hand on the other man's back. 'Don't worry. Dead women tell no tales. By the time we reach Acumwick, the wolf will have done our work for us. We'll come back and find the body in a day or two. Hagal will never know. Now let's get to the hall. I want my food. Killing always makes me hungry.'

Making jokes about what she'd do when she met the wolf and speculating on how she'd die, the pair sauntered off.

Cwenneth hugged her knees to her chest, hardly daring to breathe. She was alive, but there were many miles of inhospitable country between here and Lingwold.

She screwed up her eyes tight. She'd do it. She'd prove them wrong. She wasn't minded to die yet and particularly not to suit thieves' and murderers' schemes. She would defeat Hagal and prove to everyone that she wasn't cursed.

* * *

The air after a slaughter takes on a special sort of stillness, different from the silence after a battle when the Valkyries gather the honourable dead. Then the birds pause, but the air continues to flow. After a slaughter, even the air respects the dead.

The instant Thrand Ammundson came around the bend in the road, he knew what had happened—a slaughter of the innocents.

'Gods! What a mess.' Thrand surveyed the carnage spread out before him. An overturned, smouldering wreckage of a travelling cart with six butchered and dismembered bodies lying about it dominated the scene. The sickly-sweet tang of fresh blood intermingling with smoke and ash hung in the air.

'You would think after ten years of war, people would know better than to travel so lightly armed,' one of his men remarked. 'Halfdan maintains the peace, but there are Northumbrian bandits. Desperate men do desperate things.'

'Surprised. They thought they were safe,' Thrand answered absently as he bent to examine the first body. 'Always a mistake.'

He gently closed the old man's eyes and forced his mind to concentrate on the scene.

The bodies were cold, but not picked clean. And the fire had failed to completely consume the cart. It had merely smouldered rather than burning to the ground. Not a robbery gone wrong, but cold-blooded murder. And he knew whose lands they crossed—Hagal the Red's. Hagal would be involved, but behind the scenes. A great spider waiting for the fly to blunder in.

Thrand pressed his lips together. Everything proclaimed Hagal the Red's handiwork, but he needed more proof if he wanted to bring him to justice, finally and for ever. Something solid and concrete. Hagal had had a hand in the slaughter of Thrand's family back in Norway. Thrand knew it in his bones, but no one had listened to his proof and Hagal had slithered away like the snake he was.

'How do you know they were surprised?' Helgi, one of his oldest companions-in-arms, asked, kneeling beside him.

'Look at their throats. Cut.' Thrand gestured towards the two closest bodies. 'And this lad and that man still have their swords in their belts. Whoever did this got in and got out quickly.'

'A dirty business, this. Who would dare? Northumbrian outlaws?'

'I have a good idea who our enemy is. He won't bother us. More's the pity.' Thrand knelt beside the second body, little more than a youth. No arrows and impossible to determine the type of blade used from a clean cut. Thrand frowned, considering the options. The intense savagery of the attack sickened him, but, knowing Hagal's methods, it failed to surprise him.

There was never any need to mutilate bodies. A dead man will not put a knife in your back.

He had only discovered Hagal was in Half-dan's employ after he swore his oath of allegiance to Halfdan and had agreed not to attack a fellow member of the *felag* on pain of death.

Hagal's time would come. Once his oath was complete, Thrand would ensure it. He refused to add the shame of being an oath-breaker to his titles.

Without his code, a man was nothing—one of the lessons his father had taught him. And he had to respect his father's memory. It was all that remained of him. Thrand had shown little respect for him and his strict rules the last few months of his life, much to his bitter regret.

'If they attacked this party of travellers, they could attack us,' someone said.

'Do you think they'd dare attack us?' Helgi shouted. 'You have never been on the losing side, Thrand. Your reputation sweeps all before it. They pour gold at your feet rather than stand and fight.'

'Only a dead man believes in his invincibility,' Thrand said, fixing Helgi with a glare. 'I aim to keep living for a while.'

At his command, his men began to methodically search the blood-soaked area for clues, anything that could prove Hagal was here and had done this. He didn't hold out much hope. Hagal was known to be an expert at covering his tracks.

'A woman,' one of them called out from beside the cart. 'No longer has a face. What sort of animal would do that to a woman?'

'Any clues to her identity?'

'High born from her fur cloak. Her hands appear soft. Probably Northumbrian, but then there are very few of our women here.'

Thrand pressed his hands to his eyes. A senseless murder. Such a woman would be worth her weight in gold if held for ransom. Or if sold in one of the slave markets in Norway or even in the new colony of Iceland, she would command a high price. Why kill her? Why was she worth more dead than alive to Hagal who valued gold more than life itself?

'See if anyone survived and can explain what

happened here and why. Dig a pit for the bodies. It is the least we can do. Then we go forward to the Tyne! We need to return to Jorvik before Halfdan convenes the next Storting.' he proclaimed in ringing tones.

'And if the bandits return…they will know someone has been here.'

'Good. I want them to know,' Thrand said, regarding each of his men, hardened warriors all, and he could tell they too were shaken by this savagery. But he knew better than to trust any of them with his suspicions about Hagal. Thrand was well aware Hagal had used his spy network to escape in the past.

'This is Hagal the Red's land. Surely he will want to know about bandits operating in this area. He has sworn to uphold the king's peace,' Knui, his late helmsman's cousin, called out. 'Will we make a detour?'

'Leave Hagal the Red to me.' Thrand inwardly rolled his eyes at the naive suggestion. Hagal's way of dealing with this outrage would be to hang the first unlucky Northumbrian who dared look at him and be done with it. No one would dare question him.

'But you are going to tell him?' Knui persisted.

'We've not actually encountered any outlaws, merely seen the aftermath of an unfortunate occurrence.' He gave Knui a hard look. Knui was only on this expedition because it had been his late helmsman's dying request. Sven had sworn that Knui wasn't in Hagal's employ, but his words made Thrand wonder. 'Speculation serves no one. Our first duty is fulfilling our oath to my late helmsman, Sven, and ensuring his child will want for nothing. We gave our oaths on his deathbed. First the child and then…perhaps…once we have returned to Jorvik and the Storting is finished.'

'What do we do with her? Leave her for the eagles? Or put her in the pit with the rest?' one of his men called. 'They were far from kind to this one.'

Thrand stared at the woman's mutilated body with distaste. It reminded him of Ingrid, the woman who had caused him to betray his family and who had ended up murdered. One more crime to make sure Hagal was punished for. A senseless, wasteful crime. 'Lay out the dead before burial while I check to see if any more bodies are about. There may be some clue I missed. And we want to make sure we don't have to dig two pits.'

He left his men to their task. With a drawn sword, he went into the woods, circling about the site. He forced his mind to concentrate on the task rather than revisiting long-ago crimes. Any little signs which might give him a clue to where the attackers went, or if any of the party had survived.

He pressed his hands to his eyes. 'Come on, Thrand Ammundson. What are you missing? Concentrate instead of remembering the long dead.'

When he approached the end of his circuit, he noticed scattered bluebells rapidly wilting in the warm afternoon. Someone else had been there. The dead woman? Or...?

He frowned, annoyed with himself for not immediately considering it. Details mattered. High-born Northumbrian ladies always travelled with at least one female companion.

Someone had survived. Someone who could bear witness to what happened here. Someone who could speak in the king's court and condemn Hagal. He gave a nod. The gods had finally given him his chance if he could get the creature to Jorvik alive.

Moving slowly and paying attention to little clues on the ground—a broken twig here, a scattered flower there—Thrand followed the woman's trail. He discovered a hollow where she must have hidden for a while. There was evidence of other feet as well. Kneeling down, he felt the soil. Cold. The attack had been this morning, so she could not be far…if she had survived.

He spied a single wilting bluebell on the far edge of the glade.

'Where are you? Come out! I'm here to help!'

The only sound was the wind in the trees.

He frowned, drew his sword and slowly picked his way through the undergrowth, looking for more signs. The trail was easier as if the woman had ceased to care about being followed. The far-off howl of a wolf pierced the stillness. Wolf or Hagal's men? He knew the sort of death he'd prefer. With a wolf, the woman stood a chance of a quick death.

He entered a clearing where gigantic oak and ash spread their bare branches upward. A shaft of sunlight cut through the gloom, highlighting the strands of golden hair which had escaped from the woman's coarse dark-brown cloak as she tried to free the fabric from a thorn bush. Her fine gown was immediately obvious.

Thrand breathed easier. The woman remained alive. He sheathed his sword.

'Are you hurt?'

She glanced up with frightened eyes, eyes which matched the few bluebells she still carried and pressed closer to the thorn bush. The cloak opened slightly, revealing a gold-embroidered burgundy gown. Her long blonde hair had come loose and tumbled about her shoulders like spun gold.

Thrand whistled under his breath. He found it hard to remember the last time he'd seen a woman that beautiful.

Had Hagal finally made a mistake after all this time?

He held out his hand and tried for a gentle approach rather than his usual brusque manner. 'I come in peace. I've no wish to harm you. What happened back there? Back with the cart?'

She gave an inarticulate moan, redoubled her efforts to free herself from the bush. The cloak tore and she started to run. Thrand crossed the glade to her before she had gone three steps. He caught her shoulders and gave her a little shake.

'If you run, you die. These woods are no place for a lone woman.' He examined the fine bones and delicate features of her face. She came up to his chin. Most women barely reached his shoulder. 'Particularly not one who is gently bred.'

He allowed his hands to drop to his side and

waited. Had his words penetrated her shocked brain?

Her tongue wet her lips, turning them the colour of drops of blood on snow. 'I'm already dead, Norseman. Here or elsewhere—what does it matter?'

'Are you injured? Did they hurt you? How did you escape?'

She slowly shook her head and started to back away. In another heartbeat she'd run. Thrand silently swore. He did not have time to spend chasing this woman through the forest.

'Do you want to live?' he ground out. 'Simple choice.'

She stopped, hesitating. 'I…I…'

Forget gentleness. He had tried. The Northumbrian woman was stubborn beyond all reason. Action was required. He reached out and grabbed her wrist.

'You come with me.' He pinned her with his gaze. 'Whatever happened to you before, know that you belong to me hereafter. I'm your master now.'

Chapter Two

You belong to me. I'm your master. The words reverberated through her brain. Cwenneth stared at the large Norseman warrior who held her wrist captive, hating him. After all she'd survived today, she'd ended up a slave to an unknown Norseman. And she knew what they were capable of.

Surely it would have been better to die a quick death at Narfi's hands than to suffer this…this torture!

She had been a fool to trust Hagal the Red and his promises in the marriage contract. She had been a fool to flee from her hiding place at the sound of this man's voice. She had been a fool to try to undo the cloak when it became entangled on the thorn bush.

Time to start using her mind instead of panicking like a scared rabbit! Aefirth would have wanted her to.

'I belong to no man, particularly not a Norseman.' Cwenneth brought her hand down sharply and twisted. 'I will never be a slave. Ever.'

He released her so abruptly that she stumbled backwards and fell on her bottom, revealing more than she would have liked of her legs. Cwenneth hastily smoothed her skirts down.

'That's better,' she said in her most imperious voice, playing for time and ignoring the way her insides did a little flutter at his intense look. 'Keep your hands to yourself in the future.'

'If you want a race, so be it, but I will win.' The planes of his face hardened to pure stone. 'You are welcome to try. I will catch you before you go ten steps. And my mood will be less generous.'

He reached down and raised her up. His hand lingered lightly on her shoulder, restraining her.

'Will you strike me down if I run?' Cwenneth whispered. She'd survived Narfi, only to be killed for sport by this man? Her limbs tensed, poised for renewed flight, but she forced her legs to remain still.

'Where is the challenge in killing women?'

he responded gravely. 'I'm a warrior who fights other warriors. Playing games of chase with a beautiful woman will have to wait for another day. I've other things to attend to. Give me your word that you will come meekly and I'll release your arm. Otherwise, I will bind you.'

Cwenneth concentrated on breathing evenly. Playing games of chase, indeed! As if she was some maid flirting with him in the Lingwold physic garden! She was a widow whose heart had been buried with her late husband and son.

She clung on to her temper and did not slap his face. This was about survival until she could return to Lingwold. Once she was safe behind the thick grey-stone walls, she could give in to sarcasm and her temper. Until then, she guarded her tongue and kept her throat whole.

'Let me go and I'll give my word,' she ground out.

'Satisfied?' He lifted his hand.

She stared at the large Norseman warrior standing before her. He had released his hold, but the imprint of his hands burnt through the cloth. Large and ferocious with glacial blue eyes, a man who took pride in fighting, and the last sort of person she wanted to see. Who was he? Was it a case of things going from bad to worse? How much worse could it get? At least Thrand Ammundson was in Jorvik. No one could be as bad as that man.

'You see, I keep my word. Now will you? Will you trust me?'

Cwenneth swallowed hard to wet her throat and keep the tang of panic from invading her mouth. Trust a Norseman? A Norseman warrior? How naive did he think she was?

'Say the words now.' He pulled a length of leather from his belt.

'I'll come with you...willingly. There is no need to bind me,' she muttered, despising her weakness, but she hated to think about her wrists being bound and marked. 'I give you my word. I won't make a break for my freedom.'

'And I accept it.' He refastened the length of leather to his belt. 'You see I'm willing to trust you, but then I can outrun you.'

'How do you know how fast I can run?' she asked, watching the leather sway slightly like a snake.

'You wear skirts.' His dark-blue eyes darkened to the colour of a Northumbrian summer's midnight, but held no humour. 'Skirts tangle about your legs and catch in thorn bushes and brambles. If I have to chase you or you disobey me, things will go much worse for you.'

Cwenneth lifted her chin. She had to concentrate on small victories. She remained unbound…for the moment. It would be harder to escape if he decided to tie her up. And she planned on escaping when the time was ripe. 'I will take your word for it. I've never worn trousers.'

'A modicum of sense in your brain. Not my usual experience with Northumbrian women.' His brows drew together. 'Why are you here? Why were you left alive? Why was your entourage attacked?'

She knew then he'd found the carnage that lay back there on the road. Silently, she named the six men who had died, thinking they were protecting her. They were seared on her heart. Someday, somehow, Hagal would be made to pay. Even faithless Agatha needed justice. In this darkening glade with the bare trees towering above her, she had half-hoped that it was a dreadful nightmare and she'd wake up to find Agatha softly snoring near here or, better still, in her tapestry-hung room at Lingwold.

'The attack came from nowhere,' she began and stopped, unable to continue. A great sob rose up in her throat, and in her mind she saw the images of the bodies where they fell and heard the unholy screams. She forced the sob

back down. No Norseman would have the pleasure of seeing her cry. She straightened her
spine and looked him directly in the eye. 'I'm
sorry. I can't speak of it. Not yet. Please don't
make me.'

'You're my responsibility, and I want you
alive.' He captured her chin with hard fingers,
and his deadened eyes peered into her soul. 'As
long as you do as I say.'

'My world has changed completely.' Cwenneth forced her eyes to stare back into his.

She knew she was a tall woman, but her eyes
were merely on the same level as his chin. He
made her feel tiny and delicate, rather than
overgrown as she had in the past. Even Aefirth
had been barely taller than her. Absently she
rubbed where his hand had encircled her wrist.

'I give better protection than the men who
died, the ones who were supposed to ensure
you and the other woman came to no harm.'
He released her chin. 'Was she your mistress?'

'My mistress?' Cwenneth hesitated. He
thought her the maid! Her heart leapt. A tiny
glimmer of hope filled her. This Norseman had
made a fundamental error.

If he knew who she was, he'd return her to
Hagal who would surely kill her. A wife, even
a solemnly betrothed bride like she was, was

a husband's property. And they were fellow Norsemen. She needed to get back to Lingwold and warn her brother of Hagal's treachery rather than be delivered with a pretty bow about her neck to that viper.

'Who was your mistress? Quick now. It is hardly a difficult question.'

'The Lady of Lingwold. She was on her way to finalise her marriage to Hagal the Red.' Feverishly Cwenneth prayed that her deception would work. 'I'm her tire woman. Cwen. I'd left the cart to gather bluebells and hopefully improve the smell. After all the travelling we had done, the cart stank. The herbs in the cart gave my lady a woolly head.'

She gulped a breath of air as the words tripped off her tongue. So far, so good.

He pointed to the gold embroidered hem of her gown. 'A very fine gown for a maid to be wearing, Cwen.'

'One of my lady's cast-offs,' she said with a curtsy. 'I had it in honour of her marriage. She had many new gowns and no longer had need of this one. It was from her first marriage and quite out of date.'

He nodded, seeming to accept her word. The tension in Cwenneth's shoulders eased a little.

Cwen had a good ring to it, reminding her of Aefirth's pet name for her.

How hard could it be to play the maid? It was far safer than being herself—the woman whom everyone wanted dead or believed cursed beyond redemption, destined never to have a family who loved her.

'And, Cwen, your lady did not wish to get out of the cart and sent you instead. Did she fear bandits?' His lip curled slightly as if he disapproved of such fine women.

'She knew about the possibility of outlaws. There are desperate men about these days.'

'Even though she must have known she was on her bridegroom's lands.'

'Even then. My lady was timid.' Cwenneth gestured about her. 'It is in places such as these that man-eating wolves lurk. Or so my…her nurse used to say.'

She winced at her near slip, but his face betrayed nothing. Perhaps he didn't have that good a grasp of the language. Or perhaps… Drawing attention to the mistake would only make matters worse. But she had to have convinced him. He looked to be more muscle than brain like most of the Norsemen. Certainly his shoulders went on for ever.

The ice in his eyes grew. 'If she was in the

covered cart, how did she know about the woods, the wolves and most of all the bluebells?'

'My lady caught a glimpse of the outside through the slats in the window when the cart stopped so they could get the mud off the wheels. I went to fetch them,' Cwenneth improvised. 'She would hardly have let me go if she thought the attack was going to happen. My lady trusted her men and the promises her bridegroom gave.'

Cwenneth finished in a breathless rush. If she kept to the truth as much as possible, she should be able to fool him.

When she had her chance, she'd escape and return to Lingwold, like in the stories her nurse, Martha, used to tell. Her brother would see that justice was done. Enough warriors to make a formidable army would flock to Edward's banner when he put the call out to avenge this outrage.

'I find it hard to believe Hagal allowed his bride to travel without protection. Or did she intend to surprise him? This timid bride of his?'

'Hagal provided over twenty warriors. You would have to ask them why they fled. My lady was only allowed six of her own men.' She waited, heart in her throat, to see his response.

His stone-hard face betrayed nothing. 'Do you wish me to take you to Hagal the Red's stronghold? He will want to hear news of his bride's demise.'

Cwenneth's stomach knotted. The Norseman was leaving the decision up to her. Lingwold was a real possibility instead of a cloud-in-the-sky fantasy. She could almost see the comforting stone walls rising up before her.

'Her brother needs to hear the news first. He will give a reward for information about my lady. I know it.'

The Norseman remained implacably silent.

Cwenneth pressed her hands together and gathered her courage. 'I believe...I believe Hagal's men murdered everyone in my party.'

There, she had said it and had mentioned the possibility of a reward. Gold always motivated the Norsemen. Her stomach twisted in knots. In the silence which followed she could hear the flap of a wood-pigeon's wings.

'A strong accusation,' he said, his face remaining devoid of any shock or surprise. 'Why would Hagal's men want his bride dead? He will have spent time and effort negotiating the marriage contract.'

'Perhaps they are in the pay of Thrand the Destroyer and betrayed their master.'

'I think not,' he said, crossing his arms, and his face appeared more carved in stone than ever. No doubt he expected her to cower. 'Try again. Who attacked this convoy?'

Cwenneth glared back and refused to be intimidated. 'I speak the truth—Hagal's men did it under his orders. I overheard them speaking afterwards. He wanted her dead to fulfil a battlefield vow he made. I hope even Norsemen have a respect for the truth. The Lord of Lingwold certainly will. He'll see justice is done and Hagal the Red is punished for this crime.'

As she said the words, Cwenneth knew she spoke the truth. Edward might have desired the marriage, but he wanted her alive. Blood counted for something...even with Edward. He would take steps to avenge Hagal's actions. Even a convent without a dowry currently sounded like heaven compared to being a Norseman's slave or, worse still, murdered.

'How did you propose to get to Lingwold? It is over a hundred miles through hostile wilderness and floods. The mud-clogged roads from the recent rain are the least of your problems.'

Cwenneth sucked in her breath. He knew where Lingwold was, but then it was one of the largest estates in southern Bernicia.

'Walk!'

'Wolves and bears lurk in these woods. Not to mention outlaws and other desperate men who roam the roads.'

'I know. I was waiting until nightfall before I returned to the...' Cwenneth's throat closed. What did she call it now that murder had taken place? 'To where it happened. I hoped to find something there, something I could use on my journey. I refuse to simply sit here and die.' She clasped her hands together to keep them from shaking uncontrollably. 'Will you take me to Lingwold? Help me complete my journey? The Lord of Lingwold will give a great reward for information about his sister. I promise.'

'I've no plans to visit Lingwold at present.'

Cwenneth blinked. He was refusing? 'What do you mean? There will be a reward. A great reward. Gold. As much gold as you can carry.'

'The promise of a *small* reward for telling a man his sister is dead fails to tempt me. The great Lord Edward of Lingwold might even take a severe dislike to the man who brought him news of his sister's demise.' His mouth curled around the words as if her brother was anything but a great lord.

'You have a point. He is known to have a temper.' Cwen fingered her throat. She couldn't confess now. Not now that she knew this man disliked her brother so much that he refused to consider a reward. She'd have to come up with a different plan. That was all. 'Where do we go?'

'You go where I choose. You tell your story when I choose and to whom I choose. And not before. Like you, I know Hagal the Red did this.' A bright flame flared in his eyes, transforming his features. 'I have my own reasons for wanting him to face justice.'

Until he chose? To become his slave for ever? Cwenneth firmed her mouth and renewed her vow. 'Who are you? What shall I call you?'

He made a mocking bow. 'Thrand Ammundson.'

Thrand Ammundson. Thrand the Destroyer. Cwenneth gulped. The Norseman whose band of warriors raided Lingwold yearly. The man who loved killing so much that his name was a byword for destruction. The man who was supposed to be in Jorvik, but who was here and probably on his way to raid innocent Bernicians.

Her luck was truly terrible. Of all the Norsemen to encounter, it would have to be him, the one man other than Hagal the Red most likely to want her dead.

'You're Thrand the Destroyer?' she whispered, clasping her hands so tight that the knuckles shone white.

He was right—her brother had no cause to love him and every cause to kill him. As she had departed for Acumwick, Edward had crowed that he looked forward to having Thrand's head on a plate and his hide nailed to the parish church's door.

'Some have called me that, but they are wrong. I have never come to destroy, only to take what is rightfully mine or my liege lord's. The Norsemen of Jorvik did not start the last war, but they did finish it.'

'That makes it all right because you won,' Cwenneth remarked drily, trying to think around the pain in her head. Right now she had to put miles between her and Hagal, who definitely wanted her dead. Everything else could wait. Patience was a virtue, her nurse, Martha, used to say.

'The victor commissions the saga, as they say.'

A soft rustling in the undergrowth made Cwenneth freeze. She instinctively grabbed hold of Thrand's sleeve.

'Wolf or mayhap a bear,' she said in a hoarse whisper. 'My luck goes from bad to worse.'

Thrand put his fingers to his lips and pivoted so that his body was between her and the noise.

He started to draw his sword, but then relaxed.

'There, see.' He pointed with a long finger. 'No wolf.'

Cwenneth crouched down and found herself staring into the tusked head of a boar. The animal blew a hot breath over her face before giving her a long disdainful look and trotting off.

'That was unexpected,' she said, sitting back on her heels.

'Thor has shown you favour,' Thrand remarked in the quiet that followed. 'Good luck follows your footsteps in battle when Thor favours you.'

'I don't believe in the Norsemen's gods. And I know what those tusks can do. My stepson was gored once. It ended his fighting days and he walks with a bad limp. I wouldn't call that lucky.'

She gave an uneasy laugh. A god favoured her? Thankfully he didn't know about the curse she carried. He'd abandon her in these woods if he did. Pressing her hands together, she tried to control her trembling and breathe normally.

'You're married? What did your husband

say about you travelling with your lady to her new home?'

'My husband died and…and I found myself back in my lady's service.' A fresh dribble of sweat ran down her back. The words rushed out of her throat. 'My luck has been dreadful these last few years.'

'You're wrong.' His searing gaze raked her form, making Cwenneth aware of her angles. Her sister-in-law was one of the plump comfortable women which men loved, but Cwenneth had few illusions about the attractiveness of her body—all hard angles with only a few slender curves. 'You survived the slaughter. That makes you luckier than the corpses back there.'

Her shoulders relaxed. He hadn't noticed her slip. 'I've lingered too long in these woods. Can we go from this place?'

He made a mocking bow. 'As my lady wishes.'

'I'm not a lady. I am a maid, a person of no consequence.'

A faint smile touched his lips. 'It is well you reminded me.'

She shook her head to rid it of the prickling feeling that he was toying with her. But Norsemen were not that subtle. They used brute force to destroy farms and steal livestock, rather than cunning to discover the hidden stores. She'd bide her time and escape.

'What have you found, Thrand? Anything? There is nothing to say who did this here,' Knui called out as Thrand emerged from the woods with his prisoner in tow. 'We thought the demons who must dwell in this place had found you and conquered your soul. But then they whisper that Loki has already determined your fate at Ragnarok.'

'A witness,' Thrand answered shortly, keeping a firm grip on Cwen's wrist. Binding a woman was always a last resort. He would use her to bring down Hagal and finally revenge his parents. What happened to her after that was none of his concern.

'Will you take her to Hagal?' Knui asked with an intense expression. 'The slaughter happened on his land. He will want to find the Northumbrians who did this and punish them. A direct assault on his authority can't be tolerated. Think about how Halfdan will react when he knows. These bastards want to start the war again. Do they never give up?'

'In my time,' Thrand answered, giving Knui a hard look. With each word, Knui proclaimed that he was indeed Hagal's creature.

It was only Thrand's promise to Sven which stayed his hand and prevented him from running the man through. Sven had given his oath his cousin would be loyal with his last breath. 'I have promises to keep first, as you well know.'

'But won't she slow us down?' Knui continued grumbling, seemingly oblivious to the threat in Thrand's look. 'The last thing we need is a woman with us. It is going to be difficult enough to get in and out of Bernicia as is.'

Knui was right in one respect. The last thing he wanted on this journey was a woman, but Hagal, who loved gold more than life itself, wanted her dead. And that was more than enough justification for keeping her with them and alive.

'Let me worry about that.'

'We need to be back before the Storting starts,' Knui persisted. 'I want a say in Halfdan's successor, even if you don't.'

'You seek to challenge my authority, Knui, son of Gorm, kinsman to Sven Audson?' Thrand reached for his sword. If Knui wanted a fight, so be it. He had never walked away from a battle. He never would. 'Do so openly. I've no time for games and whispers. Are you prepared to chance your sword arm against mine? Shall we see who the victor will be?'

Knui glanced over his shoulders and saw the other men had moved away from him, leaving him isolated. The colour drained from his face.

Thrand waited impassively.

'Not I.' Knui hung his head. 'I have seen you on the battlefield, Thrand. I know what you can do. I am content for you to lead us.'

'I accept your judgement.' Thrand sheathed his sword and the rage subsided. There would be no need to do battle with Knui...today. But he no longer trusted him.

Sweat poured from Knui's forehead. 'Thank you.'

'I lead this *felag*. The woman comes north with us...unless any cares to fight me.'

'Do you think we can get a ransom for her?' Helgi called out.

'She claims to be the maid. When has anyone ever ransomed a maid?' Thrand answered, giving Cwen a significant look. Her pale cheeks became stained the colour of her gown and she kept her eyes downcast. 'What is a serving maid worth beyond her value at the slave market?'

'Yes, I am the Lady of Lingwold's maid,' Cwen called out. 'How could I be anything else?'

Thrand schooled his features as his men

looked to him for confirmation. He inclined his head, not committing himself either way. Her voice was far too fine and her gown, under the coarse woollen cloak, too well made. He'd bet his sword and a good more besides that she was the true Lady of Lingwold.

'Indeed,' he murmured, releasing her wrist. She instantly rubbed it. 'How could you be anyone but the maid?'

'You are going to bury them here? After you have taken everything of value from them? They served my lady well. She respected them,' she said, turning away from him and not answering the question. 'They deserve better than being plucked clean by the crows.'

'They have no use for their swords where they are.' Thrand shrugged as his men busied themselves with completing the pit. 'The crows have enough to eat. No point in leaving them out in the open.'

Her brow wrinkled as she pleated her burgundy skirt between her fingers. 'I...I suppose not. But there must be a churchyard near here. They should have a Christian burial. Find a priest.' She gave a tiny sniff. 'The decent thing to do.'

He bit back the words that he had no decent bones left in his body. All he lived for was war.

It had been a part of his existence for so long, he knew no other way of life. All finer feelings had vanished years ago on blood-soaked ground before a burning farmhouse in southern Viken. Burying them was the best way to make Hagal uneasy. 'This is a conversation you should have with the lord of these lands.'

She paled and took a step backwards. 'You mean Hagal the Red.'

Thrand watched her from under his brows and wondered if she knew the truth about how her bridegroom had acted in Norway and Northumbria? What had he promised her family to lure her out here so he could fulfil his vow of revenge?

'The Lady of Lingwold was meant to be his bride. Once he learns of the massacre, he will come here,' he said, willing her to confide the truth and beg for his assistance. 'He is a man who likes to see the aftermath of such things with his own eyes. Shall we wait?'

She tucked her chin into her neck. The action highlighted its slender curve and the way her golden hair glinted in the sun. He curled his hands into fists and concentrated.

The consequences of being distracted by beauty were deadly. He had learnt that lesson in Norway. No, the Lady Cwenneth in her way was just as black-hearted as Ingrid had been. And her earlier remarks about the dress being ruined showed how her mind worked—she did not care about people, but things.

'He wanted everyone dead and I'm alive,' she said in a low voice. 'He'll kill me if he finds me. He'll come after you as well once he knows.'

'I want him to wonder who is buried and who did the burying,' Thrand answered shortly. 'I want him unsettled. I want him to wonder if you are dead out in those woods or not. I want him to know fear for once.'

'Do you fear him?' She shivered and wrapped her arms about her waist, and her shoulders hunched. 'I do. What sort of man does what he did? Makes such orders?'

'Not in a fight.' Thrand's hand went instinctively to his sword. 'I have studied how he fights in battle. Utterly predictable. Always goes for the downwards thrust followed by a quick upwards one to finish his opponent off. Never varies. And he hangs to the rear rather than leading from the front.'

Her crystal-blue gaze met his—direct and determined. 'Hagal doesn't fight fair. Ever. He looks for the weakest point and goes for it. He did this with…with Lord Edward.'

'What did he promise Lord Edward to make

him cough up his sister?' he asked silkily. 'What did the Lord of Lingwold hope to gain?'

'Peace and your head.' She lifted her chin, every inch the proud lady. 'Does it bother you to know you are hated that much?'

Thrand schooled his features. Despite everything he thought he knew about Northumbrian ladies and their empty-headedness, a reluctant admiration filled him. She might be beautiful, but she also had a brain which was full of more than feather beds, ribbons and embroidery.

'How did murdering you get the Lord of Lingwold my head? Everyone thinks I'm in Jorvik with the king.' He allowed a smile to play on his lips.

Her brows drew together and finally she shrugged. 'I don't know. Ask Hagal. He was hardly going to confide his intentions to me. Understandable in the circumstances, but aggravating as I'm sure you will agree.'

She inclined her head. Thrand fought the unexpected urge to laugh. Lady Cwenneth had more than a bit of grit to her. He sobered, but it didn't mean he should trust her one little bit.

Thrand turned the matter over in his mind. The more he thought about it, the more farfetched it seemed. Marriages took a long time to negotiate. No one knew he would be in the area. He hadn't known until a few days ago that he'd be travelling north. But there was a method to Hagal's madness. He always played a long game.

Why did Hagal need the Lady Cwenneth's death? Why now? How would killing her bring Lord Edward Thrand's head? And what did Hagal get out of it? He drew a steadying breath.

The answer would come to him as he travelled north and before he arrived back in Jorvik for the Storting. Then he'd know precisely how to deploy Lady Cwenneth to destroy Hagal once and for all. For too long that particular Norseman had eluded him.

'Well?' she asked, tapping her slipper on the ground. With her set chin and fierce expression, he could almost believe she was descended from the Valkyries. 'Do you have the answer? It would make me feel safer if I did.'

'You will have your opportunity for revenge. I trust you will use it well as I doubt you will get a second chance.'

'One chance is all I will need. He will not rise when I am done.'

'And you are certain of that? What are you going to do? Plunge a knife in his throat? Are you capable of that?'

All fight went out of her shoulders. Instead

of an avenging Valkyrie, all was naked vulnerability and confusion. Lady Cwenneth was no shield maiden. 'I have no idea. All I know is he should die for what he did. Hopefully you are right about this.'

'I know I am right…this time,' Thrand muttered and tried not to think about the unquiet dead he'd failed.

Chapter Three

Cwenneth avoided looking at the pile of bodies and instead concentrated on the smouldering remains of the cart. Smoke hung in the air, getting in her eyes and lungs. Her entire life, including the future she hadn't truly wanted but had been willing to experience for the sake of her people, was gone.

'Is there anything left? Anything salvageable?' she asked.

'Either burnt or taken,' came Thrand's reply. 'Did your lady only travel with one cart?'

'There was a baggage cart as well.' She frowned. 'I should have said earlier.'

'It is all gone then. Your lady's dowry. They took anything that wasn't nailed down and burnt the rest'

The words knifed through her.

'But my things? My mother's…comb.' Cwenneth clamped her mouth shut before she mentioned the mirror and her jewellery. Since when would a maid have her own mirror, let alone rings and pendants?

It wasn't the gold she missed, although she was furious about it. What she missed most was the lock of Richard's hair, his soft baby hair. She used to wrap her fingers around it when she needed comfort and normally wore a pendant with it in to keep him close to her heart. Stupidly, she had taken off the pendant this morning and put it in the iron-bound trunk to keep it safe because the clasp was almost broken, and now it was gone for ever.

'Time to go. There is no point in sifting through ash.' Thrand put a heavy hand on her shoulder.

Cwenneth resisted the temptation to lean into him and draw strength from him. She stood on her own two feet now, rather than leaning on anyone, let alone a Norse warrior. 'The sooner I am away from this place of death, the better.'

'Take some boots. You will need them.' The glacial blue in his eyes increased.

'Why?'

It was clear from his expression what he thought of her. A barely tolerated encumbrance. Cwenneth didn't mind. It was not as if she wanted to be friends. Somehow, some way she'd find an opportunity to escape.

Escape? Back to what? A brother who saw her as a counter to be used? And a sister-in-law who hated her? Cwenneth banished the disloyal thoughts. They were family. Lingwold was home and she loved its people. Whatever the future held, it wasn't being a slave to this Norseman.

'Why do I need boots?'

'Unless you wish to walk in bare feet, you need boots. Your slippers will be torn to ribbons within a mile,' he said with an exaggerated politeness.

'From where?' Cwenneth gestured about her. 'Where are the boots stored? Where am I going to find a pair of boots?'

He gestured towards the bodies. His men immediately paused and backed away from them. 'You are going to allow a good pair of boots to go to waste while your feet bleed?'

Her stomach knotted. He wanted her to rob the dead. 'It feels wrong. They died wearing those boots.'

He made a cutting motion with his hand. 'Do the dead care? Will they rise up and challenge you?'

A faint burn coursed up through her cheeks.

She winced. He probably robbed the dead without a pang of guilt. Norsemen were like that. They took rather than respected the property of the living or the dead.

Cwenneth glared at him, hating his long blond hair, his huge shoulders and the fact that he was alive and her men were dead. 'I have never robbed the dead before.'

'Do you want to choose or shall I?'

'I'll choose.' Cwenneth walked over to where the youngest of her men lay. Dain's mother had been her nurse when she was little. She had asked for him because she thought he'd have a good future in her new household. Martha had readily agreed. 'Dain's boots. They are solid and new. His mother gave them to him before we departed. They are good leather to walk a thousand miles in, or so Martha proclaimed. She'd have liked me to have them.'

'And you think they will fit?' he asked in a casual tone. His eyes watched her as a cat might watch a mouse hole. 'Shouldn't you try them on first?'

She pressed her lips together. Perhaps she'd been too hasty at dismissing him as all brawn and very little brain. She needed to be very careful from here on out and weigh her words, rather than rushing to fill the silence.

'I have large feet for a woman.' She bent down and tore several strips of cloth from Dain's cloak. Luckily the material ripped easily. 'This should be enough to fill the toes.'

She knelt down and started to stuff the boots before she said anything more.

'You have done this before,' he remarked, hunkering down next to her.

Up close, she could see that his hair was a hundred different shades of yellow and that his features were finely made despite his overbearing size and manner. Their breath laced. Her hands trembled, and she redoubled her efforts. All she had to do was ignore her unwanted reaction to him. He wanted to unsettle her for his own perverse pleasure. Well, she'd disappoint him. She lifted her chin.

'Once at Christmas, I dressed up as a bard.' She gulped, rapidly shoving her feet into the boots before walking a few steps. 'I mean, my lady did and I helped her. She wore her husband's boots… When I get back to Lingwold, Martha will appreciate the gesture.'

'And you believe the boots will last that long?'

'I have to.' She rubbed her hands together, pushing the thought away that she might never get back. Lingwold for all its faults was her home. 'What shall I be riding in? Where is your cart?'

He appeared to grow several inches and his shoulders broadened. Barely tamed. Every inch the warrior. 'Playtime is over. You won't be riding, Lady Cwenneth.' Thrand made a low bow. 'Your ladyship will be walking. I am fresh out of carts and my horse is not overly fond of Northumbrians or women. And I'm not minded to inconvenience him for a proud Northumbrian lady like you. The only question is whether or not I have to tether you to my horse.'

She put her hand to her throat and her heartbeat resounded in her ears. He had called her Lady Cwenneth. Lady! 'You know. How?'

His lips turned up into a humourless smile. 'Did you think me an idiot? I've known since the first time you opened your mouth. It amused me to see how far you would push it and how many mistakes you'd make. You're a very poor liar, my lady, even if your voice is sweet enough to charm birds from the trees.'

Cwenneth stared at her hands. Each word knifed her heart. She had been certain that she had fooled him. Naivety in the extreme. It would have been better if she'd died in the woods. She was Thrand Ammundson's prisoner—worse than that, his slave. He knew her brother wanted his head and had been prepared to pay a high price to get it.

How could he be so cruel as to play this sadistic game? Giving her hope and then turning her over to the one man who would kill her? Her knees threatened to buckle. Summoning all her strength, she locked her knees and balled her fists.

'Will you deliver me to Hagal? Trussed up like a prize? Was that what you were always planning on doing? Why bother with the play-acting?' She stretched out her neck and attempted to seem fiercesome. 'Why not cut off my head and send it back to my brother as a warning? Go on. Do it now.'

'My enemy wants you dead. Why should I want to do that job for him?' Something stirred in his lifeless eyes—a flash of warmth and admiration that was so quickly concealed Cwenneth wondered if she had imagined it. 'The enemy of my enemy is my friend. I learnt that in Constantinople and it kept me alive.'

'We do share a common enemy, but we will never be friends. Temporary allies at best,' she said, tapping her finger against her mouth. *The enemy of his enemy...* She wanted to fall down and kiss the ground. They were on the same side. He needed her alive and unscathed.

'You take my point.'

Her heart did a wild leap. She was going to see Lingwold's grey walls again. She'd never complain about the tapestry weaving being done incorrectly again or the subjects her sister-in-law considered suitable for gossip, but which bored her senseless. She'd be back with her family and people who understood her.

'Then you'll be taking me to Lingwold.' She clasped her hands together to keep from throwing them about his neck. 'My brother will pay a huge ransom for me. I swear this on my mother's grave. He has many men pledged to him. He could send an army against Hagal, assist you in getting rid of your enemy. My brother hates being taken for a fool, and Hagal played him.'

She knew in her relief she was babbling like a brook. When the words had all flowed out of her, she stood, waiting for his agreement. The silence grew deafening. The bravado leaked from her veins as his stare hardened.

'We're allies,' she said in a small voice. 'It makes sense.'

He shook his head. 'I'll never go to Lingwold. Your brother's assurances aren't worth the spit it takes to say them. If I took you back to Lingwold, I would be truly fulfilling Hagal's promise to your brother. I know what will happen to me if I enter Lingwold with you even if Hagal has been destroyed. After I've finished with you, you may go where you please. Your fate is not linked to mine beyond that day.'

'I failed to consider that.'

Her brother could be every bit as ruthless as any Norsemen. War had brutalised the idealistic youth she'd known. He bragged about outsmarting them and leaving a band of them to die in a burning house. He proudly proclaimed that it was the only reason Thrand had left him alone for the last raiding season. Her brother might listen to her story, but only after he'd taken Thrand's head. If Thrand had acted on her advice, she'd have ended up betraying the man she depended on to save her life.

Thrand nodded towards the muddy track. 'Time to go, your ladyship. Walk—or would you prefer to have your hands bound and be tossed on the back of my horse? I'm in a generous mood after your display of courage. Not many women have asked me to take their life.'

'I'm not a sack of wool. I will walk. Where are we headed? South to Jorvik?'

'North to fulfil an oath to my late helmsmen. But I intend to return to Jorvik before the next Storting.'

'When is that?'

'Less than a month.' He made low bow. 'That will have to satisfy you, Lady Cwenneth. And you had best keep up. I have no time for stragglers, particularly when they are pampered Northumbrian ladies.'

Cwenneth touched her neck, her hand automatically seeking the reassurance of her lost pendant and Richard's lock of hair. She forced her fingers down. 'I will walk until it is time to stop. Have no fear on that. I won't need special assistance.'

'I shall be interested to see you try.' He raised his voice so it rang out loud and clear. 'Lads, the lady is for walking and reckons she can keep up. Do I have any takers? Will she be able to and for how long?'

All about her, Thrand's men began to wager on how long she'd last. Several remarked on how all Northumbrian ladies were pampered and unused to hard work. One even predicted she would not make but a few yards beyond this place before she demanded to ride. Cwenneth gritted her teeth and silently damned them all to hell.

'Do you always keep at this pace?' she asked, trying to wring out her gown as she trudged through the mud. She must have blisters on top of blisters. Every fibre of her being longed for a warm hearth, a roof over her head and a soft bed to sink down in. But with every step she took and mile she passed, she took satisfaction in proving another Norseman wrong.

'Getting through the woods and putting distance between us and the massacre is a priority.'

'We've put miles between us and…and where the massacre happened. Surely it must be time to find shelter for the night.'

Every sinew in her body ached. She hurt even where she didn't think she had muscles.

Thrand half turned from where he led his horse through a muddy puddle and lifted an arrogant eyebrow. 'We need to make up for lost time. I want to get through these woods before night falls and the rain starts in earnest. We camp in safety. Does that suit your ladyship? Or has my lady changed her mind and now wishes to become a sack of wool?'

The exaggerated patience of his tone grated on her frayed nerves. She stopped and put a hand in the middle of her aching back. 'Leave me at a farmhouse. Do your raiding or whatever you are going north to do and pick me up on your return. I'll wait patiently.'

'How would I know that you'd stay there? Waiting *patiently*?'

'I'd give my word.' She fixed him with a deliberately wide-eyed gaze, but kept her fingers crossed. If the opportunity to go happened, she wouldn't linger, but she would send a reward once she made Lingwold. 'No one has questioned it before.'

He made a disgusted noise. 'If I had taken your word earlier, I would still think you the tire woman. Underestimating my intelligence does neither of us any credit.'

Cwenneth ground her teeth. Fair point. She forced her feet to start marching again. 'A necessary deception. I had no idea if you were friend or foe.'

'Once having deceived someone like that, how do you build trust? I'm curious to hear your answer, my lady.'

'I'm not sure,' Cwenneth admitted and concentrated on skirting the next puddle. 'But you should consider the suggestion if you think I am slowing proceedings down. A good commander thinks of all his men. My late husband used to say that.'

'Consider being left at the farmhouse.' He slowed his horse slightly and kept pace with her feet. 'Hagal and his men will begin hunting you once they suspect you live. They will not stop until you are dead or you have defeated Hagal. How will you ensure that farmer's loyalty when his crops are threatened? A good commander should think about all eventualities before coming to a decision.'

Cwenneth's stomach knotted. Hagal's men, in particular Narfi, knew every farmhouse in the area. They were bound to check once they discovered the buried bodies and that hers wasn't there. Her flesh crept. Thrand was right—why would any farmer shelter her? She wouldn't be safe until Hagal was dead and she was back inside Lingwold's walls. 'I failed to think that far ahead.'

'If you want to stay alive, let alone gain the revenge you want, you will have to start thinking ahead and you will stay with me. I'm your best…no…your only hope.'

'But we are staying at a farmhouse. The thought of a bed and a pillow has kept me going for a while.'

His face took on a thoughtful expression. 'People do remember travellers and when Hagal's men come, they will answer their questions.' He gave a half shrug, but his eyes were sharp as if seeking something from her. 'A lone woman travelling with a group of Norsemen…

I doubt many fine ladies travel through this part of the country. If Hagal's men fail to find your body in the woods, they will check with the surrounding farms. It is what I would do.'

Cwenneth regarded the ground, rather than meeting Thrand's direct stare. To think she had earlier dismissed him as being all brawn and no brain. He had considered several steps ahead rather than thinking about immediate needs. She needed to start thinking smarter and stop giving in to prejudice. Thrand Ammundson was highly intelligent as well as a formidable warrior.

Some place deep within her chimed in that he was also good-looking when he wasn't scowling. She ignored it. She had not been interested in men since Aefirth died. Her very being had been encased in ice.

She narrowly avoided another muddy puddle and tried to think about what her next move should be in this real-life game of cat and mouse she was playing, rather than what Thrand looked like when he wasn't scowling. The only advantage she held was that Hagal thought her dead.

'You've fallen silent, my lady. Do we stop at the next farm? I can see smoke rising in the distance. There will be a welcome of sorts.'

Cwenneth hiked her gown up to keep it out of the mud and silently bid goodbye to all thoughts of a feather bed. The only thing keeping her out of Hagal's clutches was his belief that she was dead. 'You're right, we need to continue on and stopping at a farm is far from a good idea. The stress of today is addling my nerves.'

'Here you had dreams of a bed,' he said with heavy irony. 'Have you given up on your dreams so quickly? Are all Northumbrian ladies this weak willed?'

'Do you know many Northumbrian ladies?'

'I've met enough.'

'They weren't me.' Cwenneth made a show of placing her feet down, even as the pain from the blister seared up her right leg. 'I can keep going as long as you require it. There is no need to stop at a farmhouse or any settlement. The open air suits me fine.'

A hearty laugh rang out from his throat. 'You learn quickly.'

'Did you plan on stopping at a farm? Before…before you encountered me?'

He pulled his horse to a halt. All good humour vanished from his face. 'I've my reasons for not wishing to be remembered.'

'And they are?'

'My own.'

* * *

Just when Cwenneth was convinced they would be trudging through the dank mud all night, Thrand imperiously lifted his hand and pulled his horse to a halt. The entire company stopped. 'We will make camp here tonight. We should be safe. The ground is good in case of attack…from anyone or anything.'

Cwenneth sucked in her breath, giving silent thanks her walking for the day was done. But she was also pretty sure that she had beaten all wagers against her. It was strange—whenever she had considered quitting, she remembered the wagering and became more determined to prove them, particularly Thrand, wrong. 'Expecting trouble?'

'It is better to expect trouble than to encounter it, unprepared,' Thrand said before issuing orders to his men. 'Perhaps if your men had…'

'They were outnumbered. The outcome would have been the same,' she answered, placing her hands in the middle of her back, rather than giving in to the desire to collapse in a heap. Once down, she had her doubts about getting up again. 'I keep wondering if there was something more I could have done, but my brother was determined on the match. He threatened me with a convent of his choosing and no dowry. I considered being the wife to a Norse *jaarl* was the better bet. Without a dowry, I'd have been little better than a scullery maid. It shows how wrong a person can be.'

'And defeating me means more to your brother than his sister's life?'

She pressed her hands to her eyes. 'Edward had no part in this. He wanted to believe Hagal's assurances and saw the marriage as a way to gain a powerful ally. But he'd never have sent me if he suspected the truth. A dead sister is no use to him in his quest for power within the Bernician court.'

His level gaze met hers. 'There was nothing you could have done once the events were set in motion. The only mistake Hagal has made in this enterprise is to allow you to fall into my hands alive.'

'But...'

'He will pay for it. Now sit and rest. Women like you have no experience at setting up a camp and cause delays.'

'You have a very low opinion of Northumbrian ladies.'

'My dealings with them have been deliberately kept to a minimum.' The glacial blue of his eyes thawed slightly. 'However, you did better today than any of my men thought you would. You have earned your rest.' He shook his head. 'You are far stronger than even I thought you would be. You have made me revise my opinion of ladies. Not all are pale, puny creatures with less stamina than a mouse.'

'Good.' Cwenneth sank to the ground, rather than argue. Her feet throbbed and burnt. Sitting, being ignored, was bliss. But her journey home and back to her family had just begun. Somewhere along the way, she'd teach that arrogant Norse warrior that ladies from Lingwold were to be reckoned with. She clenched her fist and vowed it on her son's grave.

'Far from smart to provoke him, you know. His temper is legendary.'

She glanced up and saw a slender Norseman standing before her. She shaded her eyes. He'd been the one who had objected to Thrand bringing her along. Her own temper flared. 'His nickname gives it away—the Destroyer. I doubt he acquired it through being kind and gentle to his enemies.'

'Thrand is a great fighter. When a battle comes, he always wins. Halfdan's most potent weapon. They say rather than take the risk, people shower him with gold when he appears on their doorstep.'

'Have you travelled with him often?'

'First time.' The man leant forward and lowered his voice. 'I promised my cousin on his deathbed I'd come. Someone has to see right for his child as it is kin. And Thrand, he is the sort of man to lead an expedition into enemy territory and return, more than likely with bags full of treasure and gold. Sven had a good war because of his friendship with Thrand. There are iron-bound chests full of gold back in Jorvik.'

'That I can well believe.' Cwenneth said a fervent prayer that Thrand and his men would not be returning to Jorvik with more treasure looted from Bernicia.

'I want gold,' Knui stated flatly. 'Lots of it. But then you don't have any as Thrand will have already taken it. So I'm not sure why I'm bothering with you.'

Her hand hit her belt. Her rings. Aefirth would have understood. *Cwennie, survive*, he would have said. *Rely on no one but yourself.* Maybe this warrior would go to Lingwold and let her brother know she survived.

Edward would raise an army to free her if he thought Thrand the Destroyer had her. He'd march to Jorvik and make his demands heard. She had to have patience and think long term. Her hand started to fumble for the rings and her blood became alive with excitement.

A warning sounded in her gut. Why was a Norseman trying to make friends with her? Did he guess that she possessed even a little bit of gold? Why mention it otherwise?

Her hand stilled and dropped to her side. She had to proceed with caution and trust no one.

'Knui Crowslayer! Where have you hidden yourself this time?' someone called. 'I need some help with the firewood!'

'It was good to speak with you,' Cwenneth called after him. 'We must speak another time.'

She hugged her knees to her chest, oddly pleased that she didn't give up her rings at the first hint. If today had taught her anything, it was not to be blindly trusting. She would wait for her opportunity, rather than acting on impulse.

There was more than one way to get back to her old life. All she needed was patience and a workable plan. Thinking ahead rather than regretting mistakes.

'You have remained in the same place since we arrived.' Thrand's voice rolled over her. 'Is that wise? Surely my lady must have a complaint about the primitive standards of this camp.'

Cwenneth lifted her head. All of her muscles screamed with pain and the shadows had grown longer. She wasn't sure if she had slept or if her mind had become mercifully blank. Now everything came flooding back. She remained in the nightmare and it was about to get worse because they had stopped for the night. And she had no idea of Thrand's plans. He had claimed her as his woman.

Did he expect her to become his concubine? There had only been Aefirth. She knew how to be a wife, but she had little idea how to be a mistress. Refusing the position was out of the question, not if she wanted to live.

'I wait for my orders, to find out what I need to do, rather than presuming.' Muscles protesting at the slightest movement, Cwenneth struggled to stand, but he motioned she should stay seated. She gratefully sat back down.

'Are you capable of following orders?' Up close she was aware of his height, the broadness of his shoulders and the way his shirt tightened across his chest. There was power in those muscle-bound arms, but gentleness as well. She could clearly remember how he'd approached the wild boar—slowly and carefully, rather than scaring it. 'Doing whatever I ask of you?'

'If I'm going to stay alive, I have to learn.'

'Clever woman.'

'I've kept my word so far. There is no need to tie me up. I'm not going to run away tonight, not on these feet.'

His gaze slowly travelled over her, making her aware of how her hair tumbled about her neck and the way her gown was now hopelessly stained with mud. She must look like something the dog had dragged in.

His thin smile failed to reach his eyes. 'I doubt you'd have the strength.'

'I kept going today.'

He put a hand on her shoulder. Heat flooded her. She wanted to lean into his touch. 'My men wagered that you wouldn't.'

'I heard them when we started. Who won in the end?'

'I did.'

'You bet on me?'

The blue in his eyes deepened. 'My purse is heavier. But you lasted even longer than I thought you would. Impressive. I thought, back by the farm, you'd beg for a ride.'

'Giving up is not an option if I want to return to my old life. It is better to be unbound. It makes me believe that one day I will regain my freedom.' She kept her head erect. 'I have my pride. The lords and ladies of Lingwold never beg.'

'And you want to return?'

'Very much. It is my home.' Cwenneth looped a strand of hair about her ear. 'Life is good at Lingwold. The walls are strong. Food is plentiful and everyone sleeps soundly in their bed. I would even kiss my sister-in-law and stop complaining about her silly rules about how you weave tapestry.'

'If it is in my power, word will be sent after I have finished with you.' He balanced the pouch of gold in his hand. 'But you have presented me with another problem. You walked too slow.'

'I hate horses.' Cwenneth leant forward, wrapping her hands about her knees. There was no way her feet would harden by morning. 'There, I have admitted it. My fear of horses was stronger than my hurting feet. Tomorrow may be a different story.'

She had been wary of horses ever since Edward's stallion had bitten her arm when she was ten. All she had done was try to give it a carrot. Edward had laughed at her fear.

'Here.' He tossed a small phial of ointment to her. It landed in her lap. She twisted off the top and wrinkled her nose.

'And this is?'

'For your feet. An old family recipe. My grandmother used to swear by it. It heals blisters.'

She blinked twice as her mind reeled. She had thought he'd come to mock or worse. 'Why?'

A faint smile touched his features, transforming them. A woman could drown in those eyes, Cwenneth thought abstractly as a lump formed in her throat. She refused to hope that he was being kind. She doubted Thrand the Destroyer knew the meaning of kindness or simple human decency. He probably had another wager that he wanted to win.

'Put the ointment on. We will have to go miles tomorrow and I have no wish for you to hold the men back. Purely selfish. I need to be back from the north within the month.'

She weighed the small jar in her hand. The man she thought devoid of all humanity had shown that he wasn't and that made him all the more dangerous. 'I will in time.'

He made an annoyed noise in the back of his throat. 'It goes on now. Your feet need to have a chance to heal.'

Without waiting for an answer, he knelt down and eased off her boots. Her feet were rubbed raw with large blisters on the heels and base of her feet.

Cwenneth gave a moan of pain as the cool air hit them.

'You kept going on these? Impressive.'

'For a Northumbrian lady?' She held up her hand. 'Please, I did overhear banter when the men were wagering. I'm not deaf or daft. And, of course, Narfi thought I was a pampered pet who would not last the night.'

'What do you think of Norsemen?'

'That they are muscle and—' She clapped her hand over her mouth. 'And I have seen first-hand your intelligence.'

'You would do well to remember that.' He nodded towards her feet. 'And it is for anyone. I have seen young men in tears over less. And I think you do yourself a disservice. You have a stronger will than most other women I've met.'

'You met someone with a stronger will?'

His body went rigid, and the stone planes in his face returned. 'A long time ago.'

'I had no choice. You would have tethered me to that horse and made me run simply for the pleasure of it. I've heard the stories.'

'I would have slung you over the back with your hands tied behind your back to prevent you stealing my horse.' His brows drew together. 'Humiliating a woman ultimately humiliates the man more. My father taught me that.'

Cwenneth breathed a little easier. Thrand

Ammundson was no nightmare of a warrior. 'I stand corrected.'

'Courage impresses my men. You never know when you will need allies. You impressed them today. Now let's see about these blisters.'

He ran a finger along the base of her foot. For such a large man, his touch was surprisingly gentle. Warmth spread up her leg, making her feel alive and cared for. She wanted him to keep stroking, keep kneading the ball of her foot. A sharp pain went through her.

She jerked her foot back. 'That hurt.'

'The blisters can be healed. Give me the jar.' He held out his hand. 'I will show you how and tomorrow you do it yourself. Morning and night until your feet toughen. Tomorrow we go quicker.' He took the jar from her unresisting fingers and knelt down before her.

A pulse of warmth radiated from his touch. He touched first one blister, then another, spreading the soothing ointment on. Cwenneth leant back on the green moss and gave herself up to the blissful relief of the pain vanishing.

A small sigh of pleasure escaped from her throat. Immediately, he stopped and dropped the jar beside her.

She glanced up at him. His eyes had darkened to midnight-blue.

'Why do you stop?' Her voice came out far huskier than she intended.

'Finish it. You have the idea.'

'Thank you for this,' she said, reaching for the jar. A liquid heat had risen between her legs. He hadn't even kissed her or touched her intimately, and she had behaved like…like a woman of the street rather than the lady she was. He was her enemy, not her friend. Her cheeks burnt with shame. Ever since Aefirth had died, she had been encased in ice. She had been so sure she'd never feel anything like that again and now this. With this man who should be the last person on the planet she was attracted to, her enemy but also her saviour.

To cover her embarrassment, she bent her head and pretended to smell the strongly scented ointment. 'An old family recipe, you said? It is better than anything the monks could provide, but it smells so strong.'

'It is good for burns as well. Thankfully my grandmother taught me how to make it before she died or it would have been lost for ever. She used to use lavender or dog-rose petals to make it smell better, but I have never bothered with it.' He gave an awkward cough. 'It has helped me many times. Now let me see you put the ointment on.'

Cwenneth breathed easier, grateful to get the subject away from how his touch made her feel. She needed to remember who he was and what he was capable of. They might have a common cause, but he remained her enemy. She couldn't be attracted to him.

'I can see where smelling of roses would not give the right impression for a warrior.' She forced an arched laugh. 'Is it true that berserkers like you can't tell the difference between their own men and the enemy in battle?'

His face emptied of all humour and became a dark, forbidding mask. Her shoulders relaxed. A forbidding stranger she could deal with, the man who kneaded the ointment into her foot was the danger.

'I've never killed any of the men who serve under my banner, Lady Cwenneth. But then I'm no berserker, merely a warrior who has fought in many battles and proven his worth to his king.' He inclined his head. 'Can you appreciate the difference?'

Cwenneth examined a stain on her gown. She had made a mistake. 'They say... I had heard rumours. I thought it best to ask. I apologise. My ignorance about your customs is no excuse, but it is all I have. I'll try for better in the future.'

'Rumours are often lies,' he said gravely.

'They say in every rumour a kernel of truth hides,' she said quickly before she lost her nerve. 'Why are you a warrior in a foreign land, Thrand? Why did you follow that path? Why didn't you stay in the North Country?'

His hands curled into fists, but he stood absolutely rigid. 'Because it was the only way which was open to me.'

'People always have a choice.' Cwenneth concentrated on slathering the ointment on her feet. 'Do you enjoy killing? Is that what it is?'

'Killing is always a last resort. Intimidation works better.' He gave a half smile. 'But I am good at warfare. Very good at it. My sword is my fortune. I fight for gold, rather than a country.'

'But haven't you ever wanted to be something more?' she persisted. 'Both my husband and brother were warriors, but they also had another life which included lands, a hall and a family.'

'War is my life, my whole life,' he said. 'It is what I have chosen. There is nothing else for me.'

He stalked away, ending the conversation.

Cwenneth stared after him, weighing the jar in her hand.

'Curiosity can get you killed, Cwenneth,' she muttered. 'The same treacherous Norse blood runs in his veins as Hagal's. You have to think about saving your life and escaping. Keep away from him. Stop trying to see good where none exists.'

The trouble was a small part of her heart refused to believe it.

Chapter Four

Thrand concentrated on setting up camp properly in this inhospitable and rain-soaked place rather than thinking about Lady Cwenneth and the way with a few simple words she had caused him to remember long-forgotten emotions and people. But her questions kept hammering at his brain.

Why had she wanted to know his reason for becoming a mercenary? What did she hope to gain from it? Mercy? Pity? He doubted if he had any left. All the finer feelings had died when he had discovered his parents' bodies, despite Lady Cwenneth's insistence that she saw good in him.

War gave him life and a reason for being on this earth. When he knelt in the mud before the smouldering farmhouse with his parents'

mutilated bodies at his side, he had known what
he had to do.

'What are you going to do with the woman?'
Knui called. 'Now that you have won your
wager and proved your point. She managed
today, I'll grant you that, but barely. We need
to be back in Jorvik for the Storting and I want
the question of my cousin's child settled.'

Mine. Cwen is mine. The thought came from
deep within, shocking him slightly at its fierce
possession.

Thrand filled his lungs with clean air. He
lifted his brow. 'Do?'

Several of the other men turned pale as they
recognised his tone.

'She struggled. The Tyne remains several
days' walk in harsh conditions. Return her to
her people and collect a ransom. They will pay
nothing for a corpse,' Knui continued on, seemingly oblivious to Thrand's growing irritation
and anger. Thrand forced a breath, forced himself to remember his promise to Sven that he
would look after his cousin on this trip even
though Knui had the reputation of being a big
mouth and a braggart. Sven wanted his child
welcomed by one of his family. 'Best sell her
to some farmer if you do not wish to collect

ransom for her. I've done that in the past. Not as much gold, but some. She won't make it to the Tyne.'

'My pouch of gold is heavier because you bet against her.'

'She will bring ill luck to our expedition,' Knui commented.

'Thor favours her and, if she has Thor's favour, she will make the Tyne and beyond,' Thrand commented, looking at the man in turn as he explained about the earlier encounter with the boar.

'Thor sent a boar to look after her in the woods?' Helgi gasped.

'What other conclusion can I draw? The boar blew on her face as if he was anointing her,' Thrand said, fixing Knui with a hard stare. 'One ignores a gift from the gods at one's peril.'

'You're a hard man, Thrand Ammundson,' Knui said, making a low bow. 'I'd thought to spare her life, but you are the leader of this *felag*. Your word and Thor's boar must hold sway. The lady will bring good fortune to this enterprise.'

Thrand clung on to his temper with his last ounce of self-control. Knui had kept to the right side of the invisible line which separated him from insubordination.

Once the *felag* had dissolved, he and Knui would settle their differences, but for now he needed him here where he could see him. The last thing he wanted was Knui running to Hagal with the news. Lady Cwenneth's survival had to be revealed at the time of his choosing and not before. Hagal had slipped away from traps before. This time he wanted to leave nothing to chance. 'Lady Cwenneth travels with us. She will not be sold to a passing farmer or merchant. My responsibility and mine alone.'

'Where has the lady gone?' Helgi asked. 'I wanted to ask her about the boar's tusks and how they curved. It makes a difference to the destiny.'

Thrand frowned, his gaze sweeping the camp site. The steady drizzle had stopped and the sun had come out. Then he saw her, curled in a small ball beside his pack. His shoulders relaxed. She was still here. And she was his. The gods had given her to him to avenge his parents' murder. And he would use her without pity or remorse.

He walked over and spread his cloak about her shoulders. She mumbled slightly and turned her face towards him. Her lips shone red in the pale oval of her face. Innocent. Beautiful—and her chances of living were slim. An unaccustomed stab of pity went through him. 'Leave her to sleep.'

Cwen's dream were confused—to begin with it was all blood and gore mixed up with Aefirth's corpse holding its skeleton arms out to her and she started running, but could not escape. She grew so cold that her limbs shook and she doubted that she'd ever be warm again. But she knew she wanted to live, not to die. But then a heavy spice scent combined with a life-giving warmth settled over her, making her remember sensations she thought were lost to her. A peace descended along with warmth. And she watched Aefirth mouth 'goodbye, go live'. She was safe. All would be well. She half opened her eyes and saw another cloak covered her, far finer than the one she had lent Agatha. A dreamless sleep claimed her.

In the pale grey light before dawn, Thrand sat, listening to the steady breathing. He never slept long and it was easier to allow other less troubled, dream-plagued men a chance for their rest.

A slight moan turned his attention to the cloak-wrapped woman. Cwen had barely moved since he had taken her half-eaten bread from her fingers and wrapped his second cloak about her. What was he going to do with her, this Lady of Lingwold?

'You are not what I wanted or needed in my life, Cwen,' he murmured.

Cwen began to thrash about on her make-shift bed. 'No, please, no!'

He put his hand on Cwen's shoulder. Even the simple touch to waken her from her dream had his body hardening. His mouth twisted. Cwen needed to sleep, rather than be enfolded his arms. She was a complication that he could ill afford. He had to use her, rather than care about what happened to her.

'Be quiet. You will wake the others.'

'Thrand?' she whispered, panic evident in her voice.

'The very same.'

'I'd hoped it was a dream. That I would wake and find myself in Lingwold. Or failing that, Agatha snoring beside me.' Her voice faltered and her bottom lip trembled, making him want to taste it. 'But I woke here, knowing what happened and knowing that I can't go back to the same person I once was. My life divided and there's no one to guide me.'

He removed his hand and moved away from

her. Hell indeed. It had been months before he slept properly after his parents' murder. And then only because he'd killed two of their murderers. 'Unfortunately, there is no magic spell to make this go away. Lie quietly. Morning will come soon enough. You are safe here amongst my men. No dark riders will come and get you. Sleep. Close your eyes.'

He walked away from her and the temptation to hold her.

She followed him, his second cloak dragging on the ground. 'I want to talk to someone. Please. I don't want to dream. I want to know that other people are alive.'

Her words touched a long-buried wound. After his parents' death, he too had wanted company, but there had only been the sound of owls hooting in the night.

'You enjoy disobeying my orders.'

'Was that an order?' She ran her hands up and down her arms. 'It is no good lying there and pretending, knowing that you are awake.'

'You slept for most of the night.'

'You watched me?'

'I notice everyone,' Thrand ground out, annoyed he had revealed anything to her. 'Part of my job. Don't consider yourself special.'

She dipped her head, not meeting his gaze. 'I'll try to remember that.'

Thrand shifted uncomfortably. He had hurt her and it wasn't what he had intended. The words had come out far too harshly. All the more reason why starting anything with Cwen was bound to end in disappointment and heartache. He never felt comfortable around women. They either wanted too much or not enough. Even with Ingrid, the woman he'd betrayed his parents for, they had never really talked. It had been all physical.

'My men need their sleep, even if you don't.' He gestured towards his men. 'They were awake when you shut your eyes. You missed the songs and the fight when Helgi and Knui quarrelled over a game of tafl.'

'Will it always be like this?'

'Knui quarrels with everyone,' he said, pretending to misunderstand her question. 'I regret I ever agreed to his coming on this journey, but it was the only thing which would settle Sven. I wanted my friend to die easily, rather than ranting. I wanted him to...'

'You don't trust him.'

He gave her a sharp look. 'I trust very few people, but a good commander trusts his men.'

'And is Knui your man?'

'Trust is forged in battle. I've only travelled with Knui.'

She leant forward, and he could spy the pale hollow of her throat where his cloak gaped. 'Will I always see them—the corpses, I mean? I swore I could hear the sound of pounding hooves coming after me. Hunting me.'

He carefully shrugged, hating that he wanted to take the pain and suffering from her. 'Some men suffer and see the parade of the dead. Others sleep soundly.'

'And you? Do you sleep soundly?'

Her mouth trembled and it was all he could do to keep from dragging her into his arms and kissing her until the dreams fled. He clenched his fists. He made a point of not caring.

'Watching the stars helps. That and exhaustion.'

Her long lashes covered her eyes. 'Was that why you forced me to walk? You were doing me a service? I hadn't considered that. Thank you.'

'Don't go making me into something I am not. My reasoning was purely selfish. I knew my men would bet against you and I enjoy winning.' The muscles in his neck relaxed. There, he had told her a partial truth. He was not going soft or losing his edge, but there was something about this woman he admired. She had courage.

'If it helps me to sleep, then I'm grateful. It is better you didn't say or otherwise I'd have worried about the dreams.'

'You have a different way of looking at things.'

She stretched out a foot. He watched the high white curve of her instep and struggled against the urge to hold it again. 'My blisters are much better. Your grandmother must have been a very holy woman to create such a miracle cure.'

'She learnt the recipe from her mother.' Thrand put his hand on her shoulder and felt her shiver. Her words brought back long-forgotten memories. This sense of disorientation and questioning was so familiar. The memory of sitting and staring at the smouldering heap that had once been his house, knowing that he too should have seen the signs, stirred deep within him. 'My grandmother used to say the past was written in stone, but the future is written in water. I never understood it until I was forced to grow up.'

She shook his hand off. 'Then I shall have to ensure Hagal pays for his crimes. It is something I can do to honour the dead.'

Thrand's muscles tensed. A small beacon of hope. A willing witness, rather than a scared, reluctant one, would give much better testimony. 'Do you mean that?'

'Yes, yes, I do.' She tilted her head to one side, her long lashes making dark smudges against her pale cheek. 'Is there a way?'

'I want you to make a statement in front of the Storting, tell them what happened. Loud and clear, looking them in the eye and never faltering.'

'And if the king chooses to believe Hagal and return me to him? Or if Hagal kills me? Once he knows…'

'Hagal already wants you dead. It is my job to keep you alive.'

'I have been thinking. There must be a way to disguise myself, make it less likely to be remembered if we encounter anyone before…before we reach Jorvik.'

'Then you will do it?'

'Ensuring Hagal and the men who committed the murders are punished for this must become my life.'

Unaccustomed pity stabbed his heart. A beautiful woman like her should have more than vengeance in her life. Annoyed, he pushed the thought away. Cwen had the right to live her life as she saw fit and what happened to her afterwards was none of his concern. 'You have courage, Lady Cwenneth.'

'A compliment, I think.' In the grey light, he could just make out the crooked half-smile, which changed her features from pretty to heart-stoppingly beautiful.

'What do you consider your most memorable feature?' he asked, rather than giving into the renewed temptation to kiss her.

'My long, blonde hair. One true asset, according to my sister-in-law.'

'Cut it. Having it short will make you like a thrall, a slave.'

'Will you do it?' Cwenneth stared directly at Thrand and willed him to understand. 'I am afraid my hand will not be steady enough even if I can get a sharp knife.'

'Right now?'

'Before we start travelling again. Before I become memorable to any traveller.'

'Hold your head still.'

He took a knife from his belt and with one swift motion, a lock of golden hair tumbled to the ground, swiftly followed by the next one, until all about her feet a golden carpet lay. Her entire being tingled with awareness of him, the way he moved and the gentleness of his touch for such a large man and his warm, spicy scent.

Cwenneth screwed up her eyes and tried to breathe slowly. It had to be a reaction to the day's events rather than a true attraction to a man like him. She had never felt this way about Hagal or any of the other North men she'd encountered. And she knew what he'd done, even if the rumours were exaggerated.

'With the right tools, the task is easily accomplished.' He stepped back and considered her from hooded eyes. 'Your hair was too heavy for your delicate features. Your eyes appear much bigger. You were wrong—your hair isn't your most memorable feature. Your eyes are.'

Her hands paused in their exploration of her shorn head. 'My mother used to call them the window to my soul.'

His face took on an intent expression. 'They are. Windows.'

'I will take your word for it. There is no mirror around here.' Cwenneth's heart thumped. Thrand's eyes were mostly iced over. What did that say about his soul? 'I had a little silver mirror that had belonged to my mother, but it is gone now. Burnt or stolen. Lost to me at any rate.'

She swallowed to get rid of the lump in her

throat. It wasn't so much the mirror, but losing her connection with her mother.

'There is a pond where you will be able to spy your face. You can wash the dirty streaks from your skin while you are at it.'

Cwenneth scrubbed her face. 'I hate having a dirty face. You should have said.'

'You fell asleep before you ate the evening meal.' He put a hand on the middle of her back. 'Come and see the new you.'

He led the way to a small pond, keeping his hand on the middle of her back. A faint mist hung over the lake, and a solitary duck paddled.

'If you crouch down and lean out…'

'I know how to do it,' Cwenneth answered, going over to a flat rock and away from the touch which sent liquid heat coursing through her insides.

She leant out and looked, half expecting to see her usual reflection, but instead a woman with very short hair and enormous blue eyes stared up at her. Thrand spoke the truth. Her eyes were suddenly the most noticeable thing about her face. Her chin and jaw line were far stronger than she'd have liked. A very determined face, but with vulnerable eyes. Her, but not her.

She put out a hand, created ripples in the pond, destroying the image.

'Not to your liking. I can tell from the way you slap the water.'

Cwenneth concentrated on splashing cold water on to her skin before drying it. 'Far too fierce and determined. Here I always considered myself to look delicate. I wouldn't recognise me so that must be a start.'

'With short hair and the tattered gown, anyone we encounter will think you a thrall and not worth the bother of investigating your identity.'

'Until I open my mouth.'

'Keep silent.' In the pale light, the planes of his face had relaxed, making him far more approachable. 'Thralls are supposed to be silent. It is part of their charm. Is that possible for you?'

'You are teasing me now.' A bubbly feeling engulfed her. How long had it been since anyone teased or joked with her?

His face instantly sobered. 'I never tease. Ask anyone.'

She bowed her head and plucked at a loose thread on her gown. The bubbly feeling went. 'Why are you helping me? Why are you willing to shield me from Hagal?'

'You asked me earlier why I became a mercenary,' he said slowly. 'Hagal made me into one. I was a barely bearded boy when he turned me into a killer.'

'How?' Cwenneth whispered, watching him. To become a killer at such a young age. Not a warrior, blooded in battle, but a killer. 'How did he do it?'

'Along with three other men, he murdered my family. I have dedicated my life to ensuring their murderers were punished. It was the only way I could honour my parents. I slew the first of them that night. It satisfied something deep down in my soul and I discovered I was good at it.' He stood with his feet apart and hands fisted. His eyes no longer held any light, but were as ice-cold as midwinter. 'What I have done since that day I do to calm that itch in my soul. I don't fight for country or king, but because I get paid. And I've killed men because I was ordered to.'

'Your family? Did you find them slain in a similar fashion?' Cwenneth placed her hands on her head. She was so wrapped up in her own misery that she had missed the obvious point— Thrand never questioned her accusation about Hagal, a man he must have fought alongside.

Her breath caught. Thrand's desire for revenge had nothing to do with what happened back in the woods and everything to do with past wrongs. She was to be a tool, much like he used a sword or an axe. He wasn't doing this because he was attracted to her or felt some connection with her and her plight. She pressed her nails into her palms, making half-moon shapes. 'You knew, before I opened my mouth and accused Hagal, who was responsible. Hagal was involved in your parents' murder.'

'Years ago.' Thrand's mouth twisted as he stared out at the pond. 'Justice goes by a different name in Viken now that we have the current king. I left with a price on my head as that king approved of getting rid of the thorn in his flesh who was my father.'

Cwenneth struggled to understand. 'We are far from the North Country. Hagal has been in Northumbria for years, serving Halfdan, the same king you serve. His elevation to a *jaarl* shows he has served him well.'

'My oath to Halfdan forbids me from harming any in the *felag* as long as they stay loyal.' He slammed his fists together. 'I was unaware of Hagal's presence in the *felag* or I would never have given my sacred oath. A bad bargain, but a bargain it remains. And simply putting a knife in Hagal's back would not do it. I want him to suffer.'

She struggled to understand. 'But surely—'

'I honour my father by keeping sacred oaths. A man becomes worthless if he breaks his solemn oath and I am unworthy enough as is. He was one of the finest men I ever met. Honourable to a fault.'

'But strict with those who did not obey him?'

'My father died for his code.'

'Fathers only want what is best for their sons.'

Thrand stood in the glade, head up and unrepentant, but underneath she glimpsed the young man who had wept bitter tears when he found his parents. A man who was determined on revenge, but who clung to his father's code because it was all that remained of his family... because it was the only thing which separated him from his family's murderers.

Giving into instinct, she cupped his cheeks so he was forced to look into her eyes. 'Your father would be proud to have such a man as you for a son.'

Their breath laced, caught and laced again.

'You never met my father. My father had little time or forgiveness for people who failed him.'

'But I've met his son.' Her mouth began to ache. She wet her lips, not knowing what she wanted, but knowing she was powerless to move away from him. Her hands pulsed with warmth. 'You gave me that ointment and covered me with the cloak. Now you have cut my hair to help me hide and keep alive.'

'Hagal wants you dead. It is enough reason to keep you alive. It is the first time he has left a witness. The first mistake he has made in a very long time. I've been waiting for it and I plan to use you to destroy him. That is the sole reason I have helped you.'

'But you *have* helped me.' She stroked his cheek with her palm. 'The action counts, not the reason.'

With a groan, he put his arms about her and his mouth descended on hers. He tasted of spring rain and fresh air, but with more than a hint of dark passion. And she knew she wanted that passion. He made her feel alive, rather than as if she was one of the walking dead, the way she had felt since Aefirth and Richard died.

She pressed her body closer to his hardness, seeking him. She wanted him in a way she had not wanted any other man. She wanted to drown in this kiss and forget everything that had happened to her. She moaned and arched her body nearer.

Instantly, he stepped away from her. The

cool breeze fanned her heated cheeks while her body thrummed with liquid heat.

Cwenneth dropped her eyes. She had just pressed her body to a man who was a virtual stranger, inviting him to take her.

'Please say something,' she whispered, putting her hands to her head.

'Return to the others,' Thrand answered, trying to regain control of his body. He had not intended on kissing her, nor on his body reacting so violently to her nearness. He knew what out-of-control desire for a woman did to him, how he lost perspective and how easy it would be to care for a woman like Cwen.

If anything, with her hair short, she looked more desirable than she had with her long hair tumbling about her shoulders. Her mouth had become crimson from the kiss, and her eyes were dark blue. The memory of her honey-sweet taste invaded his body. 'Now! Go!'

He half turned to Cwen, knowing if she made a gesture towards him, he'd pull her into his arms and take her mouth again, plundering it for all its warmth, promised passion and the balm it brought to his soul.

His goodness had stopped years ago. He had been the one to disobey his father and to meet Ingrid secretly, even though his father had warned him against becoming involved with the woman. His desire for her had been too great, and he hadn't believed his father about her past behaviour.

All he'd seen was an ageing man who had hurt his leg in a fall and wanted to spoil his fun. It had been the first time that he had openly defied his father.

After he had found his parents, he had confronted Ingrid and she had admitted the truth— she had lured him away so that his parents could be killed, Hagal could acquire the land he coveted and she could be free of Hagal. He had left her on her knees, begging him to save her. Later her strangled and mutilated body had been discovered and he'd known if he had had an ounce of goodness in him, he would have saved her, but instead he'd left her to her fate.

Cwen did not need to know about that. Or the traps Hagal had managed to wriggle free from over the years. Or the people Thrand had failed to save.

She hadn't taken to her heels when he roared at her. She simply stood looking at him with those trusting, big eyes as if he could actually protect her.

Something twisted in his gut. He never wanted her to think him a monster. He wanted her to believe the impossible—that there was more to him than simply warfare, battles and killing.

'Did you hear me, Cwen? Go this instant!'

Her lips turned up into a sad smile, and her shoulders hunched. 'You called me Cwen. My late husband used to call me Cwennie.'

He released his breath. The crisis had passed. He had regained control of his body and pushed away all thought of drinking from her mouth. 'You can hardly be Lady Cwenneth with short hair. Cwen suits you.'

Chapter Five

The first rays of the spring sunshine broke through mist, warming Cwenneth's face and the back of her neck. Without the accustomed weight of her hair, her entire body seemed lighter. So far today, the going had been easier and her feet had hurt less.

The banter between the men bothered her less and she was beginning to figure out the individuals—which ones she liked and which ones were better avoided altogether. The thing which struck her was how little difference there was between these men and her brother's men or even the men who had served under her husband's banner.

From what she had seen this morning, she was very glad she'd followed her instincts and had not offered Knui Crowslayer her rings. He took the slightest opportunity to belittle and mock everyone. It made it easier when Helgi muttered that he had been forced on them by their dead friend.

'Today is going to be a good day. You can taste it in the air.' She inhaled a deep breath, savouring the tranquillity.

'Can you?' Thrand asked, coming to walk beside her as he led his horse.

A tingle ran through her body. After they had returned to the camp, there hadn't been any time to talk to him and explain about the mistake she'd made in kissing him like that. She had just hoped by ignoring it, everything would go away and they'd return to that ease they'd had before she'd made a mess of things.

'The air is perfumed with bluebells and the sun is shining.'

'And how do you explain the sound of horses, coming towards us? At speed?'

Nausea rose in her stomach, replacing her sense of well-being. 'Too soon. Tell me it is too soon.'

'Hands on swords.' He gave Knui a hard look. 'I speak. No one else, whatever the provocation. Farmers on the way to market, most likely. No point in borrowing trouble.'

'And me? What should I do?' Cwenneth fought against the rising tide of panic.

'Hunch your shoulders and keep your eyes down. It should suffice if you keep silent.'

Cwenneth bent down and grabbed a handful of dirt. Silently, she offered up prayers that her fears were unfounded. It was far too soon for anyone to be out hunting her.

The lead horse stopped in a cloud of dust.

The horseman lifted his helm, revealing his dark-blond hair and scarred face. Narfi. Her luck was out.

'Narfi the Black, fancy encountering you here and in full war gear,' Thrand said in a loud voice. 'Is there some problem with the locals? Not paying their tribute on time? And you are going to bully them into it? Nothing new there.'

Narfi curled his lip. 'Here is a sight that I did not expect to see today. Thrand the Destroyer and his band of merry followers. My master will wish to know why you are here.'

'No doubt.' Thrand stood in the centre of the road, his right hand casually resting on his sword.

'And your business is…? Be quick about it, man. I've things to do.'

'I travel on the king's business as usual,' Thrand said, concentrating on Narfi while he fought against every instinct in his body which told him to scoop up Cwen and ride away with her. 'What do I do but serve my king? Is there some war I need to know about? You appear dressed for battle.'

'We hunt bandits, Thrand Ammundson. There are many who refuse to accept our law. It is our task to keep the peace.' Narfi swung down from his horse. He was about half a head shorter than Thrand, stockier and with fists like ham hocks and a strut like a bantam cockerel's. 'Do you come to break it?'

'Keep a civil tongue in your head,' Thrand said, fixing Narfi with his eye. Off to one side, he saw that Cwen had obeyed his orders. She stood with her shorn head heavily bent. He released a breath.

'Hagal the Red is the lord in these parts, not you.'

'He has risen far under Halfdan's patronage. We both serve the same master…for now. Allow me and my men to go about our king's business as the land is at peace.'

'These Northumbrians need to learn a lesson.' Narfi scratched his nose. 'They grow bolder by the day—stealing sheep and cattle so that their children can be fed. Hagal has ordered me to take all measures necessary to ensure the Northumbrians understand they lost the war.'

'Halfdan desires peace in his lands for all his people. Taking food from children's mouths breeds resentment rather than loyalty. Halfdan made the same remarks only last week.' Thrand's fingers itched to draw his sword and knock the smug sneer from Narfi's face. Once he would have done so and accepted the consequences, but his years of warfaring had taught him to wait and allow his opponent to make the first and often fatal mistake. It was about taking the opportunity when presented. Narfi would give him that opportunity...eventually.

'The king would never have said such a thing in his youth,' Narfi remarked. 'We need a strong king who will put the needs of the Norse first.'

'Someone like Hagal?'

'You said it, not I.' Narfi openly smirked.

'Hagal does fancy challenging for the crown!' Thrand inclined his head. 'Thank you for the confirmation. It puts a different complexion on matters. I shall redouble my efforts to be there for the Storting.'

'I've seen you fight, Thrand. Too much the legend and too little the cold killer these days.' Narfi placed his hand on his sword's hilt. 'Your reputation as a warrior is exaggerated. Easier to have one demon than a thousand. You or rather your name does have its uses.'

His men nudged each other.

'Intriguing.' Thrand listened to the confirmation of what he'd long suspected. Others had used his reputation as a cover for their own deeds. A part of him was pleased Cwen had heard the independent confirmation. It bothered him that he wanted her to think of him as more than a mercenary.

'Hagal is worth ten of you,' Narfi muttered.

'Your words, not mine.'

Cwenneth forgot to breathe as she waited for the verdict which would allow them to pass unmolested.

Narfi stood not five feet from her, the man who supposedly had charge of her, the man who had murdered Agatha and the rest, and he challenged Thrand. She heard the genuine pleasure in his voice as he tossed off taunt after taunt. He sought a fight with Thrand.

This was going to end badly. She could feel it in her bones. Thrand and his men were outnumbered. She knew what these men were capable of and how they butchered innocent men.

Her knees threatened to collapse and the world started to turn dark at the edges. Cwenneth shook her head, trying to clear it. Fainting was a luxury she could ill afford. If she fainted, or even made a sound, Narfi would be bound to notice and recognise her. Her only hope was to remain like a statue, a statue of a thrall.

Cold sweat pooled at the base of her neck, her mouth tasted of ash and her back screamed from hunching over. The instinct to run and hide grew with each breath. She fought with all her might to keep still and hunched over. Her haircut and stained clothing had to be enough.

In her mind, she repeated Thrand's words over and over again—*Narfi would never equate a thrall with the missing Lady of Lingwold.*

Narfi cast his lifeless eyes over the group.

Pulling her cloak tighter about her, she hastily lowered her chin and hunched her shoulders even more. *Thralls kept their eyes to the ground.*

Silently, Cwenneth prayed for a miracle.

Suddenly, Narfi's shoulders relaxed and he beamed with false good humour. 'Next time call at the hall, rather than sneaking about like a thief, Thrand Ammundson. Hagal keeps a good table for men who belong to his *felag.*'

'Halfdan holds my oath.'

'It is the same thing.' Narfi made a dismissive gesture with his hand.

Cwenneth released her breath. He accepted

Thrand's word. They might get through this
without any bloodshed, or Narfi realising who
she was.

'I'll remember for the next time, but today I
decline.' Thrand gave a little cough. 'It never
does to keep a king waiting.'

'What sort of bandits are you looking for?'
Knui called out. 'I know Hagal the Red's reputation for rewarding those who assist him with
gold.'

'Did I say bandits?' Narfi's eyes narrowed.
'We're searching for a woman. Hagal's bride
has been kidnapped. Hagal wants her released.
If any of you discover her and brings her to the
stronghold, he will give you gold. You have my
solemn oath on it.'

Cwen curled her fists and concentrated on
the ground. Surely Thrand's men would keep
silent. Thrand had made it clear that she belonged to him.

'We will keep it in our thoughts and, should
we discover such a person, I will be sure to let
Hagal know,' Thrand said smoothly as he gave
Knui a hard stare. 'You will have to be content
with my word, Narfi.'

'How much gold?' Knui called out.

'More than you could carry, Knui Crowslayer.' Narfi gave an evil smile. 'As you have

given us information in the past, you know he is a man who keeps his words in these matters.'

Before Cwenneth could make a sound, Knui had reached her and shoved her forward. She stumbled and fell at Narfi's feet. 'Here you go. Here's your missing woman. Now I want my gold.'

Cwenneth concentrated on Narfi's mud-splattered boots, praying for a miracle. Thrand and his men were outnumbered and Knui had turned traitor.

The tip of Narfi's sword jabbed her cheek, pricking her and forcing her face upwards. Her gaze locked with Narfi's dark one.

'You thought, my lady, to hide. Pathetic disguise, cutting your hair. You should have stayed in your cart and had a quick death. Better for everyone.'

'Why?' Cwenneth asked in a trembling voice. 'Why better for everyone?'

'Because your husband slew Hagal's close kinsman two Aprils ago.'

'The woman belongs to me,' Thrand thundered and his sword knocked the blade from her cheek. 'I've claimed her. I'll not give her up easily. I will deal with the traitor later, but for now this is between you and me, Narfi.'

Cwen scrambled on her hands and knees

away from Narfi. When she reached the other side of Thrand's legs, she stopped, put her fingers to her cheek and wiped a drop of blood away. Her stomach roiled. Thrand had come to her defence but for how long? Thrand was a warrior, a warrior like her husband and her husband had died of his wounds.

'This woman belongs to you? Since when?'

'You marked her. No one marks my woman.' Thrand concentrated on Narfi as he struggled to keep control of his temper. The small trickle of blood on Cwen's cheek nearly sent him over the edge and in order to survive a fight with Narfi, he had to remain in control. But Narfi would fight him or be branded a coward for ever. 'Given my mood and the brightness of the day, I was prepared to overlook your insolence about my mission, but not this. You will pay and you will pay in blood.'

'Make her a present to Hagal.' Narfi took a step towards where Cwen cradled her cheek on the ground. 'He will be most interested to know where his errant bride has been. He'll arrange a special welcome for you, Thrand, as you discovered her.'

'Over my dead body,' Thrand said, moving between Cwenneth and Narfi.

'That can be arranged.' Narfi lifted his

sword. 'Shall we see if the man matches the legend after all?'

There was a hiss of swords as Thrand's men drew their weapons. Thrand held up his hand, checking their movement. They obeyed him in an instant. Knui looked over his shoulder, suddenly unsure. Thrand glared at him. Knui's reckoning would come. He would see to it personally, but first Narfi.

'A fair fight between you and me, Narfi, with Lady Cwenneth as the prize. Winner takes everything. No need for our men to fight.' Thrand paused, allowing his words to sink into Narfi's puffed-up brain. 'Unless you are all talk and no sword arm.'

'I welcome the opportunity to prove the man is much less than the legend.'

Instantly, the air became alive with the men making wagers on who would win. Thrand caught Helgi's eye and nodded. Helgi moved towards Cwen, helping to clear a space for the fighting, but being there to protect her if Narfi's men decided to act before the fight was through.

Narfi made a mocking bow towards where Cwen crouched on the ground. 'You should have stayed in the cart like you were supposed to, my lady. Your death would have been quicker. I intend to take my time after your so-called champion dies.'

Cwen paled to ghost-white. Hot rage poured through Thrand's blood. Narfi enjoyed baiting her and making her feel uncomfortable. The man deserved to die. 'Does your arrogance know no bounds?'

'When you lie dying, you will know what folly it is to believe in the legend of your greatness.' Narfi lifted his sword.

Thrand thrust his sword downwards, catching Narfi on the thigh. 'I defend what is mine!'

Narfi responded with a swift blow which Thrand easily deflected. The two men circled each other, trading blows, but nothing decisive. A probing of strength and skill to learn as much as possible about his opponent.

In the early days, after his parents' death, Thrand had engaged in many of these fights. It had been the only way to get to two of his parents' murderers. And he had nearly lost his life by being too quick and impatient. He had learnt to sit back and wait for the opportunity. They always overreached in time.

Thrand crouched, tossing his sword from hand to hand, enjoying the faint thrill of combat against a good opponent.

Thrand moved to his right. Narfi stuck out

his foot. Thrand rolled, avoiding the blow, and rose to catch Narfi's elbow.

'That passes for fighting, Narfi? My grandmother would have done better.'

'Is that who taught you? I had wondered.'

Thrand narrowed his eyes, watching the movement of the sword. Narfi would try again. He fought dirty, relying on the trip and trick, rather than any real skill. But Narfi also left himself exposed every time he tried it. A question of patience and not giving in to frustration or anger.

Thrand gave Cwen a quick glance. Her face except for the streak of blood was completely white. Thrand's blood boiled anew. He choked it back with difficulty and blocked another blow from Narfi, but Narfi also kept his distance, preventing Thrand from delivering the killing blow.

Sweat streamed down Thrand's eyes, blurring his vision. The time was right. Risky, but he could force the issue. He pretended to sway and stumble as if he were disoriented and tired.

Unable to resist, Narfi came closer and once again stuck out his foot. Thrand deliberately crashed down. Narfi's sword caught his back, sending a pain jolting through him but Thrand forced a roll and jammed his sword upwards.

With one fluid motion, Narfi fell, gave a gurgle. Thrand kicked the body to free his sword.

His men and Narfi's were arranged about in a circle, silently watching. Thrand pointedly turned his gaze from Knui. Promise or no promise to Sven, the man had betrayed him and defied his leadership. A swift death was too good for him.

'Lady Cwenneth is mine. Mine. Does anyone else fancy trying their luck?'

The cowards who passed for Narfi's men started to back away, looking to save their hides. Thrand concentrated on breathing. Get them gone, before he dealt with Knui. And he wanted to know how many other of his men might betray him. In the silence which followed, the others began to beat their swords against their shields and proclaim their loyalty to him. The noise grew until the woods rang with sound and Narfi's men had taken to their heels and fled.

'Watch your back!' Cwenneth called out. 'Knui!'

Thrand pivoted and swiftly dispatched Knui, who had crept up on him with a drawn sword. Knui gave a soft gurgle and fell on top of Narfi.

'I owe you a life debt, Cwen,' he said, looking straight at her. The bleeding had stopped on her cheek. He wanted to enfold her in his arms and taste her lips again. 'You saved me from having to execute him. Sven was blind to his defects.'

'We are even, then. Narfi would have killed me, and the death he had planned would not have been quick or easy.'

'We're even,' Thrand confirmed, bending down and cleaning his sword, rather than reaching out to her. Little things to occupy his mind and hands. He had come far too close to losing control and it had been his anger at what could happened to Cwen which spurred him on, rather than his desire for revenge or the knowledge that his men depended on him to get it right. And that scared him half to death.

Cwenneth rose unsteadily to her feet. Somewhere in the top of the tree, a bird started singing again, filling the air with joyous sound.

Knui and Narfi lay dead on the blood-soaked ground. They were the first men she had ever seen die violent deaths. Knui had betrayed her and would have killed Thrand. And Narfi would have tortured and murdered her.

Several violent shivers went through her. She lived, but the man who had started the slaughter breathed no more.

'Are you all right, Cwen?' Thrand asked.

'You seem miles away. We need to get going before they return with reinforcements. Narfi will be left for the crows to pick over.'

'And Knui? What happens to his body?' she whispered, keeping her eyes averted from the bodies.

'I regret that I ever allowed Knui on this expedition. I thought to honour my friend's request, but Knui had the black heart of a traitor and deserved a traitor's death.'

'He tried to kill you.'

'He knew that he had to or I would have killed him.' Thrand's face became hard. 'Once he had allowed his greed to get the better of him, he was doomed.'

'You suspected him.'

'I distrusted him, but I never expected him to betray me or my men in this fashion. Sven would never have asked me to have Knui on this *felag* if he had suspected the full extent of his treachery. Some would say that Knui's death was far swifter than he deserved.'

'He had betrayed others?'

'Hagal pays gold for betrayal, not out of the goodness of his heart. You heard Narfi the Black. They had done business together before.'

'Narfi took pleasure in killing,' Cwen said slowly, concentrating on the bodies rather than on Thrand's hard face. 'He spoke about getting a large meal after the slaughter. Do you ever feel like that? That killing makes you hungry? Do you need to eat?'

She wasn't sure why she asked except Narfi's statement yesterday had truly revolted her. Maybe if she knew Thrand was like Narfi, then this longing for Thrand would go. Maybe she would feel like she should find a way to escape from Thrand and get back to her old life, instead of having this small thrill that he had claimed her as his woman and had fought for her.

'My appetite goes for days,' Thrand replied. 'The last thing I feel right now is physical hunger. All I feel is sorrow that two warriors are dead and all because of the greed of one man.'

Cwenneth nodded. A small piece of her rejoiced. He was not as depraved as Narfi. But it still did not make him safe or any less her enemy…her very temporary ally. 'I'm trying hard to find pity in my heart for them, but I can't. Goodness knows what sort of person that makes me.'

'The line between revenge and justice is as fine as a hair.'

She bit her lip, hating that part of her had rejoiced at Narfi's death. She never considered that she would be someone who enjoyed another's demise.

'I should be better. The priest at Lingwold would tell me I was wrong and any death diminishes me, but Narfi needed to die.' She shook her head. 'I suppose at least the worst one is dead. Justice of a sort for my men.'

'No, the worst one remains alive,' Thrand corrected with a stern gaze. 'Do you think these men would have done what they did if Hagal hadn't ordered them to? He keeps his hands clean, but his heart is black. I've no idea how many other warriors he has corrupted with his gold, but I can make a guess.'

'Have I put you and your men in danger?' she asked, putting her hand on Thrand's sleeve. 'They know you are in the area now. When I overheard Narfi and the other man speaking back in the woods, it was mentioned that they could not spread the rumour you had done this because you were in Jorvik with the king. But now Hagal will know before night falls. They will say you did it, not Hagal. They will make you into an outlaw.'

'Only if we fail to make the Storting.' Thrand slammed his fists together. 'When they have reinforcements, they will come looking for us, in particular you. We go now.'

'Why would they listen to me? All Hagal has to do is proclaim it was Narfi acting on his own and—'

'Narfi would have slit his own mother's throat if Hagal asked him to,' Helgi called out. 'Everyone knows whose creature he was. There are many in the Storting who reckon that he'd never bed a woman without asking his master's permission.'

Cwennneth pressed her lips together. 'Is that supposed to be reassuring?'

'You are more of a threat to Hagal then ever. You know too much. You're the proof that Hagal planned this. The king will listen to you and hear the truth in your words.'

'I heard Knui say that he had taken Hagal's gold previously for information,' Cwenneth said. 'There must be others who have taken gold. Surely they should be exposed.'

'Exactly!' Helgi said. 'This woman of yours, Thrand, is more than a pretty face. She has a quicksilver mind. Thor has favoured us indeed.'

'The proof of what?' Cwenneth stared at him. 'What does Hagal intend?'

'The proof he intends to move against the king. Or rather the king's chosen successor when the king dies. Halfdan is gravely ill. Hagal knows that most of the inner circle distrust him. It is why he was sent to Acumwick, rather than being kept close in Jorvik. I suspect he intends to use your brother and his men in some way to assist his cause.'

'My brother made peace with the Norsemen so he would not have to go to war again. This was what my marriage was about—a weaving of peace. He wants to remain at Lingwold for the birth of his child.'

'Your brother is no stranger to war, though. The Lord of Lingwold can command an army. Hagal wants that army.'

'Or maybe just the dowry he stole to pay off his bribes.'

'If he needed that, he would have kept you alive so he could have had you beg your brother for more gold. How big was your dowry?'

She sucked in her breath. Norsemen politics sounded as precarious as Bernician. But Thrand was wrong. Edward had more respect for his men than to move directly against Halfdan. He still counted the cost of the last war.

'More than it should have been,' Cwenneth admitted with a sigh. 'My sister-in-law grumbled about it, but my brother thought it was a small price to pay if he no longer had to worry about paying Danegeld every year to you.'

'Your brother has never paid me Danegeld.'

Thrand leant down and picked up his sword, cleaning it on Knui's cloak. 'We met in battle and that was all. I went south and killed for my king there. It is where I collected my gold.'

'He swears he pays it to Thrand the Destroyer. Grumbles every single time. "That misbegotten Norse raider" is probably the kindest thing he has said about you.'

Thrand frowned. 'Hagal has held the north since the end of the last war. If anyone demanded payment, it will be one of his men. They simply used my name to extract money.'

'Yes, that bothered Narfi.' Cwenneth shook her head. 'And my husband would have slain Hagal's kinsman in battle, rather than in cold blood. It is the fortune of war. There is a difference.'

Thrand stilled, listening. 'Our time grows short.'

He turned away from her and barked several orders in Norse. His men looked unhappy, but agreed. Two quickly mounted their horses and rode off in the opposite direction. Another three followed suit going another way. Within a few heartbeats she and Thrand stood alone in the glade with the bodies and two horses— Thrand's and Narfi's.

'What is going on?' Cwenneth asked as her stomach knotted.

'Change of plan.' He put a hand in the middle of her back. 'You stay with me. My men have other jobs to do. If we split up, there is more chance they will follow one of them. Hagal will think that I will make straight for Jorvik and that is where he will concentrate the search. We need to go north. I will fulfil my oath.'

Cwenneth regarded the deep and menacing woods, rather than leaning into his touch. She had no idea how she was going to run, let alone walk. Her legs were like jelly. But if they stayed, Hagal would return with more than enough men to deal with Thrand.

'How far do we have to go before we can stop? Before we are safe?' she asked, moving away from his touch.

His face grew grave. 'You won't be truly safe until Hagal is defeated. It would be wrong of me to lie to you, Cwen. Helgi and Ketil are going to Jorvik to tell the king what happened here. Halfdan will listen to them and stall any request for blood money for Narfi the Black and Knui Crowslayer's families until the Storting begins and I have returned. He owes me that much. The others go to warn various other warriors whom I know are loyal to Halfdan. They need to be on the lookout for the traitors, men who have accepted Hagal's gold and are prepared to forsake their oaths.'

A great hard lump of misery settled in her breast. She pushed the thought away and concentrated on her immediate problem. 'How far do you expect me to walk?'

'I don't.' He leapt on his horse. 'Your walking days have ended. They will expect me to take you south, but we are going north. It is the best way to keep you safe.'

'But I can't ride!' Cwenneth gasped out. She looked at Narfi's horse. There was no way she could do it. The brute bared its teeth at her. 'I've no idea of how to ride and now isn't the time to start.'

'Your education has been singularly lacking then. We remedy it—now.' He caught Cwenneth by the waist and hauled her up on his horse, setting her in front of him. He kept her in place with one arm while the hand held the bridle. He made a clicking noise in the back of his throat and his horse lunged forward.

Under her bottom, Cwenneth felt the power of the horse. It amazed her that he could handle such a big animal with ease, but it was as if he and the horse were as one. Liquid heat rushed through her. This man had fought for her.

'Would Hagal beat you in a fair fight?' Cwenneth gave an uneasy laugh and tried to concentrate on other things besides the warm curl in the pit of her stomach. She'd get over this attraction to him. He had made it very clear where his feelings lay. His interest in her was as a weapon against his enemy. He did not care about her as a person, or more importantly as a woman. 'Or is he like Narfi? All talk and pride.'

He increased his grip on her waist. 'Hagal fights better than any man I know. But he prefers to play the spider and allow his victims to blunder into his web.'

Cwenneth gulped and concentrated on the horse's ears. She'd hoped that Thrand would dismiss Hagal as not very good and overrated, but Thrand respected his skill.

'Where are we going if not to Jorvik?'

'To the north. Near Corbridge.'

The north. Corbridge. In Bernicia. Still many miles from her home, but reasonably close to her stepson's lands. Cwenneth's breath caught.

Only yesterday, she would have been trying to figure out a way to escape and get to her brother. Everything had changed now. She had seen the personal risk Thrand had taken to save her life. She knew what Narfi was capa-

ble of and she had to believe that Hagal was a
thousand times worse. Hagal had to be stopped
before he caused the whole of Lingwold to be
destroyed.

'What is in the north?'

'I made a promise to my best friend. I will
ensure his child is well looked after. Before all
things. I owe Sven my life many times over.
He was the closest thing I had to a brother. If
something should happen and my life were to
end before this was done, I know Odin would
forbid me entrance to Valhalla.'

Cwenneth bit back a quick retort. Thrand
knew he might not survive the coming battle
and he wanted to do right for his friend. More
proof if she needed it that he was very different from Narfi and Hagal. He was a good man.

'Will you be taking the child with you?' she
asked. Her mind reeled as she thought about
how a child would cope amongst the Norsemen.

'Why would I want to do that?' Thrand
sounded genuinely shocked and surprised.

'Because it is your friend's child.'

'The child has a mother. I will make sure the
child is looked after, but my life has no room
for children or any sort of family.' This time
there was no mistaking the finality in his voice.

'Until my vengeance is complete, I don't have room for anyone in my life.'

Cwenneth hated that her heart ached.

Chapter Six

Thrand concentrated on keeping his body upright and in the saddle and ignoring the increasing pain in his back. Narfi's final blow had cut deep into his back. With each pound of Myrkr's hoof, the wound protested. Years of battle had taught him to bury the pain and attend to the task at hand—escape.

Cwen was a weapon, nothing more. His destiny was not to have a family. He'd lost his family through his own mistakes. He wouldn't risk it again.

He shifted in the saddle. White-hot pain shot through his back. An involuntary moan escaped his lips. He tightened his grip on the reins and on Cwen's waist.

'Something is wrong!' Cwen half turned in the saddle. A frown came between her delicate brows. 'Are you well?'

'I'm perfectly fine,' Thrand answered between gritted teeth. If they stopped, he doubted if he could get back on Myrkr and be able to lift Cwen up as well. Already his vision was hazy. 'Far too soon to stop. Myrkr has a good few miles left in his legs. He is just slowing because of the extra burden.'

She put her hand against his chest. 'Do you really think that or are you simply saying it, hoping I will believe it?'

He concentrated on the road ahead, rather than how Cwen's curves felt against his body. 'Few dare question me.'

'Perhaps more should. Stop being arrogant and inclined to believe the legend of Thrand the Destroyer.' She gave an uneasy laugh. 'You're really Thrand Ammundson, a seasoned warrior, but still human.'

'You are wrong. We are the same.'

'I beg to differ.'

Cwenneth glanced back at Thrand's face when he didn't give a quick retort in turn.

Over the past few miles, all the colour had drained from his face, making it more like a death mask than a living countenance. His arm about her waist now resembled a dead man's grip.

She gasped. She should have checked Thrand

for wounds before they left. She knew how quick Aefirth had been to dismiss any wound as trivial. Why should Thrand be any different?

Even Myrkr had sensed something was wrong. The horse was moving slowly and kept glancing back at Thrand.

'We need to stop,' she said. 'Right now. You must stop.'

'Go farther.' Thrand drew a shuddering breath. 'Need to keep you safe.'

'May God preserve me from stubborn warriors.' She reached for the horse's bridle. 'We stop now!'

The horse halted immediately. Thrand listed to one side, and his arm abruptly loosened. Cwenneth made a wild grab for Mrykr's mane and barely stayed on the horse.

'What do you think you are playing at, Cwen?'

Cwenneth let go of the mane and slid off the horse. She mistimed it and fell to the ground. Not the dignified dismounting that she'd hoped for, but it would suffice.

'Making sure we stop before you collapse and die.' Cwenneth stood up gingerly and stretched out her hands and legs. Nothing seemed to be broken. Her heart beat so fast that she thought it would burst out of her chest.

'Measures had to be taken. You're badly injured. Stop playing the legend and pay attention to the man.'

'Leave it.' His jaw jutted out, making him look more like a stubborn boy than a fearsome warrior. 'I don't need any of your help. Anyone's help. Now are you getting back on the horse? Or do I leave you to fend for yourself?'

'An empty threat.' Cwenneth tapped her foot on the ground. 'You need me alive.'

'Cwen!' He slid off the horse and winced, putting his hand to his back. His mouth was pinched white with a bluish tinge.

'The fighting was intense. Two men died. My price for continuing on is examining your wound.' She held out her hand. 'Please, before you get us both killed.'

'I can take care of myself,' he muttered, not meeting her eyes. 'I have been doing it for long enough. And if I have survived this many battles, I reckon that I will survive a bit longer.'

She held her hand. 'I can help. Together we can bind the wound so you can travel. You look half-dead.'

His brief look of longing nearly took her breath away but before she could actually register it, the mask had come down. 'Far too stubborn.'

Cwenneth put her hand on her hip. She had always deferred to Aefirth and her brother, not wishing to risk their wrath, but Thrand was different. He was not the sort of man to use his fists on a woman whereas her brother had always been quick with his if he didn't get his own way. 'My late husband died because he ignored his injuries. I won't allow you to do the same.'

'Why would you do that for me?'

'Self-interest. I need you alive to keep me alive.'

He gave a great sigh. 'If you insist…but no fussing.'

'I do insist. There seems to be a deserted hut over here. Shelter, as the sky threatens rain.' Cwenneth pointed to a little building with its roof in desperate need of repair. A small stream ran alongside it. Shelter and water—what more could she want? Providence. A small boar was carved on the lintel over the door.

Cwenneth's heart leapt. If she ever returned to her old life, she'd make sure she incorporated the boar in any device she might have. Did women in convents have devices? Her brother was likely to make good his threat and send her to one. Whitby, if she was lucky. Or further up the coast if she wasn't. But she'd deal with that once it came about. Right now, there was no guarantee she'd reach Jorvik.

Thrand lifted a brow. 'You have no idea who uses it. Or when they might return.'

'We'll stop here for the night.'

'We need to get up north and back to Jorvik as swiftly as possible. Time is of the essence. I promised my men.'

'Your men will wait for us.' She marched towards the hut. 'Are you coming? Or do you leave me to die? Your one weapon against the man who killed your family?'

'How do you know my men will wait?' His smile was more like a grimace of pain. 'They are mercenaries. They will go with whosoever pays them the most amount of gold. There is adventure for the taking at the moment. Ireland, Iceland, even the trading routes to the east require men with strong backs and stronger sword arms.'

'You would wait for them,' she said with sudden certainty. Thrand would wait because he was that sort of person, because he honoured his word. 'Only Knui spoke out. The rest remained silent. And none bet against you.'

He tilted his head to one side. 'You appear to know my men very well.'

'They're men of honour.' As the words left

her mouth, she thought of the irony. Two days ago, she would never have thought she'd utter those words about any Norseman, but she knew they were the truth. Honour didn't only belong to the Bernicians. 'I am going into the hut. You may follow if you wish, but we are not leaving this place until I say.'

She marched into the hut. Her heart thudded in her ears as she heard Thrand's horse whinny. She clenched her fists and hoped that Thrand would not challenge her any more.

'The hut appears derelict, but it has been used in the recent past,' Thrand said from the doorway. 'Whoever used it will be back.'

'Take off your top and stop being difficult.' She put her hand on her hip.

'A masterful woman. How refreshing. Most of the Northumbrian ladies I've encountered faint at the sight of blood.'

She rolled her eyes. 'I make no comment on the women you might have encountered previously.'

'I spoke of ladies. Northumbrian ladies.' His soft words skittered over her flesh.

'Then as you know I am no longer a lady. I am a woman. You claimed me.' She snapped her fingers, hating the sudden flash of jealousy which struck at her core. Which other ladies had he known? It wasn't any of her business. Truly. She wasn't interested in him. Not in that way. She was only with him because she wanted to survive.

A voice deep within her called her a liar.

'I will have no more of this nonsense about me being a gently bred lady who faints at the sight of blood. I am a widow and have seen the male torso before. I attended my husband during his last illness.'

'You are wrong there, Cwen. Your breeding oozes from your pores.'

'Stop stalling. Strip.'

He pulled off his top and exposed his torso. His skin was a golden hue except where a network of scars gleamed white.

Cwenneth sucked in her breath and hastily averted her eyes from the faint line of hair that led down his chest and disappeared into his trousers. She'd had enough humiliation with his rejection of her kiss earlier that morning.

'Have you seen enough, my *lady*?'

'I'll let you know.'

She walked slowly around him, hoping that he didn't notice the flame in her cheeks. The removal of his shirt had dislodged the slight scabbing. Fresh blood oozed from the cut on his lower back. It was a wonder that he had remained upright, let alone was able to ride a horse, hanging on to the both of them. Cwenneth swallowed hard. The debt she owed him grew with each passing breath.

'Before I take another step that wound will be cleaned and stitched,' she said, opting for a practical tone. Her stomach roiled. 'Hopefully Narfi's sword was clean.'

'Can you stitch wounds?'

'One thing I can do is sew. I embroidered my gown, not that there is any gold left on it,' she commented drily.

'But have you sewn flesh?' His fingers brushed hers. A jolt of fire ran up her arm.

'I've seen worse,' she said, avoiding the question. She had watched the monks sew up Aefirth three times—the first time he came home after a battle, after an accident in training, and the final time. But now wasn't the moment to confess her lack of practical experience. 'The wound doesn't gape and no vital organs are touched or you wouldn't have been able to ride for so long. You have lost blood and the wound still seeps. Sewing rather than burning. A simple enough task for me.' After what had happened with Aefirth and Richard, her confidence in her abilities to heal were next to nil. She had promised her sister-in-law to always call for the monks and never to attempt anything on her own again. But Thrand needed help immediately before he lost more blood or the wound festered.

His hand captured hers. 'You tremble.'

She pulled away from him. 'I can do it.'

'We could find a monastery. A monk would stitch me up. They have in the past. Honour bound, even to help a pagan sinner such as me.'

'Once Hagal knows you fought Narfi, he will check every church and monastery in the vicinity just in case. He is not a man to respect sanctuary.'

He closed his eyes for a long heartbeat.

'My husband died from a wound that went putrid.' She kept her gaze on the walls of the hut. Her nails made half-moons in her palms as she felt moisture gather in the back of her eyes. 'He should have gone to a healer straight away, but he was eager to get home. By the time the monks and I had a chance to look at the wound, it was too late. The poison had spread. They tried to burn it out, but failed.'

He placed a heavy hand on her shoulder. 'How would you have felt if he had died elsewhere?'

She spun around and looked into his face.

His mouth was pinched and his lips were more blue than red. 'Do you have a choice?'

He closed his eyes and his pallor increased. Sweat now cascaded down his face and his arms began to shake.

Cwenneth clamped her lips together and waited, silently praying that he would see sense and stop being stubborn. Men.

He bowed his head. 'I give in. Tomorrow morning we go. My pack and saddle will need to be brought in. Myrkr stabled. I've no wish for some thief to take them while we are messing with my back.'

'Remain here.' Without waiting for him to reply, she walked out of the door. Myrkr bared his teeth at her. Normally, she'd have backed away and not even tried. But that wasn't an option. She advanced forward and gripped his bridle.

She tugged, but the horse remained still and unmoving. He gave a low whinny and shook his head, determined to wait for his master.

'Move it,' she growled and shoved her shoulder against the horse. 'You have to so I can save his life. Do this for Thrand.'

To her astonishment, Myrkr allowed her to lead him to the small lean-to she'd spied at the side of the hut. There was a manger with the remains of some oats in the bottom. 'You see—food.'

While the horse ate, she rapidly undid the saddle and removed Thrand's gear. 'I'll return later. Let you know how it went. Give you some more food.'

The horse lowered his head and pawed the ground twice as if he understood. She pressed her hands to her head. Talking to horses and expecting them to understand—she must be losing her mind. But her nerves eased slightly to think she was not alone.

She staggered back into the hut and dropped the pack down with a thump. 'Myrkr is safely stabled and your pack is here. Your saddle can wait.'

In her absence, Thrand had started the fire. The flames highlighted the increasing pool of blood on his shirt.

Cwenneth clenched her fists. God save her from self-sufficient men. She put down the pack with a loud and satisfying thump.

'Be careful with that. If it was too heavy you should have said.'

'What is in there? The takings from your latest raid?' she bit out.

'Enough gold to provide for Sven's child as well as healing herbs and a little food.' He sank down to the ground. 'I think I might have over-done it after all.'

'What healing herbs do you have?' Cwen-neth's mouth went dry. 'My late husband al-ways used to have a few supplies, just in case there was no monastery available. Hopefully you use the same herbs.'

He motioned towards his pack. 'There are some. Valerian root, knit bone and a few oth-ers. No poppy seeds. Those who have served in Constantinople swear by it, but it gives me strange dreams. And I do have silk for sew-ing up. Linen stitches do not hold as well. And there is some ale for washing the wound. Or drinking. I don't have any linen for bandages. My shirt will have to do.'

The tension in her shoulders relaxed slightly. She would have preferred wine or something stronger, but ale would do. She simply had to hope that he would either keep still or pass out once she started sewing. 'Valerian is good. It will help you to sleep if it is mixed with alco-hol.'

'Afterwards. I'll drink it afterwards.' His eyes burned fiercely into her soul.

'Can you hold yourself steady?'

'I've withstood worse.' He raised his chin, and his blue gaze pierced hers. 'Our healers are not known for their gentleness. When I can, I go to a monastery as the monks are better at healing than our so-called healers. They are as apt to murmur a spell as to sew you up.'

'Interesting, since you have sacked monasteries.'

'I've never made war against the monks. There is no sport in killing an unarmed man.'

Her eye bulged. 'And you fight for the sport?'

'That and other things.' His eyes blazed. 'It is what I am good at. The only thing I am good at…in case you hadn't heard.'

Cwenneth concentrated on the hollow at the base of Thrand's throat. Narfi had made it clear that he had spread rumours about Thrand, but Thrand was also a seasoned Norse warrior with all the horror it entailed. He was her brother's enemy, but there was more to him than just being a warrior. He could have easily turned her over to Narfi for gold, but he hadn't. He had made sure that they put miles between them and any pursuer. And he valued his friends. He was keeping his promise to Sven. 'I had heard.'

'Good.' He closed his eyes. 'Whenever you are ready…'

Cwenneth bent her head and concentrated on threading the bone needle. 'I'm ready now.'

'Get on with it.' Thrand lay down on the pallet on his front, exposing his back.

'Please let the curse be gone. My life depends on him,' she murmured as she started cleaning the blood from his scarred back.

Cwenneth sat back on her heels and examined her handiwork. Once she had started sewing, the rhythm had begun to flow and her stitches had become neat, pulling the flesh together. The wound wasn't as deep or complicated as she had first feared.

The main problem had been its length. Thrand would bear the scar for the rest of his life. Another one to add to the series of silver and purple lines that criss-crossed his back. Unable to find any rags, she sacrificed the bottom third of her gown to make a satisfactory bandage. His shirt was far too bloodied for any purpose but feeding the fire. She had enough for two changes of the bandage before she would have to start finding more cloth.

That was a problem for another day. Right now, it was about making sure the blood stopped.

She reached over and gave the coals a stir. The fire blazed brightly for an instant, consuming the last of his shirt before subsiding into a pile of coals.

'Thrand,' she said softly, ignoring the tighter and tighter knot which had taken up residence in the pit of her stomach. 'I've finished. But I'm cursed, you see.'

Silently, she prayed that Thrand would answer. He lay so still that she had to wonder if he even lived. She wished she had her mother's mirror to check his breath. She pushed at his shoulder and turned him onto his side.

Thrand gave a soft groan and then started to splutter. 'I don't believe in curses.'

Cwenneth brushed away an errant tear from her cheek. He lived and now all she had to do was to keep him alive.

She went to the fire and retrieved the potion of valerian root and ale she had made. 'Drink this.'

His eyes were unfocused. He grabbed her hand. 'Is it over? Have we won? Tell me that.'

'Yes, we've won,' she confirmed softly and prayed that she spoke true. This time she would defeat the infection or die in the attempt.

Chapter Seven

The world about him rose rugged and unspoilt, tall snow-covered peaks and dark rich soil, lit with a flat, unnatural light. A hard land, but a good one. Thrand knew without being told where it was. Iceland, the new colony where Sven had once joked that a man could be free to live his life as he saw fit.

Thrand had visited it several years before when he had signed on to a trading vessel for a season. He had arrived to discover the man he sought had died two months before. Thrand had silently marked the name off as one less he had to kill and had left. But this was the first time he had dreamt of the place.

He knew he was dreaming by the light and the lack of breeze. But he also knew he wanted to remain there. He knew he could remain if he wanted to.

Thrand bent down, running the soil through his fingers, like he had seen his father do a thousand times. A simple action to determine if planting time was near, but one he'd never done as an adult. The earth felt good in his hand, a living thing rather than the cold, hard, lifeless touch of steel.

The longing to have a place of his own struck him deep in his soul. Once he had thought he'd spend his life planting and harvesting, rather than earning his keep by his sword arm, as his mother had longed for him.

He looked back towards the longhouse with its gabled roof. It reminded him of his boyhood home, but it was set back on a hill, not too near the water. To the right sat a pen filled with horses. Their different-coloured manes shone in the light. One pawed the ground as if to say, *come, train me, if you are man enough.*

He gave a crooked smile. As a boy, he had thought he'd spend his time training horses for a living. His father had laughed and told him to pay more attention to his fighting skills. His gentle mother, though, had smiled and quietly encouraged him.

Thrand's heart ached. He missed his mother's sweet smile and the way her long fingers were always busy with something, from spinning to weaving and even shelling peas. She had never sat still and she had always taken time to help others in their hour of need. For many years it had hurt too much to remember, especially the cruel way her laughter had been silenced. But here, the memories made him long for something else. Here he had hope.

A woman came out of the house with two children clinging to her skirts. Her face was turned from him, shadowed. She held out her hand, beckoning him in, welcoming him. He started to go towards her and ask her name and if those children could be his. He wanted to know who else was there. Somehow, he knew if he went further, he'd be part of a family again.

'Thrand, Thrand, wake up.' A hard hand shook his shoulder. He fought against it, wanted to stay and see if he could have a family again, if he could find peace at last. 'Thrand! I know you can hear me. Give me a sign. One little sign.'

He fought against the voice, fought to remain in his dream land, but the woman and her children had vanished, leaving him all alone on a windswept plain. He was at a crossroads. A great part of him longed to rejoin the woman, but the clear voice kept calling him, making it impossible for him to go farther.

'Thrand, wake up! Make some sign! Show me that you live. You have to live!'

The dream had vanished as if it had never been. Leaves and straw poked through his cloak, and his nose itched. But most of all he was aware of the woman beside him.

He opened one eye and saw Cwen crouched down beside him, a worried frown between her perfectly arched eyebrows. Her slender hand hovered above his shoulder. The flickering light of the fire highlighted her cheekbones.

He would have almost considered her a goddess or one of those angels that the Christians believed in. But she wrinkled her nose and sneezed. And he knew she was real. Angels or goddesses did not sneeze.

Cwen had called him back from the dream land. He swallowed hard, remembering how Sven had spoken about a journey to an empty country before he died. How he looked forward to starting a home there with his wife and child. To having a life beyond war.

'Cwen?' he whispered between cracked lips. His entire body was drenched in cold, clammy sweat and his arms felt as weak as a newborn babe's. 'You stayed. I thought you might go. Escape back to Lingwold.'

'Where would I go? I gave you my word.'

She put a hand on his forehead. 'Your temperature has broken. It is a good sign. I think you will live to fight Hagal after all.'

Her blue eyes sparkled in the firelight. Had she been crying? He dismissed the idea as impossible. No one cried for him...not since his mother died.

His mother had spent most of the year before her death weeping over him and his imagined failures, as his father raged and predicted dire things. Until in the end, he had figured that he might as well be as bad as they both seemed to think. He started to take pleasure in goading his father and getting a reaction. His dalliance with Ingrid had driven his father wild and that had been part of the fun.

To his eternal shame, he had proved worse than either parent had ever imagined. His actions had led directly to their deaths. He had tried to change and to become the sort of man who would was worthy of his parents. But still he failed; he had not been able to take his revenge. So far, Hagal had always slipped away.

'It will take more than a little wound like that to kill me,' he said to distract his mind from the past and his failure.

Instead of Cwenneth answering him, her eyes turned unbearably sad and her bottom lip trembled. Something inside Thrand broke. He had meant to give her a compliment and he had made a mess of it.

'Cwen, what is wrong?'

'Nothing is wrong.' A single tear trembled in the corner of her eye.

He started to lift his hand to cup her face, taste her lips and kiss the shadows from her eyes. Then he remembered what she had said about her husband and his death. His hand fell back.

He'd been foolish. She wasn't weeping for him. She was weeping for her dead husband. It should have made him feel better, but the thought was like a hot knife in his stomach.

In that instant he hated the man and that his widow should weep for him so long after his death. If he died, no one would weep. No one would ever weep. He wanted it that way, didn't he?

'Then why are you crying?'

She hastily scrubbed her reddened eyes. 'Smoke from the fire.'

He nodded, allowing her lie. 'I told you— you are stuck with me for a while yet. I have had worse wounds and have lived to tell the tale.'

'Are you suffering any pain? I can get you some more valerian.'

Only around his heart. His hand fell back to the makeshift bed, rather than bringing her head down to his lips.

'I heal quickly. The wound isn't deep.' His mouth tasted foul and his body ached with new pains with each breath he took. His life was supposed to be very different, but protesting about it would not change his destiny.

It bothered him that he wanted her to feel something for him. When had a woman ever felt something for him? Like Ingrid, they had all wanted something from him.

It was fine. It was the way he wanted things. His life held no room for the gentler aspects of life—a woman's loving touch or a family. The longing from his dream was the product of a fevered mind. The thought failed to ease his pain.

'I need to change your bandage. Your thrashing about has loosened it.' Her hands pushed him down. 'Lie still. On your side. Allow me to work.'

His fingers picked at the linen bandage. The cloth was far finer than his shirt. 'Where did you put my shirt?'

'I have had to burn your shirt as it was blood-soaked beyond what a simple wash could do.

We should never have ridden as far as we did. Are you always this reckless?'

'What did you use?' He clenched his fist and tried to think of the garments in his satchel. The most likely cloth was Sven's last gift to his former mistress—a fine linen shift. It annoyed him that he was bothered. 'What did you use?'

'A bit of my undergown. It is strong linen and clean. I had no idea where the clothes in your satchel had been.'

He forced his body to remain still as her cool hands worked. She had sacrificed part of her undergown for him. She had not taken Sven's token to his former mistress, the woman who had borne him a child. Sven had insisted that his woman must have it, with practically his last breath. It made him feel worse—beholden to Cwen, rather than angry with her. 'I will replace it when we get to Jorvik.'

'The wound has stayed shut. I used the remaining blister ointment on top of the stitches.'

'It helps with healing,' Thrand confirmed.

'As long as it keeps infection at bay...' She didn't pause in her ministrations but continued to tighten the bandage.

Her fingers brushed his skin, causing an agony of a different sort. Thrand practised breathing steadily.

Impersonal. She probably would have done it for anyone. He had to stop hoping that she harboured some feeling for him. Or that he could have a future which was very different from his past.

The dream had been simply valerian-induced with no hidden meaning.

He tried to get up. To his shame, he seemed to have no more strength than a kitten. A wave of tiredness washed over him. He collapsed back down on to the pallet, rather than resisting it as he would have done normally. He rubbed his hand across his jaw. He sported some bristles but not many and not too long. 'How long have I been asleep?'

'The entire night, most of a day and all evening.'

The clouds from his mind vanished and his muscles were suddenly on high alert. 'Entire day and night? Why did you let me sleep that long? Has the fire been on all this time?'

'I gave you valerian root mixed with the ale. The infection... You had to be kept warm.'

'We need to travel. We've stayed here far too long.' He redoubled his efforts to stand, but her hands pushed him back down.

'You need to sleep.' Her voice soothed him.

'Who travels during the night? Drink some more valerian and ale and take the pain away.'

He shook his head. The scar under his eye itched. The first time it had happened, Ingrid had just told him to sleep in her arms and then two armed men had burst into the barn. His instinct never played him false. They had tarried far too long here as it was.

'No, we go.' He heaved himself up from the pallet and his back screamed in agony. 'Now, before morning.'

'No one has passed by. I heard some jangling of a cow bell last evening, but there was nothing more. No one knows we are here. Whoever used this in the past is long gone.'

'Smoke from the fire will have been visible. For miles. Particularly if you had the fire going during the day.' He put his hands on her shoulders and steadied himself. The room swam slightly before righting itself. The hardest part was always the getting up. Thrand focused on the smouldering coals.

Two bright patches appeared on her cheeks. She stepped away from his touch. 'You said Hagal would search to the south, towards Jorvik.'

'We've no idea where they're searching. And the smoke has been rising long enough for someone to take notice. Smoke from a deserted hut always attracts attention.' He ran his hand through his hair. 'It was only supposed to be for the operation in case you had to burn the wound to stop the bleeding.'

'It kept you warm.'

'You were supposed to smother the fire once the operation was done!'

Cwen pursed her lips. 'Obviously, I missed that instruction in my concern for your health.'

'Sarcasm fails to alter the situation.'

'Neither will yelling at me.'

Thrand kept his back rigid and took three steps forward. The pain nearly blinded him, but he could move. 'We go now, before we have to entertain unwanted visitors.'

'Will you be able to get on your horse? You can barely stand.'

She put her hand on his arm. It took all of his willpower not to cling on to her for support. She had to think he was fine if he was going to save her life.

'All the more reason for departing.'

'My late husband used to say…'

'Preaching your late husband's words won't alter the situation.'

The way her face fell twisted his gut. Thrand pressed his hands to his eyes and attempted to regain control. What was it about Cwen that made him want to obliterate any man who had touched her? She wanted her late husband, not him. Natural. Why would a lady like her care about a Norse warrior like him?

He gulped a mouthful of life-giving air and regained control of his emotions. Task at hand, not longing for something which could never happen.

'We walk very slowly, but we put a distance between this place and us,' he said with exaggerated patience.

'I am a lady, not your slave. I dislike being ordered about.'

'Humour me, Cwen. Please.'

Cwenneth pressed her lips together, hating that Thrand was being logical. They had stayed here for far too long, but she had not had a choice. Keeping him drugged had been the right thing to do. She could not face losing him to an infection, not after seeing how Aefirth had suffered.

She watched as Thrand kicked dirt over the fire, extinguishing it, then tested it for heat and putting more dirt over. A hard lump settled in her stomach.

She wished she had thought of the risk of

being seen, instead of staring into the flames
and thinking about Aefirth's last days.

She picked up her cloak and concentrated
on shaking it out. 'I will bow to your superior
wisdom—after all, you must have experience
at escaping.'

He turned back to her. 'If you give me the
pack, I will see about Myrkr.'

'I will handle the pack and the horse,' she
said between gritted teeth and shouldered the
heavy bag. 'I'm hardly some useless lady who
can't lift more than a feather.'

Thrand slowly turned back towards her. The
planes of his face softened, making him human.
'I have never considered you weak.'

A warm glow infused her body. He thought
her strong. Aefirth had always considered her
helpless. She hated the disloyal thought.

'We take frequent breaks. I refuse to have
you act like a martyr.' She glared at him. 'Do
you understand? I can give orders as well.'

A muscle twitched in the corner of his cheek.
'Few would dare order me about like that. My
reputation precedes me.'

'I know the man, I don't fear the legend.'

'Truly?'

'The only thing I care about is getting to Jorvik and making my statement to Hagal. You are a means to an end. That is all.'

Her heart protested at the necessary lie. She wanted him to live because…he'd saved her life. Cwenneth balanced the pack on her shoulder and refused to think beyond that reason.

'It is good to know where your priorities lie.'

'There. Is the pack on Myrkr to your satisfaction this time?' Cwenneth's entire being was aware of Thrand standing directly behind her, watching her every move, but he had listened to reason and allowed her to put the pack on the horse. He had just made her do it three times until he was satisfied.

He put a finger to her lips. 'Hush. Listen.'

A faint jangle of a bridle sounded on the early-morning breeze.

'Sounds travel far in the mist,' she whispered as her muscles froze. 'They are not coming this way…'

'Caution saves lives.' He placed his hand on her shoulder. His breath tickled her ear, causing her stomach to swoop with an altogether different emotion. Cwenneth concentrated on breathing steadily.

'Caution?'

'We hide until they leave.'

'How do you hide a horse like Myrkr?'

Thrand led the way farther into the woods, stopping beside a small knoll. He gave Myrkr a slap on his hind quarters and the horse obediently trotted off. 'Like that. He will come when I whistle.'

'What's your secret?' she asked in a low voice.

'My secret?'

'Myrkr obeyed you instantly and without question.'

'He trusts me. You should try it some time. It could be a good habit to get into.' Thrand turned back to her. 'Get down and wait. Whatever happens, keep your head down and keep silent.'

Her heart thudded in her ears. 'I can be quiet.'

'With any luck, they will ride on past without investigating if the fire remains warm now that the smoke is gone.'

'And if they don't?'

'We face it when it happens. But my sword arm has never failed me yet.'

Cwenneth gulped hard. 'We need to stay together. Going off scouting will increase our chances of being seen.'

His large hand covered hers. The sim-

ple touch eased her and she found she could
breathe again. 'There is no need to give in to
panicked fear.'

'I'm not afraid,' she lied, hoping he'd believe her.

'That makes one of us then. It is fine to be
afraid, Cwen, but use it, rather than panicking.'

Cwen pressed her lips together. 'I'll remember that.'

He lay down in the hollow, stretched out,
but his hand hovered over the hilt of his sword.
'Let's hope Thor still favours you.'

Cwenneth manoeuvred her body so that their
shoulders were just touching. Even that innocent brush sent a pulse of warmth throughout
her body. 'Aren't your gods supposed to be
fickle?'

He put his finger to her lips. 'All will be well,
Cwen. It is far too dark for them to want to go
into the woods.'

The cold dew seeped up into her body as
they lay there in the grey mist of dawn, waiting. The jangling of the bridles came louder
and stopped.

'Anyone there?' a Northumbrian voice called.
'Answer us or we are coming in.'

Cwen glanced at Thrand, who quickly shook
his head.

She crouched lower, tried to make her body smaller.

'I don't know what your lad saw,' came another voice, rougher but with a lazy authority. 'But nobody ever uses this hut, not since Simon the Fat died. His ghost haunts it.'

'There was someone,' a young boy's voice protested. 'I saw the smoke when I brought the cows in from the far field. Ghosts don't cause smoke.'

'Do you think it was him? With our new lord's lady?'

'Wherever Thrand the Destroyer is, it won't be here,' an older, rougher voice said. 'Why would he be going north? There ain't nothing for him. You've roused me from a warm bed and a willing wench for this! Your lad thought he saw wolves circling the sheep the other week and it were nothing.'

Several men agreed with him. Cwenneth risked a breath. In the grey light, she counted five shapes. Five against one. The odds were terrible.

'We should check,' the first voice said. 'My lad knows what he saw and where.'

The door of the hut creaked.

'The coals are warm…barely,' someone called. 'But they ain't here. No telling who it was. Could have been the Destroyer and his men.'

'In your nightmares!'

The uneasy laughter followed the swift retort.

'Only one horse,' someone else shouted. 'Doesn't the Destroyer always travel with more men?'

Cwen and Thrand exchanged glances. Thrand eased his sword out of the sheath. She nodded and resumed praying, more in hope than expectation.

'We should search for them. They won't go far.' The boy started towards where Cwen and Thrand hid. Cwen shrank deeper into the hollow. Her muscles tensed, ready for flight.

'I didn't see anyone as we rode in,' someone shouted and the boy halted inches from their hiding place. 'If the Destroyer has left here, our farms are in danger. Our women.'

'They will have left before it became dark. Stands to reason.' Rough Voice gestured to the boy, calling him back. The boy scampered back to the others. Cwen breathed again.

'And if it is the Destroyer, he won't be alone. He will have his men with him. Hardened warriors, not farmhands. And more than one horse. Do you want to face them?'

'But we should let the Norseman know. He promised a substantial reward.'

'And you are a Northman's lapdog now?'

'I know what is good for me and mine.'

'What do you think will happen if they find him here? Do you think they'd reward you with gold? Or take all your crops like they did last year?' Rough Voice snorted. 'I know what Norsemen's rewards are like. He is as likely to rob you blind as fill your pockets with gold. Best to keep your head down and out of their affairs. You don't want them to have any knowledge of treasure you might have.'

'He'll come back to it later!'

'I hadn't considered that. I don't want any trouble.' The man drew his boy closer.

'I'm not minded to do any Norseman's bidding,' Rough Voice said. 'Even if he was here, what business is it of mine as long as he leaves my crops and gold alone?'

Others murmured their agreement.

'Let them find the Destroyer themselves, I say,' Rough Voice proclaimed in ringing tones. 'A plague on all greedy Norsemen.'

'And if they return?' the boy piped up.

'If they return and ask, we tell the truth—we checked but no one was here. But why bother trouble if trouble ain't bothering us? I have lambs to birth and cows to milk.'

After a pause which felt like a lifetime, they all agreed with Rough Voice.

The tension in Cwen's shoulders eased as Thrand released his grip on his sword.

Discussing the perfidy of Norsemen, the likelihood of an early raiding season and the state of lambing, they departed.

Cwen rolled over on her back and stared at the rose, dawn-streaked sky. Her blood fizzed as she drank in mouthfuls of life-giving air.

'They have gone. Truly gone.'

He put his hand on her shoulder. 'I told you—you have Thor's favour. It could have gone either way and it went in ours. Thanks to you and your luck.'

She propped herself on one elbow and regarded his face. His dark-blonde hair streamed out across the ground and bristle shadowed his jaw.

'I'm pleased you didn't have to kill that boy.'

'I'm a warrior, not a suicidal maniac. I only fight when I have to.' He expelled a long breath and stood up without touching her. 'The odds were not in my favour and as long as our hiding place remained undetected, there was no need. But I wouldn't have hesitated.'

'I know.' Cwenneth stood up and brushed the dirt from her skirt.

Thrand gave a low whistle which sounded more like an owl than a human. True to his prediction, the horse returned within a few heartbeats. Thrand leaned over and rubbed the horse's nose.

'They've no appetite for the search. You heard the one with the rough voice. Do you think we will be safe on the road?' she asked.

He raised a brow. 'No more roads. And we skirt all settlements. The fewer people who know about our business, the better. We've no idea how far Hagal's rumour has spread.'

She held back the words saying that, despite everything, she had found a little bit of peace in this hut. She had proven that she could heal, that some of the more damning things whispered about Aefirth's and Richard's deaths were untrue. Not everyone she tried to heal died. But that would be revealing too much of herself to this man. 'And your stitches? Are they up to a long ride?'

'You sew a fine seam. I'd expect no less from you.'

'A compliment?'

He shrugged. 'You're a strong woman,

Cwen, and a lucky one. Never allow anyone to tell you differently.'

Their gazes caught and held. She cleared her throat. 'How do you propose me getting on that horse?'

Her voice was far more breathless than she would have liked.

He jerked his head towards a stump. 'Use that as a mounting block. The sooner we are away from Hagal and his men, the better. Every day we delay is another day that Hagal has a chance to spread his poisonous lies about me kidnapping you. And the next time, the farmers might not be as wary of Norsemen as that lot was.'

Cwenneth hugged her arms about her waist. She had been foolish to think that he might want an excuse to hold her. And she had nearly embraced him after the men left. What sort of person was she that she needed to face the humiliation of rejection more than once?

Chapter Eight

Desire. What he felt for Cwenneth was nothing more than desire. He had been without a woman for months now. He had intended finding a willing woman the night Sven had died, but after that there had not been time. He had learnt his lesson after Ingrid—not to allow his heart to become involved. Purely physical and avoid complications.

Cwen was not the sort of woman one used and discarded. She was the other sort, the sort his father had told him that you protected and looked after, a woman like his mother. Strong and full of integrity. Thrand pushed the thought away. Cwen was his means of achieving revenge for his mother's death. That was all.

'Shall we stop here?' Cwen said, half turning. Her delicate brows puckered into a frown. 'Here beside this stream is as good as any place to camp for the night. Stopping before it gets too dark.'

The small wooded glade with a stream running through it would serve for the night. And his back was on fire. 'You have a good eye. It will meet our needs. I will take the first watch. You look exhausted. We've gone far enough away from any pursuers.'

She put her hand on his arm. 'And if you think to fool me by saying your back doesn't hurt by agreeing to my request, I must warn you, your brow is creased with pain and you winced when you mounted Mrykr the last time. You need to sleep. After all we've been through I won't lose you to an infection.'

Thrand drew his upper lip over his teeth. She had noticed his discomfort. He struggled to remember the last time anyone had noticed how he was, rather just accepting his bland words. Probably his mother. What would she have thought of Cwen?

Thrand shook his head, trying to clear the thought. He knew what his mother had hoped for him—a wife and children—but that would have to wait until he had avenged her death. He couldn't do both. He'd seen the terrible things that happened when men became distracted.

'The last thing I need to do is sleep.' He

gave a crooked smile as she slid down from the horse. 'I spent enough time the last few days asleep. Someone has to keep watch.'

'I can take the first watch.'

'When were you trained in swordplay, my lady? It will be safer for all if I remain alert.'

'I never had the chance to learn.' Cwen tucked her chin into her neck. 'My late husband considered it beneath my dignity, or rather beneath his wife's dignity. Perhaps I should have questioned his authority, but he was much older than I and much wiser in the ways of the world.'

'He made a mistake.'

'How hard can it be to use a sword? All you have to do is to remember which end to strike with.'

'There is more to it than that.' Thrand paused and silently vowed that he would teach her to fight before they reached Jorvik. For her own safety, she needed to learn. He didn't want to think about her being alone and vulnerable, dying like his mother had done. She, too, had not known how to use a sword and believed that there would always be someone there to protect her. 'My dreams are troubled ones. I'm used to getting by on little sleep.'

'I hate dreaming.' A vulnerable light shone in her eyes. 'I worry about your wound becoming infected. I lost my husband to one and if I lose you...how will I survive?'

A sudden stab of jealousy went through Thrand. He only hoped her much-older late husband had deserved her. 'It wasn't your fault he died. Destiny. We can't chose the date of our birth or the date of our death. Warriors die of infections all the time. I'm very tough.'

'Aefirth said the same when he lay there. He absolved me of all guilt. He was old, and I had my whole life ahead of me. It didn't make it any easier.' Her fist balled. 'And you're wrong about me being lucky. Any who seek my help will die. My stepson's nurse called out a curse when I put her from the hall and now I'm destined to lose everything I love.'

'And because your husband died, you believe an old woman's words?'

'More people died.'

'Who?'

'Our son. He was two,' she said, turning from him. Her shoulders hunched. 'He died days after Aefirth. Of a fever. I wanted to die as well, but it didn't happen. I have had to live with the knowledge of how I had failed. If I'd been a better person, I would have saved them both. But I'm wicked and so was punished. My stepson didn't even allow me to lay flowers at Richard's grave. He was afraid of the curse spreading.'

Thrand sucked in his breath. Cwen had had a son. She had had a life before now. She had been a mother. She had had a child. The emptiness of his life grated. Never once had he had the joy of holding his own child. In the stillness of the evening he envied her.

He shook his head, trying to rid himself of the feeling of wanting something more to his life. He knew what he did and why. It was the only life he had known since his family was slaughtered. It had to be until he had disposed of Hagal. Longing to have anything else led to a dulling of his sword arm and his appetite for fighting. There was no room in his life for anything but hate and killing.

'You're not cursed,' he muttered.

'You've never lost a child. It was as if my heart had been torn from my body. I prayed to God to let me die, but here I am. In the woods that first day, I found that I wanted to live. Even the thought of being with my son held no comfort.'

'We cannot control when people die. The Norns of fate are tight-lipped crones and only they know what sort of thread they have spun for a man's life. You are a good person who experienced bad times.' He knew the words were inadequate and far too harsh. He had never been good at the soft words. Even Ingrid had teased him about that. Actions for him were always more important than words. 'But it is how you respond to those times which is important. My mother used to say that to me.'

At Cwenneth's anguished look, he ran his hand through his hair. He hated having to provide comfort. He always said the wrong thing. 'What I mean is that it is a tragedy when a young child dies. Far harder than when a man does. But to think we have a say in it is wrong. Outrunning your fate is impossible. Whatever words I say, it won't make your burden any easier.'

She bowed her head. 'Richard was the light of my life and my husband's. He was such a bright thing, always into mischief, and his laughter... I wanted to take his place, but here I am.'

'How did it happen?' He hesitated. 'If you want to talk about it...'

'One moment, he was alive and well, laughing and having a game of tag with the cook. I was grateful for a little peace as Aefirth's funeral had been two days earlier. The next he complained of a stiff and hurting neck. He had a high fever and a rash. I had gone to get a poultice and when I returned, all the life had vanished. And to make matters complete, I lost any hope that I might be carrying another child. Before it started, I'd been so sure that I'd felt the baby quicken. When I had confided in Aefirth in those final hours before he died, he seemed so happy.' She looped a stray tendril of hair about her ear. 'And then…I felt like such a fool.'

'Why did your stepson behave as he did?'

'My stepson accused me…well, we never were going to be close in any case…he said that his nurse's curses were strong. He told me that I had destroyed his family, but they were my family as well.'

'Old men and children die all the time.'

'But they were my family, not strangers. I wanted them to live. Desperately.'

He reached out and laced his hand with hers. Inside him, something curled up and died. Cwen had lost not only her husband, but her son. He couldn't imagine the pain she must have gone through. It had been hard enough to leave his parents' grave. 'It was wrong, that. Not allowing you to lay flowers or mourn your son properly.'

She pulled her hand from his. 'I think of him every day. I nearly came to blows with my sister-in-law when she said that I'd get over it. Why would I want to forget my son?

'Not that it is any help…people said that to me, but there wasn't anything anyone could do to take away the pain.

'At least you could fight against someone. How do you fight against an illness?' She stood up. 'The priest said…that…it showed I'd done something wrong. A punishment from God… but I was following his orders. He had told me if I didn't dismiss the nurse, he'd withhold communion from everyone.'

'It seems to me that the priest should be blamed rather than you.' Thrand reached over and covered her hand with his. This time she kept her hand in his. 'He was trying to deflect his guilt when he blamed you.'

She raised shimmering eyes to his. 'Do you think so?'

'I know so.' He tilted his head to one side and saw the diamond gleam of a teardrop on her cheek. 'Some day you may have another child. After this is over.'

'Drink the tea,' she said shoving the cup forward. 'I don't want to talk about it any more. My heart was buried with Richard. No more children for me. Ever. I can't take the pain.'

'Why did you agree to the marriage with Hagal?'

'Not to regain a family.' She crossed her arms. Her eyes threw daggers, all sorrow vanished. 'If you must know, I was taking the lesser of two evils. My brother had threatened to send me to a convent of his choosing without a dowry. I doubted if I'd last long there. What can a cursed woman do in a convent?' She shrugged. 'Now the only future I know about involves destroying Hagal. Sometimes I want to think beyond that moment. I want to believe that there is more for me.'

'Do you want another marriage?'

'I want a life. I want to believe that I'm not cursed.'

He stared at the tea, suddenly desiring the oblivion it would bring. Maybe when he woke, he'd stop longing for things he had no business wanting—a family, a life without war and the taste of Cwen's mouth.

He drained the cup in a single gulp. 'Keep the sword across your knees. Sit over there as it will give you the clearest view. Scream if you see any movement at all.'

She sat down with the sword awkwardly placed on her lap. 'Like this?'

'You need to learn to defend yourself,'

Thrand said, closing his eyes. At last a way to repay the debt he owed her. He could ensure she knew how to defend herself. 'We begin tomorrow at first light.'

'And you won't make it easy for me? Make concessions?'

Thrand opened his eyes. 'Why would I?'

'My husband used to make things easy for me…even when I told him that I may be a lady, but I wasn't a child.'

The orange light from the sunset highlighted her height and the slenderness of her build. She certainly did not look the type, but she was tough, far tougher than he had first imagined. His eyes grew heavy. Already his mind was slipping back to Iceland and its possibilities. Somehow Cwen and Iceland were connected in his mind, but he couldn't figure out how or why.

'Your husband probably would have bet against you walking all that way on the day we met.'

'He would never have allowed me to attempt it.' She gave a laugh. 'For too long I have depended on other people. I want to stand on my own two feet. I've finished cowering. I'm tired of feeling helpless and dead inside because of something which I could not stop. You're right—some parts of your destiny you can't change.'

'Knowing the difference can be difficult.'

'Thank you for saying you will teach me how to use a sword. We're friends now.'

He raised himself up on his elbow and fought against the wave of tiredness. Friends. He wanted her friendship. He wanted to see her come back to life and not be one of the walking dead. And it scared him. 'I've never been friends with a woman before.'

She spun back around. 'And I want to learn to ride. Properly. Aefirth never allowed me to do that either. How hard can it be? I managed to stay on today without falling off. A start, yes?'

Thrand released his breath. The dispassionate part of his mind told him that he should be rejoicing. She was going to do what he wanted. He was finally going to be able to destroy the person who had been involved in his family's slaughter. He would fulfil his oath to his father. And if it meant her death…he'd lose a friend. It bothered him that she had become important to him and that his desire for her showed no signs of abating.

'Most people are afraid of me and my horse,' he said, not bothering to hide his bitterness. All the women who had shied away from him crowded his mind. All the whispers which followed him throughout the years. 'Why not you?'

He had to lance this hope before it started. He'd seen too many men lose their focus over a woman. He needed to keep his mind on what was important—revenging his family. He pressed his lips together and struggled to ignore the pain in his heart.

She stood and turned away from him. The curve of her neck highlighted her vulnerability, but also hinted at her strong backbone. 'What do they fear?'

'They fear my reputation,' he explained as gently as he could.

She stared directly back at him. Her tongue wet her lips, turning them a dusky pink in the sunset. 'I stopped being afraid and became your friend.'

He caught her hand and brought her knuckles to his mouth. A simple touch which nearly undid him. He could understand why her husband had wanted to keep her safe. Trouble was, if he was going to honour his pledge to his parents, he was going to have to risk losing her. 'Stay that way.'

Cwenneth sat with the heavy broadsword balanced on her knees. The night was far too cold. She brought her cloak tighter around her body and tried to watch for anyone who might harm them. Enemies. Even Northumbrians who might have once been her friends, but who would not be friendly to Thrand.

The irony stuck in her throat. Thrand had become more than a temporary ally. He thought enough of her to give her the first watch and he was going to teach her how to use the sword in the morning. Aefirth would never have done that. He preferred to keep her...as a child. Cwenneth frowned, hating the disloyal thought. But it was true and she had fought bitterly with Aefirth about it, before he had left the final time. But she had discovered that she liked being treated like an adult, like an equal.

Never again would she allow her brother or anyone else to bully her. Or proclaim it was for her own good.

Her teeth chattered slightly. She looked over to where Thrand lay, seeming sound asleep. She ran her hands up and down her arms and stamped her feet. The sword started to tumble off her lap, but she grabbed it before it hit the ground.

One of his eyes opened. 'Come here.'

'Why?'

'You are cold and don't deny it. The sound

of your teeth woke me up. The last thing I want is for you to catch a chill.'

'I'm fine, and you should be asleep. I'm taking the first watch.'

'Be sensible, Cwen. How can I sleep if you are making that noise?'

'Fine.' She picked the sword up and brought it over to him. 'Do you truly think I can learn to use a sword? Properly?'

'You can do anything, if you set your mind to it.'

She blinked. 'How...how do you know that?'

'You are the woman who walked.' He took the sword from her and indicated where he had been lying. 'My turn to stand guard. Close your eyes and sleep.'

She snuggled down into the warm spot. Her limbs immediately stopped shaking. She faked a yawn to keep from asking him to hold her. 'I hadn't realised that I was so tired.'

He put his cloak over her. His spicy scent wafted up, holding her. Cwenneth's blood thrummed. She concentrated on breathing steadily, refusing to beg. If he wanted to touch her, he would have done so. They were friends, not lovers.

'Do you have someone waiting for you in Jorvik?' she asked. 'Some woman?'

'There is no one. I travel alone. I live alone. Always.'

'You are travelling with me now.'

'Only through necessity.' He cleared his throat. 'You will be returned to Lingwold after you give your testimony. But my house is fine enough for any lady.'

Cwenneth balled her fists. 'I was just curious.'

'Less curiosity, more sleep.'

'And if I can't sleep?'

'Watch the stars. It is what I plan on doing.'

Thrand watched her in the grey light, intensely aware of her every move, fighting the urge to gather her into his arms. His body throbbed to the point of agony. Deep within his soul he knew he was the wrong man for her.

If he seduced her out here, it would lead to complications. She was not the sort of woman you bedded and walked away from. He had not really understood what his father had been saying about Ingrid until now—there were women you wanted to spend a few hours with and others who deserved to have a man's entire life. Cwenneth deserved eternity, but he had no room in his life for such a woman. His entire life was war and killing.

He reached out and smoothed her cropped

hair. She gave a soft sigh and turned towards him, her lips gently parted, eyes firmly closed.

It was going to be hard enough to forget her when the time came as it was.

'What are you doing to me, Cwen?' he asked. 'I need to remember who I am and what I want in this life.'

'You want to start teaching me how? Lifting the sword over my head?' Cwenneth asked. She had woken up to Thrand on the other side of their camp, full of plans of how he could teach her to use the sword, rather than holding her as he had in her dream.

She was instantly glad that she hadn't begged him to hold her last night when she was so cold. He had made it very clear: they were companions. He wasn't interested. Aefirth had taught her not to be bold and not demand. A man liked to be the pursuer, not the pursued.

'Is there a problem, Cwen?' Thrand said, coming over to where she stood. 'You have been standing there for a long time, looking at the sword. You would have been cut down a dozen times over. In order to fight, you need to be able to lift the sword. Concentrate on lifting with your stomach.'

'Is there anything lighter?' she asked as she

lifted it gingerly in front of her. The sword slipped from her grasp and fell to the ground with clunk.

'You can lift this one if you concentrate.' Thrand gave her an intent look. 'You are capable of more than you think. Lift it over your head while I count to ten. One last try before we go.'

Capable. Thrand believed she could do it. She spat on her hands and redoubled her efforts. This time, she lifted the sword above her head.

Sweat pooled on her forehead and the back of her neck, but she kept her arms straight. All of her muscles screamed, and she wondered if she could hold it for more than a count of five.

Slowly, Thrand counted to thirty. Each number seemed to take longer than the last. 'You may let go now. Try not to drop it, but let it down slowly. Controlled. You can do this, Cwen.'

Rather than dropping the sword as her muscles screamed they wanted to do, Cwenneth forced her arms to relax and placed the sword at her feet. 'I did it. For a count of thirty. You said I could do it and I didn't believe it. But I really did it.'

His eyes reminded her of the summer sky. 'That I did. You will be able to use a sword in

next to no time. Your arms will get stronger.
But you have to be able to use a sword like
mine. You never know what might be to hand
when the time comes.'

'Perhaps we can use something lighter until
my arms get strong enough.' She swung her
arms, trying to get the feeling back. 'Standing there with a sword over my head as
Hagal's men attempt to cut me down won't do
me much good.'

Myriad blue lights danced in his eyes. Cwenneth sucked in her breath. When his face was
relaxed, he was so handsome. She banished the
thought. The last thing she wanted to spoil was
this new-found ease with him.

'I doubt I've ever met a woman as determined as you,' he said, returning the sword to
its sheath. 'We'll make a legend of you yet.'

'For too long, I have let other people take
charge and have been content to hide if trouble
came.' She made a stabbing motion with her
hand, banishing all thoughts of his looks and
the shape of his mouth. 'I have no wish to be a
lamb to Hagal's slaughter. If that makes me legendary, I will take it. Is the lesson over with?'

His gaze darkened. 'We start with a stick.
When you are practising, you don't want to
injure the person so you use wooden swords.'

Something in his tone made her pause. 'Did you ever hurt anyone in practise?'

'I didn't start with the intention of hurting him. He was the one who chose to use real blades. He thought to end my life.'

'Were you an experienced warrior?'

'No. It was only a few months after my parents' death. And he sought to make an example of me.' He handed her a stick, ending the conversation. 'Remember to keep it between your body and the other person.'

'I'm not sure.'

He put his hand under her chin and raised her face until he looked deeply into her eyes. 'You can do this, Cwen.'

Her breath stopped in her throat. Her heart started to beat wildly. 'I want to, but I'm not sure I'm holding it right.'

He adjusted her grip with a cool impersonal touch. She forgot how to breathe. Did he know how much he affected her? She swallowed hard and concentrated on the stick.

'Do your worst, shield maiden. See if you can land a blow on my body.'

'Shield maiden?'

'Occasionally women fight with us for one reason or another. They are called shield maidens. The best of them become Odin's Valkyries.'

She moved her stick upwards, and he easily blocked it. The impact shuddered through her arm. Cwenneth redoubled her efforts, but each time he easily blocked the move. A bird started singing right behind her, making her jump and breaking her concentration.

Thrand's stick hit hers and sent it spinning out of her hand.

'How did you do that?'

'You left yourself open. First rule of swordplay is never to be distracted. Block everything out except for your opponent and where his sword is moving.'

'That must be impossible.'

'You have to do it in order to be any good. Concentration grows as you get better.' His eyes softened. 'With practice, you can be aware of other things but your main focus has to be on where that next move is going to come from. A heartbeat's lapse is all that stands between life and death.'

'What should I be doing? How can I improve?' Cwenneth put her hands on her knees.

His brow knitted. 'My father used to say that it just happened, but my mother suggested that I empty my mind and concentrate on my opponent's shoulder. Where the shoulder goes, the arm must surely follow.'

'Was your mother a shield maiden?'

'Her mother had been, but my mother had different skills.' His mouth took on a bitter twist. 'Neither my father nor my grandfather considered the skill necessary.'

'And all the Norsemen have this focus?' she asked, wanting to learn more about his family. 'Or is it something unique to your family?'

'Sven used to swear that Hagal lacked concentration, but he has won far too many bouts.' Thrand's full lips turned up in a reflective smile. 'Sven liked to talk nonsense after he had taken ale.'

'And Hagal has always avoided fighting you.'

'Despite my challenges, he has found reasons to decline.'

'Are you ready to try again?' Cwenneth lifted the stick, watched his shoulder and blocked the downward thrust of his stick. Once. Twice. Three times. With each successful block, her confidence grew and she noticed that Thrand made it more difficult.

Sweat gathered on her brow. She glanced at Thrand. A faint sheen of sweat glistened on his forehead. 'We should stop. We need to travel today and you are injured despite what you think. Someone needs to be sensible.'

He caught her sleeve. Her entire body tingled with an awareness of him. Her lips ached to be kissed.

'I am not used to being looked after,' he said finally, making no any attempt to capture her mouth and moving away from her. 'War is all I know, Cwen. It is all I will ever know.'

Cwenneth's heart felt an odd pang. His eyes were so sad when he said it. 'You must know about other things like planting crops and keeping livestock.'

'The last time I helped with the sheep, I was fourteen. My father sent me up to the meadows for the summer.' He gave a half smile. 'It was the last peaceful summer I knew. When I returned, the problems began.'

'Did you give up singing and dancing as well?'

'I can feast with the best of them, but I don't want you harbouring any illusions.'

'Why would I harbour illusions about you? Your reputation is well known.'

He caught her sleeve and pinned her to the spot. 'You're right. You are more dangerous. Hagal has underestimated you. We will win, Cwen.'

In winning, she was going to lose him. What they had right now, the ease between them, was temporary. Cwenneth pressed her aching lips together. It was wrong that she wanted more. 'We need to get to Corbridge and fulfil your vow before we can destroy Hagal.'

If she told her heart enough times, maybe she'd stop thinking that there had to be another way.

Chapter Nine

'This is as good a place as any for the night,' Thrand said, gesturing to a small cave in a hillside. In the distance, Cwenneth could hear the faint gurgle of water.

They had not encountered anyone, and Cwenneth felt more hopeful that they would reach their destination without any trouble. Surely Hagal would not risk sending his men this far into Bernicia.

'Shelter and water. What more could a woman ask for?'

'I'm pleased you approve.' Thrand slid off Myrkr.

Cwenneth had noticed that today he had kept his body from touching hers as they rode. Whenever he could, he found reasons to walk.

The ease of this morning's sword lesson had vanished and Thrand seemed preoccupied, answering her questions in as few words as possible.

'If you can gather some firewood, I will go and fetch the water.' Thrand stretched. 'I could do with a wash and Myrkr a drink.'

Cwenneth froze—half on and half off Myrkr, the image of Thrand's naked skin gleaming wet imprinted on her brain. She forced her feet down, nearly tripping.

'Do you have a problem with that?' he asked, taking the pack and Myrkr's saddle from the horse.

'No, no problem. I am perfectly capable of tending to Myrkr. We have reached an understanding.'

Cwenneth carefully set the pack and saddle inside the mouth of the cave before she went about finding some firewood. Anything to keep from finding an excuse to check on Thrand and see if he was truly bathing. He had made it very clear that he did not think of her in that way. They were friends, not lovers.

When would she learn that he wasn't interested in her, not in the way she wanted him to be?

He probably saw her as a skinny stick of a thing with very little sex appeal, the same as her sister-in-law's assessment of her charms right before she departed from Lingwold. And since then he had been careful not to touch her. She had thought he might kiss her when he taught her this morning how to use the sword, but he hadn't. And she refused to be pathetic and beg. Men disliked pushy women. Aefirth had told her that enough times, but her mind kept whispering that Thrand was not Aefirth.

She gave a wry smile. Only a few days ago, she had worried that he might force her, now she worried that he wasn't touching her. She was being ridiculous.

'Come on, Cwenneth, stop stalling,' she muttered. 'You need to find dry wood, instead of dissecting what Thrand might or might not feel for you. Maybe if you are lucky, he will catch some fish and you can have a hot meal instead of the hard bread.'

She gathered three more armloads of firewood and started to lay a fire in the entrance to the cave.

There was a distinct rustling inside.

'Thrand?' she said. 'That took you much less time than I thought it would.'

The rustling stopped, but there was no answer.

From somewhere behind her, she heard

a snatch of song in Thrand's off-key voice. Thrand was clearly still at the stream.

Cwenneth pinched the bridge of her nose. Whoever was inside wasn't Thrand and they could easily take Thrand's sword and the gold before she returned from fetching him.

'Come out right now!' she called. 'We mean no harm, but we will not let you rob us blind.'

She waited in the afternoon sun. The only response was more rustling.

Her hand gripped the knife she now always wore in her belt. There wasn't time to wait for Thrand. She had to act.

'Stop being a coward,' she muttered. 'Whoever it is, he doesn't have a horse. You just need to keep him there until Thrand arrives.'

A large owl flew out, beating its wings against her face. Cwenneth screamed. The owl did not stop, but kept on going, flying high into the sky.

She sank down on the ground outside the hut and started to laugh. An owl. She had been frightened of an owl.

'What do you think you are playing at, screaming like that? You could have let half the countryside know where we are.' Thrand towered over her, the thoroughly enraged warrior. His hair gleamed dark gold in the sunlight and a few drops of water from his bath in the stream clung to the strong column of his throat. Enraged, but still breathtaking.

Silently, she cursed her attraction to him. She smoothed her skirt down so her limbs were covered before twisting over.

'What is your explanation for this?'

'I heard a noise and thought someone might be trying to rob us. But it was an owl, only an owl.' Cwenneth rose and tried to brush the dirt off her skirt. She concentrated on the blossom on the nearest plum tree. 'I overreacted.'

'What did you intend to do with that knife?'

'I was going to make sure whoever it was did not run off with our gear. All I had to do was to keep them in the cave.'

'You should have come for me first when you suspected something.'

'I wasn't going to lose our things.'

'I forbid it.'

Cwenneth blinked twice. 'You forbid?'

'Next time, you get me before you attempt anything foolhardy. Your life is too valuable. After we are finished, you can do what you like, but until then you obey me.'

'I finished with being a cosseted lady, Thrand, when Narfi murdered everyone in my party. It is why you are teaching me to use a sword. I can defend myself.'

He stepped closer to her. She knew if she reached out a hand, she would encounter his broad chest. 'Most people think twice about provoking me, Cwen.'

'I am not most people.' She made the mistake of glancing up into his dark forbidding face. It could have been carved from stone, but she saw something more in his eyes. Concern? Caring? It was gone so quickly she couldn't tell. 'Your temper doesn't bother me. Shouting and standing there with clenched fists will do nothing.'

'Cwen!'

'I deemed it necessary. Time was running out. I acted.' She ran her hands through her hair, plucking bits of grass out. So much for looking desirable or attractive—she undoubtedly looked a mess. 'You were having a wash.'

'Overconfidence can kill.'

'So can sitting around and waiting to be rescued.'

He grabbed her arm. The touch sent a warm tingle coursing through her. She slipped out of his grasp and glared at him.

'The key to this exercise is to stay alive, not go confronting anyone,' he continued in a quieter tone.

'I confronted an owl!'

She glared back him. His angry face was inches away from her. Their breath interlaced and a warm curl started in the middle of her stomach. Every particle of her was aware of this man.

'Do not do it again!' he said, giving her shoulders a little shake. 'You could have been hurt.'

'Or what?' she asked, her heart beginning to race. 'What will you do?'

She moistened her lips with her tongue. She knew she was playing with fire, but it was also hugely exciting. The last time he had been un- balanced, he had kissed her. And she wanted him to kiss her. Badly. She advanced towards him, but he retreated until his back was against the side of the cave.

'Cwenneth!' The word was torn from his throat as he stood rigid. The muscles on either side of his neck bulged. 'You go too far.'

'Thrand, I haven't gone far enough,' she whispered, not moving away from him and lift- ing her mouth towards him. 'That is part of the trouble. I need to go further. I am strong and it is time I started acting like it. Or else I might as well have died in the slaughter. I'm tired of waiting, Thrand. I want you.'

'You don't know what you are asking.'

'I do know. I want to feel alive, Thrand. Make me feel alive.'

With a long groan, he lowered his mouth to hers. The kiss was savage in its ferocity, demanding and taking. She returned the kiss, looping her arms about his neck and pulling him closer. This time she was not taking any chances that he might pull away. She wanted to see what would happen when the kiss ended.

She could not remember if Aefirth had ever kissed her this passionately. There was something about the wildness of the kiss that called to a dark place deep within her soul—utterly new and unexplored. What was more—she wanted to be kissed like this, like he was branding her with his mouth and stamping his possession on her.

Their tongues met, tangled and teased. With each passing heartbeat she knew one kiss would be too little. She needed more, much more.

His hands came about her body and pulled her close. She felt every inch of his hard, muscular body. He wanted her. A bubble of happiness infused her. After what happened she had been worried that he had no desire for her, but he had, and she intended to use it to assuage the heat which had built up inside her.

She tightened her grip on his neck and tilted her pelvis towards his as her tongue delved deeper into his mouth. His hands slid down her back to cup her bottom and hold her there, unmoving against the hardest part of him. She wriggled slightly, feeling him press against the apex of her thighs and knowing she needed more.

His tongue slid round and round in her mouth, gently pulling and tugging. Warm and wet. What had been a curl of heat in the pit of her stomach grew to a wildfire in the space of a few breaths.

She found it difficult to remember when she had felt this alive. Her whole word had come down to this man. And she knew she needed more than a simple kiss. She wanted to feel his skin against hers. She wanted to feel alive. His tongue drove deeper into her. She pressed her body closer and felt his arousal meet the apex of her thighs. She rocked against him.

'You are playing with fire,' he murmured against her lips as his hips drove against her again.

She answered him by arching towards him, allowing her breasts to brush against his chest. 'I'm a grown woman. I know what I am doing.'

He groaned in the back of his throat and

switched their positions so that her back was against the wall as his hands roamed over her body, cupping her breasts and teasing her nipples to hardened points. First over her gown and then, after he tugged slightly, slipping inside the cloth and touching her bare skin.

The ache within her grew.

His mouth nuzzled her neck as his hands played. Hard-working hands sliding over the smooth skin, pulling and squeezing. Each fresh touch sent a wave of fierce heat through her, melting the ice which had encased her since Aefirth's death, leaving her molten and quivering, but alive. Oh, so alive.

Giving in to instinct, she tugged at his trousers and encountered the hardened length of him. Hot, but silk-like smooth. She closed her fist around him and felt him, knew she needed more. She wanted him in her, giving her the release she knew her body craved.

'Please.'

His mouth returned to hers as he moved her skirts, picked her up and settled her on him, driving in deep.

Her body welcomed him in. Fire meeting fire. Hot and fierce. She tightened her legs about him, held him within her as he drove deeper.

Their cries intermingled.

Slowly, slowly, she came back to earth. She touched his face. Droplets of water still clung to his hair. Tiny diamonds shining in the light.

He withdrew from her and pulled up his trousers. Her skirts fell about her limbs.

'Say something, Thrand. Tell me what you are thinking.'

'That should not have happened. I didn't mean for it…Cwen, did I hurt you?'

'Why not?' Her hands went to her top and automatically began to readjust it. 'What was wrong with it?'

'Nothing was wrong.'

'Then what is the problem?' Her heart drummed so fast in her chest that she thought he must hear.

'Because,' he said, putting his hands on her shoulders and pinning her to the spot, 'someone has to be sensible. I have no idea what you want, what you expect from this.'

'I wanted you to do this. I was a willing participant.' She put her hand on her hip. 'You might have the courtesy to say you enjoyed it.'

He ran his hand through his hair. 'That goes without saying. You were… You are amazing. Cwen, I always get these things wrong.'

She breathed easier. He did want her, but for

some reason he was treating her like she was
a fragile object. Or a lady with marriage pros-
pects. She drew in her breath sharply. That was
it. Her heart expanded a little. He still thought
of her as someone who mattered. The truth was
that she didn't. Not to her brother and certainly
not to Hagal. The only person she had to worry
about pleasing was herself.

'We are both adults, Thrand. Not every
coupling ends in marriage. I'd have to be very
stupid if I remained in ignorance about that.
What is between us…it is about the here and
now, not some far-off future. I'm asking for no
more than today. This afternoon.' She forced a
crooked smile. 'The last man who wanted me
for a bride wanted to kill me. The whole experience has made me question the value of
marriage.'

He groaned in the back of his throat. 'Don't
do this to me, Cwen. I am trying to give you a
choice. My self-control is in tatters where you
are concerned. If I lose it, I may lose you.'

'Why?'

'I may frighten you. I have frightened women
in the past. I may mark you without meaning
to. Other women have complained about me
being more interested in war than them. I am
not good at making small talk about gowns and

210 Saved by the Viking Warrior

hairstyles. I get bored at feasts. I like blood-soaked sagas rather than the romances which have the women sighing. And...and I value your friendship.'

Relief flooded through her. He was trying to protect her and worried about appearing less than a hero in her eyes, rather than not desiring her. She hated the unknown women who had made him like this.

'You found my touch unpleasant? My kiss distasteful?' She pretended to consider the possibility before running her hand boldly down his front. 'Is this why you are so hard again? So quickly? I have only known my husband and he was a great deal older than you, but he was never aroused like this after we made love.'

Her breath caught at her audacity. Proof if ever she needed it that she had changed. She would never have dreamt of touching Aefirth like this, but it felt right with Thrand. With Thrand she could be who she wanted to be. She allowed her hand to linger for a heartbeat.

'Cwen...' he said, standing completely still.

'I believe your body, not your mouth.'

'I can't make you any promises. I...I have seen women turn away from me before. I don't want to hurt you, Cwen, but if you only mean to tease, tell me now and neither of us will get hurt.'

'Who hurt you, Thrand? Who made you doubt all women?'

'Her name means nothing.'

'It means something to you.'

'Ingrid,' he admitted. 'She made me all sorts of promises when I was young. That summer before my world changed. I had slipped out to meet her that day my parents were killed.'

'Go on. Tell me the whole story. I want to know.' Cwenneth hated how her mouth went dry.

'There is little to tell. It was a young man's lust. I refused to listen to my father's commands or my mother's entreaties. I wanted to marry her. I thought we had something special. I went to where we were supposed to meet, intending to ask her, but was met by Hagal's friends. They beat me and left me for dead. But not before Ingrid had told me the truth. Rather than thinking I was the love of her life, I was a monster in the making. Ingrid had used me to get back at Hagal because she knew he feared my prowess at fighting. He had seen it as an opportunity to ruin my family.'

'Did you love her?'

'I thought I did.'

'What happened to her?'

'I found her hanging in the barn where we were supposed to meet. The day after my parents' funeral. There have been other women, but…always war called to me. I needed to fight.'

Cwenneth struggled to hang on to her temper. Suddenly she knew what Thrand was doing and why. 'I'd walk away from you now, but that is what you want me to do. And I am in no mood to oblige you.' She put her hand on his chest and grasped his shirt. 'I'm staying. I want to explore this thing between you and me if you are willing. Not a wild windswept passion, up against a tree, but something where we both take our time and enjoy it. I'm a widow, not some blushing maid. Pretending this attraction between us isn't there won't make it go away.'

'I have no room in my life for anything but my work.'

She closed her eyes and knew what he was saying—purely the physical, no pretence towards finer emotions. She needed to feel his hands and mouth on her. She wanted to feel alive in the way that his kisses made her feel. She couldn't remember feeling this alive ever.

'There are no promises in life,' she whispered, putting her fingers over his lips and gathering her courage. Doubts were for the woman she used to be. 'If anything, the last few days have taught me that. And I have not seen a monster. I have seen a very brave man who risked his life to save others, including me.'

'You talk too much.' His mouth descended and drank from hers, long and hard, sending pulses skittering through her body. And she knew that her passion was definitely not spent.

She tore her lips from his. 'This time, we should be more comfortable.'

He ran his hand down her back, sending a wave of fire coursing through her. 'A woman with authority. I like that.'

'That is good. I have discovered that I like being independent. It means I can do this without having to wait.'

She captured his face between her hands. In the afternoon sunlight his eyes had become deep pools of blue.

'Why did you think you had to wait?'

'My husband…' She shook her head. 'You bring your ghosts, Thrand, and I bring mine.'

'Hush. A woman who participates makes it more interesting than a woman who lies there, hoping it will be all be over.'

Slowly, she brought his face down to hers,

taking her time and tracing the outline of his lips with her tongue. 'Good to know.'

'You smell of grass and sunshine,' he murmured against her hair.

'Here I thought I might smell of horse.'

'Always the practical one.' He lifted her chin. 'We can take a bath together…later. There is a pond. I left Myrkr tethered there…'

She raised his hand to her lips. 'Later. He can enjoy the grass.'

He ran his hand down her back, stopping to cup her bottom. 'You appear to be overdressed. I have longed to see what you look like unclothed, but…'

'My choice?'

'Precisely. You do have a choice, Cwen. I want you to enjoy this.'

She stared at him. No one had ever seen her naked. Not even Aefirth. They had been very conventional in their lovemaking and she had always waited for him in her bed. She had never shed her clothes in front of any man, let alone shedding them in the sunlight, but Thrand was very different from Aefirth.

Cwenneth assessed Thrand under her lashes. He was asking, and she knew she did want him to see her naked. She wanted this relationship to be different. She wanted to be the new Cwen, rather than the old restricted Cwenneth. 'Undress me.'

'My pleasure.' He slowly undid the laces of her gown, loosening it, then raising it above her head. Then he took off her under-garments.

She stood in the mouth of the cave, naked with the afternoon sunlight warming her shoulders and back. She crossed her arms over her breasts and hid her puckering nipples.

'You should not be shy.' He ran his hands lightly along her arms. 'Far better than my imagination.'

'Do you mean that?'

'I lied.' A smile split his face. 'Much, much better than my imagination.'

For such a large man, his touch was incredibly gentle. He made her feel cherished. Her insides twisted. Cherished as if he actually cared about her.

'Now you,' she said, pushing away the thought. Finer feelings were unwelcome. Purely physical was what she had agreed to.

She undid his shirt and lifted it above his head, exposing his golden flesh. The linen bandage stood out from his smooth skin.

She reached out and touched his shoulder, mimicking his move, exploring the contours of his skin. With Aefirth, she had always been the passive one, waiting for him to be the first as she thought a proper wife should. But with Thrand those considerations counted for nothing. There were no rules or customs. She was free to do as she chose.

She wanted to touch him and be an equal participant. She wanted to explore every muscle and sinew of his body. She wanted to feel him moving inside her again.

She let her hand explore the line of hair which ran down to his groin.

He groaned in the back of his throat and pulled her to him. 'Slow this time. If you go further, it will be the same as last time and I want to give you pleasure.'

'I liked it fast and furious.'

'Then you will like it even slower.'

Their bodies collided, skin touching skin, and he drank deeply from her mouth as his hands roamed freely over her back. Gently, he lowered her to the cloaks he'd quickly arranged on the ground. For a brief heartbeat he loomed over her, but she reached up with a hand and pulled him down beside her.

She tangled her fingers in his shoulder-length hair, pulling his face to hers, reclaiming his lips and probing the depths of his mouth with her tongue.

He moved his mouth down the column of her throat, nibbling and tasting, sending fresh licks of fire coursing throughout her body. She tried to tell her heart that he was vastly experienced and knew how to play a woman's body the way a bard would pluck a tune from a lute. But her heart refused to believe it. There was something more, something which had been missing from her couplings with Aefirth.

His fingers captured one of her breasts and rolled the nipple between his thumb and forefinger. A gasp burst from her mouth.

'You like?' he rasped in her ear as he played with her nipples, pulling and stretching them.

She tugged at his shoulders, needing him inside her again. 'Please...Thrand.'

'I want to make it good for you. Please allow me to do this. I want to show you how good slow can be.'

She gave a nod. His mouth went lower, following the trail his fingers had blazed. He captured first one nipple and then the other, making swirling patterns with his tongue and licking them into hard pointed peaks while his fingers played between her folds, sliding in and out of her, making her warm, wet and needy.

Her body bucked upwards as wave after wave of pleasure rolled through her until she thought she could stand no more, but also knowing she had to have more. She wanted the ultimate release.

She tugged once again at his shoulders, needing to feel him inside her. This time he relented and settled himself between her legs, driving forward. She opened her thighs and welcomed him in, feeling her body expand to take the length of him.

They lay there for a timeless moment, joined, and then she began to move her hips, giving into the ageless rhythm.

He responded and they were swept together on the crest of a wave.

Much later, Thrand came back to earth and regarded the woman now sleeping in his arms. She had given herself to him unstintingly. Twice. Once fast and furious up against the side of the cave and the other slow, an exploration of their bodies and how they could move in time with each other. Even now, his body hardened at the mere thought of having her again. He wanted to experience all her possibilities. Amazing. He frowned, unable to remember if he had ever felt this way before with a woman whom he barely knew.

He ran his hand over her short hair. For the

first time in a long time, he felt at peace, as if the hungry wolf inside him had become tame and no longer looked for revenge. He remembered how his mother used to caution his father against revenge and where it would lead. She used to say that there were other ways of punishing a man. He'd never been able to think of one, but now he wondered. Could there be?

'What have you done to me, Cwen?' he whispered softly. 'I want to believe in a future which holds only peace. I have stopped only having hate in my heart. Do you know how impossible that is for me? My family needs to be honoured. Fighting is my life. I lose my edge and I lose everything.'

The soft sound of her sleeping was the only reply.

He made a face. It was dangerous to hope or to think beyond the next day. Battle and war kept him alive. He'd seen good men die because they lost their concentration. And Cwen wanted to return to her former life. She didn't want his sort of life.

When his revenge was complete and his time of battle done, then he could think about acquiring a family. Until then he travelled light. What was the point in complications and roots when the ghosts of his father and mother still begged him to do the right thing? And the right thing had to be killing Hagal. A life for a life.

He hated how his insides twisted. He wanted to be worthy of her and protect her for ever, but he knew what he was like and what lurked inside him. How everyone he'd ever loved had ended up dead because of his actions. He envied Sven's simple solution of starting again. Cwen would need another reason than just him.

Cwen said that she saw good in him, but there was also the warrior who killed and the boy who had failed his parents. She needed someone better than he was or could ever be.

'I'm sorry,' he whispered. He gently removed her head from the crook of his shoulder and slid out.

Cwenneth woke to an empty cave and a cloak covering her nakedness.

'Thrand?' she called out. 'Is there a problem?'

'Getting things ready to leave,' came the answer from outside. 'We need to go, Cwen. Sooner rather than later. Time is slipping from our fingers. There is a full moon tonight. We can start once it rises.'

She gulped hard. They were going. He had slaked his pleasure and now he was ready to go. What had passed between them was in the past. Had she expected anything different? He was a Norse warrior.

'I thought we were staying the night. Or was that just pillow talk?'

'Instinct.' His bulk appeared in the mouth of the cave, but the shadows made it impossible to see his face. 'If I ignore it, we are both dead. It served us well in the hut.'

She wished he would come over and touch her. Was he disappointed in what had passed between them?

A tiny knot started in the pit of her stomach. She had made a fatal mistake and had started caring about a Norse warrior, the sworn enemy of her family. In his arms, she had dared to dream that they might make a more lasting alliance. Funny how the dreams went when she woke.

'Do you regret what happened?' she asked before her courage utterly failed her. 'Be honest with me, rather than feeding me some lie about following your instinct.'

His eyes widened. 'Regret? How could I regret something like that? You were magnificent. Better than that—a healing balm.'

Her breath came a little easier. She had to

follow her instinct and not lose her temper. Thrand was panicking about something.

'You left me to wake up on my own.'

'I never sleep very much. I went out to watch the stars.' He shrugged. 'I wanted to let you sleep. You needed it. But we have to go. We can cover miles before the sun comes up.'

'The countryside remains still. It is at least another day's journey to the Tyne and your friend's child. We can spend more time to-gether...more time for...' She made a little gesture with her hand.

'I've been thinking. It might be best if we forget this.'

'Why?'

'As pleasant as it was, it should never have happened. You and I. I can't give you what you want.'

Cwen put her hand on her hip. 'How dare you presume to know what I want!'

His voice became cold. 'I've had enough women.'

Cwenneth flinched, but then she clenched her fists. He wanted her to turn away. 'Stars.'

'What?'

'You told me to watch the stars if I couldn't sleep and I have spent most nights watching the stars, willing the sleep to come.'

'What does that have to do with anything?'

'Being in your arms beats watching the stars. I actually slept. It is a start, Thrand. I felt alive, rather than one of the walking dead and I've been one of them for so long.'

She wished his face wasn't in shadow. She wished he'd walk over and take her in his arms. Anything to stop the terrible pounding of her heart. A faint breeze rippled over her skin.

'There is a chance you will survive. A very good chance.'

'Hagal wants me dead. There is no getting around that. He knows I live and made his vow to avenge his cousin's death through mine. I fear closing my eyes. Why watch stars when I can find peace in your arms? I'm asking for no more than that.'

'I'm tired of watching stars as well.' His arm went around her. 'And when we are done, no regrets.'

'No regrets. This is about the here and now.' She put her hand on his cheek. Her insides felt hollow. Her heart had been buried with Aefirth and Richard, hadn't it? What she felt for Thrand was desire, not love, not something lasting and true. When they parted, she would remember the time with fondness, but would live the sort of life she was born to. She would return to being a Northumbrian lady.

She hated that her old life no longer held any attraction.

Chapter Ten

The farmstead stood unobtrusively near the river Tyne. It was not much to look at, but Cwenneth could tell with a brief glance that it was prosperous. The walls were well maintained and the sheep grazing in the meadow looked fat.

'This is where the child is,' she said to break the uncomfortable silence which had grown up between them over the past few miles.

'So I am given to understand,' Thrand replied, pulling Myrkr to a halt.

Without waiting, Cwenneth slid off. They had stopped briefly to sleep beside a stream. Her dreams had featured death and destruction. Only when she woke and had Thrand's arms about her did she relax. It had felt right to wake up in Thrand's arms. But she also knew that the farm marked a turning point. Every mile after this took her closer to her destiny and near-certain death. Was it wrong of her to wish for a reprieve? And to hope that Hagal could self-destruct without her being involved? Did she have to appear in person?

'What is the woman's name?' she asked, trying to stop thinking about the future and her own cowardice.

'Maeri,' Thrand said slowly. 'Sven was wild about her. He wanted to marry her once he found out about the child.'

'What are you going to do?'

'Make sure the child is well looked after. I will make sure Maeri knows that he should be brought up as a proper Norseman and that several men have volunteered to foster him when the time comes. Knui would have formally welcomed him into Sven's family, but I will have to perform the ceremony instead.'

'The child is a boy?' Cwenneth asked.

'The message gave no clue to the sex. It has been passed from Norseman to Norseman.'

Thrand got off the horse and started to walk beside her. Cwenneth noticed how he evenly matched her stride. There was a steady companionship between them now. Her heart clenched. What was between them was temporary. Temporary allies, friends and now lovers.

Believing otherwise was to slide back into the same fool's paradise she'd inhabited when she thought marrying Hagal the Red would bring peace. Even if he wanted to marry her, where would they go?

'How old is the child?' she asked, trying to keep from examining her feelings.

'A year or so, I believe.' Thrand looked straight ahead, watching the curl of smoke from the farmhouse rise in the crystal-blue sky. 'We have been in the south, keeping peace, not the north. It took a while for the message to reach Sven.'

'Then do you know if the child is even alive?' she asked gently. Someone had to say it and prepare Thrand for the worst. The farm appeared peaceful and prosperous. The last thing they would need was a rampaging Norseman bent on destruction simply because something had happened which was beyond everyone's control. Children were fragile blessings. Her hand went instinctively to where her pendant had been.

She shook her head. Why was it so easy to believe this about another's child and not hers?

'Sven wanted to know his child was looked after. He wanted to make it right for the mother and the babe.' He stroked Myrkr's mane. 'We had gone out to wet the babe's head when the fight occurred. He took a knife in the back which was meant for me.'

Cwenneth reached out her hand. It made sense now why Thrand felt such a sense of responsibility towards this child and its mother. Even if he refused to see it, there was much that was good and honourable in him. She would be hard pressed to name other men who would do as much for a fallen comrade. Aefirth possibly; probably not her brother, Edward. 'Sven's death wasn't your fault. You couldn't know. Were you the one who started the fight?'

A muscle jumped in his jaw. 'I finished it. They were drunken fools who objected to Sven looking at their women. But he wasn't the one interested in getting his leg over. I was. I often have a woman when I am in Jorvik. A different one each time. The black-haired woman had been flirting with me. Nothing had been decided. No coin had passed hands.'

'Then you're not to blame for another's fit of temper,' she said, trying to keep her voice light. 'I, for one, am very glad you didn't die. Who would have saved me otherwise?'

She waited for his laugh. His face settled into its old harsh planes.

'Sven had so many plans for the future. He

wanted to go to Iceland and start afresh with his Maeri. He thought they could be free there to live the way he wanted to live. There is land for the asking and no king. Iceland had become an obsession with him. He'd half convinced me that I ought to go, but I've promises to keep.'

'Had he talked about Maeri before he knew about the baby?' Cwenneth enquired gently. Iceland where people could be free had nothing to do with her. Like Thrand, she needed to destroy Hagal. 'The message took a long time to reach him. Surely if he felt deeply about her, he would have gone to see her. He had to have known how babies were created and that there was a possibility.'

'On and off. And it is not that easy. We had a job to do in the south.' Thrand gave a little shrug. 'We used to tease him about it. He nearly had me killed when he left her the last time. He used to say he owed me for saving his life that day, but he was my comrade-in-arms.'

'He sounds like he was a good friend.'

Thrand's face became set in stone. 'He was like the brother I never had. If not for him, I would have lost my life a dozen times over on the battlefield.'

'And how many times would he have lost his life?'

'That is not the point. I failed to save him. And I've killed the man he sent to welcome his child into his family.'

'You're far more of his blood than his cousin could have ever been.' Cwenneth shuddered, remembering the way Knui had talked. 'He would have sold that child for gold.'

'I'll make it right for Maeri. There is enough gold to give her a comfortable life and I have Halfdan's promise that the child can enter the king's service when the time comes, if it is a boy. If it is a girl, a suitable marriage partner will be found.'

'And she will be content with this?'

'She will have to be.' Thrand frowned and a muscle twitched in his jaw.

'What is it, Thrand? What is wrong? You've been worse than a bear with a sore head today.'

'You will help me break the news? I can't stand a woman's tears,' he admitted, running his hand through his hair. 'I'd far rather face a horde of angry Northumbrians armed to the teeth than one woman's tears. And Maeri is a weeper. The way she clung to Sven the last time…'

'I shall have to remember to keep my eyes dry when we part,' Cwen said, forcing a smile. She knew the instant they parted for the last

time, the tears would flow, but she would refuse to cry in front of him. She wasn't going to
stoop to trying to hold him. Allies, friends and
lovers, but they would go their separate ways.

'Cwen!'

She reached out and gave his hand a squeeze.
'I will be at your side, but you'll find the right
words. I have faith.'

He nodded with thinned lips. 'That makes
one of us.'

Thrand fixed the farmer with a hard stare.
He was hiding the woman, or at the very least
knew where she could be found. His refusal
to meet Thrand's eyes and shifting feet gave
him away.

Years of experience collecting Danegeld
from men who wanted to cheat had taught him
to pay attention to the little clues. He would get
there without actually resorting to violence, but
the farmer would understand the consequences
for his continued refusal.

'I wish to speak to Maeri, the woman who
used to work on this farm,' he repeated the
words slowly, taking care to emphasise each
word. 'Fetch her.'

The farmer went red and then white. Thrand

flexed his hand close to the man's face. 'She...
she isn't here. You are wasting your time.'

'Where is she?

The old woman standing behind the farmer
shifted uneasily, but remained silent. Thrand
gave Cwen a helpless glance. He didn't want
to beat the information out of the farmer, but
he had little choice if they continued to defy
him like this. She shook her head and mouthed
no violence.

'Where is her child?' Cwenneth asked, moving between him and the farmer. 'Can you tell
us that much?'

'Aye.' The burly farmer clicked his fingers.
'Fetch Maeri's brat.'

A rat's-tails-for-hair girl raced across the
farmyard towards where the animals were kept.
After a few heartbeats in which the farmer and
his wife looked more and more uncomfortable
under the heat of his glare, the girl emerged
with a little boy dressed in rags and covered
in dirt. His fetid stench wafted towards them.

Thrand frowned. Children should smell of
fresh air and sunshine, not reek of manure.

But he immediately saw a likeness to his old
friend in the boy's nose, chin and hair. He had
the mother's dark brown eyes, but there was a
definite look of Sven about him.

A wave of sorrow passed through Thrand. It should be Sven standing here, viewing his son, not him. His friend lived in his child. Sven would have loved this moment and would have known what to do and how to put this right.

Could he trust these people, including the absent mother, to look after Sven's son?

He dismissed the thought as pure folly. He had done what was right by coming here. And Sven had always proclaimed what a wonderful mother Maeri would be and how she longed for children. Perhaps these people's idea of looking after children was different from his own.

'And the boy's name?' Cwen asked, kneeling down and holding out her hands to the children. 'Come here. There is no need to be afraid. This man knew your father. He is here to make sure you are properly looked after.'

The girl came hesitantly forward, half carrying and half tugging the little boy. Closer, the boy appeared more like a wild animal than a child. 'Pretty lady, is that Aud's father?'

Thrand's heart thudded and he leant forward to hear what Cwen might say about him.

'His father's friend. His father sent him because he was prevented from coming. But he'd intended on coming and claiming the child as his own.'

Thrand's heart twisted. Trust Cwen to come up with the right words. She seemed to possess the knack of it. When the time came, she would say the right words to Halfdan and destroy Hagal for ever. She had to. He couldn't bear the thought that she might die or worse, be under Hagal's control. He pushed the thought away and concentrated on the girl. Focusing on the far-off future was never a good idea.

'His mam's dead, pretty lady,' the girl said with a curtsy. She jerked her head towards the couple and whispered. 'They didn't want to say on account of what he might do. They know his reputation. He wintered in these parts afore like.'

Cwen gave him a warning glance over the boy's head as the news thudded through Thrand's brain. The boy was an orphan. It changed everything and nothing.

He gave Cwen a nod and made a gesture that she should continue with the questioning.

'What is the boy's name?' Cwen asked.

'Maeri called him Aud.' The old woman made a clucking noise in the back of her throat. 'Too unchristian for the priest. We call him Adam when necessary.'

Thrand nodded. Maeri had named him after Sven's father. She'd expected Sven to come back. That was a good sign at least. Once again, he wished that he had taken the knife, instead of Sven. Pure luck. A little voice in his mind whispered *but then he'd never have met Cwen and would never have experienced peace in her arms.* He silenced it. Sven was a good man. He didn't deserve to die in the way he had. And now the proper arrangements for the child had to be made.

'Is there a reason for the child's filth?' he asked, eyeing the child warily. Although he was used to the stench of war, he knew the difference between a battlefield and a farm.

'He sleeps with the pigs,' the girl said, releasing Aud and coming to stand in front of him. Her dress was dirty, there was a smudge on her face and she was far too thin. 'I'm not afraid to tell the truth. He sleeps there because it is the warmest place and he can get a few scraps.'

'Keep quiet,' the old woman scolded. 'Please, sir, Hilde works in the kitchen for the scraps. We took her in as a charity…when…my niece died…' Her voice trailed off at the farmer's look.

'Pigs,' Aud said proudly, lifting his chin and looking in that instant precisely like Sven. 'Pigs. Pigs. Pigs.'

Thrand frowned. Sven's son should not be

sleeping with the pigs. Once his temper would have exploded, but with another warning look from Cwen, he struggled to contain it. Her soft words appeared to be yielding the information required. 'It certainly smells like he has rolled in pig dung.'

'We can clean him up, sir,' the young girl said. 'He is a good boy. Does what he is told most times.'

'Do that!' he ground out. He pointed to the old woman. 'You help. That child smells of manure and rotten food. Children should be clean. They should smell like children, not dung heaps.'

The old woman rushed off, dragging the protesting child with the girl not far behind, chattering about how they were going to bathe and look proper for the Norseman.

Thrand breathed deeply, urging away the feeling that he wanted to tear the farmer limb from limb for treating children like that. 'I wait for an explanation.'

The farmer's colour rose, and he refused to meet Thrand's eye. 'We had given up hope of anyone coming. It has been such a long time since Maeri sent the message.'

'When did she die?' Cwenneth asked, placing herself between Thrand and the farmer as her mind raced. Anyone with half an eye could see the child was neglected. Something had to be done, but Thrand had refused to consider taking the child when they had spoken about it earlier. And she didn't trust the farmer to look after the child or the little girl. But Thrand losing his temper and striking the farmer would inflame things, rather than improve them.

'Two months ago,' the farmer admitted, his cheeks becoming ever redder under Thrand's fierce gaze. 'Maeri died two months ago. Very sudden like.'

'From what?' Cwenneth fixed the farmer with her eye. 'Why did she die? Sickness? An accident?'

'She'd just married.' The farmer tugged at the collar of his shirt as if it was suddenly too tight. 'A good man. It was a good match in the circumstances.'

'What happened?' Cwenneth placed her hand on Thrand's sleeve. He put an arm about her and pulled her close. She laced her hand through his, and he clung to it as a drowning man might cling to a spar.

'She miscarried.' The farmer adopted a pious expression. 'The priest said it was a judgement from God as she'd lived a loose life. There is nothing you can do if someone strays from the path of righteousness.'

Cwenneth longed to crack the priest over the head. It was easy to pontificate and make judgements. Miscarrying a child had nothing to do with piety. Her sister-in-law spent hours on her knees praying and still she had lost two babies. And Cwen had thought she'd been doing God's work when the old woman cursed her and she lost any hope of a baby. It still hurt.

'But this *good* man she married didn't want to look after her child.' Thrand's nostrils flared.

'Can you blame him for returning the child here?' the farmer answered with a shrug. 'He only took Adam because he wanted Maeri. She was a good cook and kept a tidy house. She wouldn't be parted from her son. So after her death, my wife pitied the poor bairn.'

Cwenneth went rigid. *So sorry for him that she allowed him to sleep with the pigs.*

'Did she have any family?' Cwenneth asked when she trusted her voice. 'Did they turn their back on the child as well?'

The farmer shook his head. 'Her parents died a few years ago. Her mother had been my late wife's sister, which is why we took her in. Adam will be a good worker in time.'

'Thrand,' Cwen whispered, tugging at his

sleeve. 'You have to do something. That child will die if you do nothing. If you simply give gold and walk away. There has to be a way of giving him a better future than what he will have here.'

Thrand said nothing, simply looked straight ahead. But his face became ever more thunderous and his fingers clenched even tighter.

'I will leave you two,' the farmer said, flushing red. 'I need to see how the boy is getting on. When he is cleaned up, he is a right bonny lad.'

He scurried off, leaving them alone in the farmyard.

'Before you say anything,' Thrand said, holding up his hand. Every particle of him bristled with anger. 'What you are about to ask is impossible. Keep quiet and we won't fight. We remain friends. I have no wish to quarrel with you over this, Cwen.'

'How do you know what I was going to ask?' Cwenneth tapped her foot on the ground. Thrand had to see that the child needed their help. She refused to leave, knowing the child might die. Somehow, she'd find a way to save that innocent little boy.

'My life doesn't have room for anyone else, let alone a child who is little more than a babe. That child needs a mother.' His jaw jutted out, and his shoulders broadened, making him look every inch the fierce Norse warrior that he was. 'Do I look like a mother? Do I look like the sort of person to wipe his nose or his tears? Or to clean up his sick? Or even make sure he is properly fed?'

Cwenneth's heart thudded, sinking to the pit of her stomach. He didn't want anyone in his life. He wasn't willing to change to save this boy. 'No child.'

'No child. No one else. I've seen the sort of life camp followers and their children lead. What is more, I have seen what happens to them when their warrior dies. I would not wish that on my worst enemy.' He placed his hands on her shoulders, and the harsh lines of his face softened. 'I am a warrior, first, last and always. Have I ever said anything to make you think differently?'

'The war is over. Others are settling. You could ask the king...' Her voice faded as she realised what she had said... Her cheek grew hot under his stare.

'A man such as me? With my reputation? Who would want me for an overlord?' He shook his head. 'Halfdan heaved a sigh of relief when I took gold over lands. I've no desire to have a large estate or be a great lord. Forget it. I know what a snakepit Jorvik politics are. They are nearly as bad as Viken politics. And it was precisely because my father angered powerful lords that Hagal was able to murder with impunity.'

Drawing on years of experience, Cwenneth schooled her features, but in her heart she mourned. Against all logic, she had been hoping that he would say something about her staying with him and perhaps asking the king for Hagal's lands once he had been unmasked as the villain.

'You can't leave him, Thrand Ammundson,' she said around the lump in her throat. 'It would be tantamount to cold-blooded murder of an innocent child. And whatever else you are, you're not a murderer of children.'

His look would have made a lesser woman faint with fear.

She clenched her fists. She had been so stupid asking. It wasn't as if she had asked him to marry her. She understood there were no guarantees in their relationship. It was temporary. But this was not about them, it was about the child. She had to get past the battle-hardened warrior and reach the man who had held her in his arms last night and who had whispered encouraging words when the nightmare had woken her.

She closed her eyes, gathered her thoughts and started again.

'I know what happens to bastards, particularly if the priest has taken against them,' she said slowly. 'That he has survived this long is a testament to his mother and his own robustness.'

'What would you suggest?' he enquired with narrowed glacial eyes. The ice in his voice cut through her heart.

'We could take him to Lingwold.' Cwenneth wrapped her arms about her waist and tried to keep her insides from trembling. That child needed her protection, but she had no power. 'I know the priest there. He will make room for him and will treat him with honour. He is a good man. He will ask few questions. Aud will thrive with enough food and he will get an education.'

'You want me to send Aud to Lingwold with a message—please look after this child?'

She held up her hands and willed him to understand. 'It would save his life. I...I could take him. I would return. I give you my word.'

'No!'

'No?' Anger coursed through her. Even now,

he failed to trust her. 'What is wrong with my idea? Father Aidan will educate him. He has done so with many orphans in the past. They've become monks, useful members of the community.'

'Sven's son is not going to go into a monastery. He hated monasteries and monks.'

Cwenneth rolled her eyes. 'You don't want him to go to a monastery. You won't have him with you and leaving him here is not an option. What do you intend to do with him? How do you intend on honouring your friend?'

Thrand put his hands on either side of his head. 'I know this! Give me time!'

'We have little time! You must decide!'

Their quarrel was interrupted by the farmer returning with Aud in his arms. 'You see the boy can be made to be tidy.'

Aud had been hastily washed and dressed in clean clothes. His damp white-blond hair curled in little ringlets and his big brown eyes made him look like an angel.

'There,' the young girl said with a pleased air as if Aud were her own. 'He cleans up right lovely.'

She too had changed into clean clothes and her hair was neatly brushed.

'Yes, he does,' Cwenneth answered softly,

thinking about Richard and the fresh smell he had always had after his wash. She wanted to smell that again. 'You both look lovely. May I hold him?'

The farmer started to hand him over, but Aud wriggled free and toddled over to Thrand, holding up his arms.

'Up!' he cried.

Cwenneth started forward to take possession of the boy before Thrand rejected him and the wailing started. If Thrand disliked a woman's tears, he'd like a toddler's even less.

However, rather than shying away or pretending he hadn't noticed like Aefirth had once done with Richard, Thrand knelt down so his face was near to the boy's. He stuck out a finger and ran it down Aud's cheek.

'You look remarkably like my friend, your father, Sven, Aud Svenson,' he said in a tender voice. 'With you alive, he lives on. My old friend would be so proud to be your father. He wanted the best for you.'

Aud threw his arms about Thrand, and Thrand hugged him back. Cwenneth bit her lip, wondering if this was the first time any child had ever been that open with the warrior.

'We would like to invite you to eat with us. My man and I discussed it,' the old woman said, coming forward. 'Maeri would have wanted it. She always said that her man would return for her. I feel so guilty now for having pushed her into that marriage. It brought nothing but trouble.'

'We would be delighted,' Cwenneth said quickly before Thrand had a chance to refuse. There had to be a way of giving that little boy a life, but she needed time to think of an idea which Thrand could embrace.

The remains of the simple meal lay on the table. The pottage had not been fancy, but it was nourishing and there was enough for all.

A huge lump rose in Thrand's throat. He found it difficult to remember the last time he had sat down to a supper with ordinary people. The taste of the stew and rough wheat bread brought back memories of sitting down with his parents and eating after a day working in the fields.

Aud sat next to him, seemingly oblivious to the fact that children generally feared him and kept away from him, hiding their faces whenever he approached. Throughout the meal, Aud kept jumping up to get one of his treasures such as a bird's feather or an interesting stone.

With each new offering, Thrand was aware

of his hollow words to Cwen earlier. He couldn't leave the boy and walk away. He, too, knew what Aud's fate would be, even if he left gold—ignored at best and actively abused at worst. Aud would be used like an animal, not treated like the bright boy he was.

A monastery was not going to happen, not for Sven's child. Lingwold would mean he could not maintain contact with the child. Cwen's brother wanted his head on a platter. The battlefield was no place for a child. But he could hardly bring up a child on his own. Where would he leave him when he had to go on the king's business? In Jorvik? Who could he trust?

He slammed his fist against the table. The conversation ceased. Everyone turned toward him with a mixture of apprehension and fear in the farmer and his wife's faces. Cwen's showed mild irritation. Only Aud seemed oblivious to the tension. He jumped up again and toddled off.

'It is all right,' Hilde said with a bright smile. 'He does it because he likes you. He doesn't mean to get you angry.'

'I'm not angry with him,' Thrand mumbled. 'I enjoy his company.'

'Then what is the problem?' Cwen asked, lifting a delicate eyebrow.

Thrand swallowed hard. How could he confess the agony he was going through? After he told her that he didn't want anyone? How could he confess to caring about the boy's future? And caring about her future, but knowing his current life had no room for either?

'Nothing is wrong.' He pushed his trencher away. 'I suddenly missed Sven. He would have liked to meet his son. He liked children. They never hid their faces when he appeared.'

He patted Aud on the head as he returned bearing yet another gift. The boy beamed up at him and handed him another feather. This time from an owl. He released another breath. The boy hadn't shrunk from him despite his thumping of the table.

'For you,' Aud said.

'He likes feathers and birds,' Hilde said helpfully. 'That one was one of his very favourites.'

'I'm sure Thrand will treasure it,' Cwen retorted with a determined look on her face.

Thrand forced a smile, but all the while his heart ached in a way that it hadn't for years. He wanted a different future.

'Aefirth often ignored Richard's offerings,' she said in a low voice as she leant towards him.

'I'm not your late husband.' Thrand carefully tucked the feather in his belt. 'I'm honoured the boy has given it to me.'

Cwen stood and straightened her gown. 'We should leave these people.'

'Leave?'

'They will have chores to do and we have a long way to go.' There was an incredibly sad dignity to her bearing, reminding him of the statues he'd seen in Constantinople. Thrand found it hard to reconcile this closed-off and dignified woman with the vulnerable one he'd watched over last night in case the bad dreams returned, the one who had turned to him with a soft sigh as she nestled her head against his bare chest.

Thrand frowned. He wanted to spend more time with the boy and get to know him. But it also seemed like he had reached a turning point in his life. What he did next had the power to alter his life for good or ill and it frightened him far more than the prospect of facing a horde of angry warriors.

'Please stay,' the farmer's wife choked out. 'It is good to see Adam…Aud so content and happy. He has spent weeks crying for his mother and driving me to distraction. The pigs were the only creatures which stopped his tears.'

'It won't be long before dark,' the farmer said. 'Stay here where it is safe.'

'Only tonight. We can sleep in the barn,' Cwen said, her look challenging him to say differently. 'We will need to be off at first light. Thrand has fulfilled his oath to Sven Audson.'

'We will stay,' Thrand said, touching the feather Aud had given him.

Somehow he'd find a way to solve his dilemma. Fresh air always made him think better, particularly when the sands of time slipped through his fingers. He needed to make the right decision, rather than one he'd regret for the rest of his life. 'Cwen, will you come for a walk around the farmyard with me? I should like to investigate Aud's home and the animals they keep here. Sven would expect that of me.'

She gave a small nod.

He held out his arm. By the end of the walk, he knew he had to have a workable plan for Aud's future.

Chapter Eleven

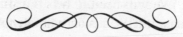

Thrand led Cwen out into the low afternoon light. Together they made a circuit of the farmyard and its buildings. He noticed how he automatically adjusted his pace to suit Cwen's. He could remember how his father had done the same for his mother and how they too had walked about the farm at this time of day.

The sky was beginning to be streaked orange and crimson. A certain peace hung over the place, but Thrand's thoughts kept circling back to his future, one which currently did not hold Aud or even Cwen. The prospect of not having Cwen depressed him, but how could he make her want to stay with him? She'd been very clear on the boundaries of their relationship. A tiny voice nagged that he had forced them on her. He frowned and tried to silence it.

'If he had lived, what was Sven planning on

doing?' Cwenneth asked as they stopped beside the large barn for the second time. 'If Maeri had been free?'

'Does it matter? It is useless to speculate.' The words came out harsher than he'd intended.

She pleated her travel-stained gown with her fingers. 'I suppose not. I was curious. Sven Audson sounds like a man who always had a plan.'

'Iceland. He wanted to take his family to Iceland.' Thrand abruptly let go of her arm.

The lowing of the cattle, mixed with the snuffling of the pigs, took him back to his boyhood. He went into the barn and breathed in the straw-scented air. He shook his head. He had no business remembering that easy time.

The last time he had been in a barn like this one was when Ingrid had led him there. He knew what had happened afterwards and he had avoided them ever since. But now he suddenly realised that he had missed the utter peace and tranquillity that went with them.

'What did he want to go there for? Surely he could have started a new life in Northumbria.' Cwenneth asked, putting her hand in his.

He closed his fingers about hers, grateful that he did not have to explain. She seemed to understand his distress. She led him away from the barn and towards the green pasture. In the distance he could see the blue-grey waters of the Tyne.

'He wanted to leave this place of war and go to a land that had never seen conflict,' he said when he trusted his voice.

Cwen frowned. 'And there is no war in Iceland?'

'A man can be free from his past there, or that was what Sven claimed. He was tired of the political intrigue that surrounds Halfdan now that he is ill. He had no great love or loyalty for any of the rivals. He wanted out.'

'If the other Norsemen are like Hagal, I can understand that sentiment.' Cwen's mouth turned up into a sad smile.

'Halfdan is an excellent warrior. He looks after his men, but the others? They are after their own glory.'

'Why not go back to the north where you all came from if he had made his fortune?'

'He had no wish to return to Viken. I never enquired too closely why he left. We all had our reasons. He wanted a life free from his past where his child could grow up innocent of all feuds.'

She tapped her finger against her mouth, and

her eyes turned thoughtful. 'A life free from your past. Is that something you would want?'

Thrand stopped. His entire being stilled. Iceland! He had been blind. It was the perfect solution. But would she agree? Did he dare ask? He knew what they had agreed, but the more he knew Cwen, the more uncomfortable he was about having her face Halfdan and the pit of snakes which passed for the Storting. Anything could happen, particularly as Hagal had started spreading rumours blaming him for the events.

He wanted to keep her with him, rather than sending her back to Lingwold where she could be used again as a pawn in her brother's quest for power.

'A man can have his reasons,' he said cautiously, trying to think how best to put it without making it seem like he cared for her. 'Thor knows Sven must have had enough. He saw it as a chance for a fresh start and the opportunity to show Maeri the man he could be.'

'Is it a good land?' He detected a slight note of wistfulness in her voice. 'A fertile land where you could grow crops free from…well… free from the threat of war and the necessity of paying Danegeld? It sounds silly. Ever since Aefirth died, I have spent nights standing at the window, longing for such a land. I didn't think it existed.'

'It is a hard land, but it can be good. The valleys are fertile. Trade is good with Norway.' At her questioning glance, he added. 'Sven and I visited it a few summers ago. There are crystal waterfalls and springs which run hot. One of his cousins settled there. Now he tends his sheep and horses instead of risking his life on the eastern trade to Constantinople.'

'It sounds lovely.'

'Would you like to see it?' he asked before he lost his nerve. The meaning of his dream when he woke from the fever suddenly became crystal clear. It was not about dying alone, but living with a family. He could have a family again. He could protect them. He would not repeat his father's mistakes or his own. He could outrun his past. All he had to do was to emigrate with Cwen.

Travelling to Iceland would give him a chance for a new start in a fresh, clean land. He could leave his past behind him just as Sven had planned to. He could stop being a warrior and become a farmer.

'What did you say?' Cwen stopped pleating her gown and stared at him.

'I am willing to take you there. You would

like it, I think. Boats take some getting used to, but the journey is done in stages. You will adjust.'

Her eyes widened as his words sank in. 'You want to take me to Iceland? Why?'

He gathered her hands between his. He had to get the words right. He wanted to put them in such a way that she could not refuse. If she refused, he didn't know what he would do.

He knew she did not want him for ever. She had made that perfectly clear the other day when they had first made love. What woman would? He had too much darkness inside him. But she was a natural mother. He'd seen the longing in her eyes when she held Aud. Once in Iceland, he'd prove to her that he was worthy of her. 'Cwen, come with me. Let's go to Iceland and take Aud with us. Fulfil Sven's dream because he can't. Aud is an innocent child. Why should he have to suffer for something which has nothing to do with him? Are you going to allow Hagal to destroy another life?'

'What are you asking me?' she gasped out.

Thrand took heart from the fact that she didn't attempt to pull away. He tightened his grip about her slender fingers. 'Marry me, Cwen, and provide Aud with a mother. That little boy needs a mother desperately. He needs you.'

Marry him? Thrand wanted to marry her, move to Iceland and put their pasts behind them. He wanted her to go to Iceland with him and be Aud's mother.

Cwenneth stared at the large Norseman standing before her, holding her hands as the giant sky began to darken all around them. The ground tilted under her feet. She forgot how to breathe. She had to have heard wrong. Had that innocent child with his treasures touched his stone-cold heart in a way she couldn't? She'd seen how they were together. It was wrong of her to wish that it had been her.

'Please say something, Cwen. Have you lost your voice?' The raw note in his plea tore at her heart.

'Did you just ask me to marry you?' she whispered finally before he turned away from her and this chance slipped away.

He put an arm about her shoulder, bringing her close to his body. 'Yes. You can be Aud's mother. You saw how he was at dinner. A little care and he will blossom. He has the makings of a fine warrior. Did you see the treasures he kept bringing me at supper?'

'Aud's mother.' She shook her head. It was wrong of her to even offer when she knew she was almost certainly facing death in Jorvik.

'But I'm the wrong woman. I let my child die alone. I should have stayed with him. Aud deserves better. He deserves a mother who will stay with him.'

'Your son died because it was his time. And this boy's mother died also. Are you going to say it was his fault?' Thrand's lip curled. 'The priest implied it was. Maybe you believe it too, but don't wish to say. Do you believe the boy is cursed?'

'Of course not! You are being ridiculous.'

'It is you who are being ridiculous.' He put both hands on her shoulders, and his summer-blue eyes looked deep into her soul. 'You have a great capacity to love, Cwen. You need to lavish it on someone who will appreciate that love rather than waste it.'

Cwenneth broke away from him and pressed her hands to her temples, trying to think around the sudden pain in her heart. Capacity to love and not wasting it. 'Are you saying that I am some sort of lovelorn female who wears her heart on her sleeve, just hoping for any creature to love me back?'

'I am not worthy of your love!' Thrand's words echoed round and round the pasture.

'You think I love you?' White-hot anger coursed through her veins. She couldn't love

Thrand. What they shared was passion. She knew it would end and had planned for it. She had kept her heart out of it. 'Of all the arrogant, pig-headed assumptions! Simply because we have shared passion, I am supposed to love you? Have feelings for you? What utter rubbish!'

'My mistake.' Thrand inclined his head, which once again wore his warrior's mask. 'I thought I had best warn you...in case you agreed to the marriage. What love and finer feeling I had died years ago. It is futile to hope. I don't even know how to begin to care for someone. I've no practice in it. You are right. The women over the years have blurred. I find it hard to put a name or face to one of them. But I know I will always remember you. If you want to call it caring, you can.'

'Why are you telling me this?'

'It is important that I'm honest with you, Cwen, in all things. I wouldn't want to marry you under false pretences. Or have you become disappointed in me. But I know that Aud will never let you down. Like you, he hungers for someone to love.'

Her heart shattered into a thousand pieces, hurting in a way that it hadn't since Richard's death. She had not realised until he said those words how much she did care for Thrand.

Over the past few days, she had come to like him—no, *like* was too mealy-mouthed of a word. She had kept telling herself that it was desire and passion but it was more than that. She admired his courage, his ability to think on his feet and the way he reacted so calmly to each new threat. And how he gave her confidence to try new things. She considered him more than a friend. But what she felt for him was very different from the quiet and uncomplicated love she had had for Aefirth.

Cwenneth drew an unsteady breath and moved away from the comfort of his body. She wrapped her arms about her waist. She had to get this right and understand what he was offering, not be seduced by the nearness of his body. 'You mean after Jorvik and speaking to the king about Hagal. Things have to be done in their proper order, Thrand. It is foolish to speak of such things until then. Aud has already lost one mother.'

The words *if I remain alive and am not returned to Hagal* hung in the air between them.

Thrand's eyebrows drew together. He made a cutting motion with his arm. 'I mean not bothering to speak to the king about Hagal and departing immediately for Iceland to begin a new life. The rumour of the kidnapping will work against you. Hagal would claim I seduced you and a woman's words are not to be trusted. I can see the purpose in his rumour now. He seeks to discredit your testimony. And we have become lovers, Cwen. How could I lie about that?'

Cwenneth closed her eyes. He was right. She should have considered Hagal would seek to blacken Thrand's name once he learnt who had rescued her. He certainly had wasted no time in spreading the rumour that Thrand had kidnapped her. 'Will he try to get you blamed for the slaughter as well?'

Thrand made an annoyed noise. 'He can try, but Halfdan knows what I am like. I've never kidnapped a woman before, nor have I murdered in cold blood.'

'But those murders need to be avenged.'

'Narfi, the man who committed the murders, is dead. Is it necessary for you to risk your life for something which will not change the course of history or bring the dead back to life?'

Cwen pleated her gown between her fingers. 'And when we are in Jorvik, waiting for the ship to be ready? Hagal knows that I am alive and with you. He wants me dead because of what Aefirth did to his cousin.'

'Hagal would have to fight me, something he has avoided doing for years, despite my attempts at provocation. Your brother has me gone. Everyone is happy. Just not in the same way we had planned. Plans can change, Cwen. For the sake of the child, they should.'

His words thudded through her. 'But the marriage contract? My dowry?'

'Betrothals are put aside all the time.' Thrand made a cutting motion with his hand.

'It seems a shame just to allow Hagal to have my dowry. He will use the gold for bribes.'

'Your brother can sue Hagal for it. It is what the courts are for. I've more gold than I could ever spend in ten lifetimes.' He put his hand on her shoulder. 'We have to think about saving an innocent child's life. It is what my mother would have wanted.'

Cwenneth stared at Thrand as the enormity of what he offered washed over her. Her dreams lately had been full of what would happen once she reached Jorvik. The only thing which had calmed her was waking to have Thrand's arms about her and watching the rise and fall of his chest.

She knew deep in her heart that she'd never

truly relax until she had proof that Hagal was dead. But Thrand was right—Edward could try pursuing Hagal through courts for the dowry. She could send word once she was in Iceland.

A tiny smile crossed her lips. Edward would not be able to do anything about her living the life she wanted to lead. No more threats of a windswept convent. Or marriages to further Edward's power.

'It is very tempting to believe we could do this.'

Thrand stepped closer and laced his hand through hers. He brought their knuckles up to his lips. 'Seize this chance to give that boy the perfect mother and a new start in Iceland away from all the politics and killing.'

'Flattery. And you have no idea what I was like. Far from perfect.' Cwenneth's cheeks flamed, and she pulled away. If he touched her again, she'd agree to everything. She scuffed her boot against the packed dirt of the barn floor and tried to stop her imagination from building longhouses in the clouds. 'Sometimes I was far too impatient, too concerned with running Aefirth's estate, rather than attending to my child. I should have done more when I had the chance... There are nights I wake up in a cold sweat, remembering all the chances I once had and neglected.'

'You need another child in your life. If you and your husband had had another child, you would not have proclaimed you could not mother that child because Richard had the misfortune to die. Whatever else happens, Aud needs a mother and he likes you. Even I could see that.'

Cwenneth's throat closed. Somehow it had felt right to be holding a little boy again. She had savoured his little-boy smell and the way he kept finding things for Thrand to look at. It made her remember Richard, but in a good way, rather than in the heavy regretful way she had fallen into. 'I like him very well. I could come to love him.'

Thrand's face clouded and his shoulders hunched slightly. 'Then it is me who is the problem. You have no desire to be married to me. I understand. War and battle have made me, but I will try to be a good father. I swear it on my parents' grave.'

'I never said that!' Cwenneth protested before he had a chance to leave. She knew if she let him walk away, her one opportunity for a life would slip past. He might not be offering marriage for the reason she had hoped, but he was offering. And he was right. Jorvik could be very dangerous for the both of them. Thrand might dismiss Hagal's threat to him, but she couldn't. Iceland could save his life.

He turned back to her. His eyes grew wide. 'Then you will do it? You will go to Iceland with me and allow Hagal to dig his own grave.'

She swallowed hard and did not give herself a chance to think.

'Yes, I will do it. I will marry you, Thrand, and be Aud's mother. We will leave for Iceland as soon as possible.'

He caught her hands and twirled her about, lifting her off the ground.

Round and round until she was dizzy.

All the ice vanished from his face. He seemed years younger, eager and excited. The way he looked caused her heart to turn over. It was no good telling her not to love him because she already did.

'We should bring the girl Hilde with us,' she said when he set her down and the world had stopped spinning.

'Why?' he asked. 'Why should we take her? She seems well settled here.'

'She looks after Aud and I don't think they look after her very well either,' Cwenneth explained with a smile. 'It will be good to have another female to balance the two males in the family.'

He turned his face to her palm and kissed it. A great warmth flooded through her, but it was also tinged with regret. She wanted him to kiss how he'd kissed her at night, as if he desired her and only her. She knew he only asked because of the children.

'Then it is decided. We will go to Iceland,' she said briskly. She refused to mourn things she couldn't have. 'You, the children and I. We will live our life away from kings and politics. We will be free. Our freedom and a life well lived will be the sweetest revenge.'

He threw his arm about her shoulders and hugged her close again. She leant her head against his chest and savoured his warm, spicy smell. 'Sounds like a good plan to me. Freedom to be the person I am is something I have always sought. My father refused to bow before an usurper. I could never return to Norway as long as the current king and his heirs are on the throne.'

'What happens next?' she asked, trying to be practical and not think about the thousand reasons why this might be a bad idea. 'How do we get to Iceland? I have never considered it before. There must be a way.'

'We will go to Jorvik and meet my men. Some of them may wish to join us. Helgi has often expressed a wish to settle in Iceland. He had made plans to go with Sven. It is only right that I extend the offer to him. I will buy a boat and hire any men we might need. It will be done before you might think. We will be there by midsummer at the latest.'

She laid her head against the broad expanse of his chest and listened to the steady beat of his heart. She tried to keep the sudden wild leaping of her heart at bay. Somehow against the odds, she might actually live to see another Christmas and then the new year and the spring beyond that. She had a future. It felt good— better than good.

He pulled her close, resting his chin on the top of her head. 'It is time I rested my weary body and found another occupation for my arm. My father farmed after spending years as a warrior. I can do the same. My mother would be proud of me.'

'But…but…'

'We will buy a large tract of land and build a fine house as well as getting the right sort of boat for the voyage. Not a dragon boat, but a trader, a sturdy one which can carry livestock as well as people. I refuse to leave Myrkr behind. The horse has been a faithful companion for many years.'

She looped her arm about his neck and pulled his lips down to hers. 'You talk too much, Thrand.'

'Most people say I hardly speak.'

'They don't know you like I do.'

His mouth descended on hers, and she drank from it. Their tongues met and tangled. She allowed her body to say things that she knew she could never admit. His arms tightened about her and she could feel his arousal. A part of her rejoiced. He did desire her. She would make this marriage work. Even a mother like her was better than no mother. She wasn't sure she could love them, but she could give them a better life. She had to stop wishing on clouds for things that were impossible, like Thrand actually loving her.

Thrand wanted her to look after the children. And she shared his bed. Many marriages started on a far worse basis.

A small cough sounded in the back of the barn, bouncing off the walls. They jumped apart. Cwenneth silently gave thanks that the interruption had not been a few heartbeats later. Even now, she knew she looked well-mussed and thoroughly kissed.

She turned her head towards the sound. Hilde stood there, with the rough shawl thrown over her shoulders. She had a worried look on her face and carried a torch. Her intent face relaxed slightly when she spied them.

Cwenneth gave Thrand's hand a squeeze and went over to Hilde.

'Aud wanted to know where you had gone. I promised him that I would look out for you. He likes you both. Aud doesn't like many people. He misses his mother dreadfully.' Hilde gave a disapproving frown. 'Too many people have gone from his life. It isn't right. He is a good boy. He tries hard. Was he born unlucky? Is that the problem? Father Athlestan says it is.'

'Hilde.' Cwenneth knelt down and took the girl's cold hands in hers. 'We have decided to take Aud and you, too, if you like. We will give your master some gold to compensate him for the loss of two such fine children.'

She glanced back at Thrand. He gave a brief nod. 'Your master will be well compensated,' he confirmed.

The young girl's face broke into a wreath of smiles. 'Where would we be going?'

'To Iceland to start a new life.'

'I don't know where that is, but I would like that very much,' Hilde said without hesitating. 'I am a hard worker. Everyone says that about me.'

Cwenneth put her hand on the bony shoulders. She had wanted to have a little girl for such a long time, someone to teach to sew and to do so many things. She had never anticipated it ending like this. 'I am sure you are.'

'Shall we go and inform your master?' Thrand said.

'And Aud? Can I tell him?' the girl whispered. 'He never liked sleeping with the pigs. He is going to be part of a real family.'

Cwenneth regarded the stall where Mrykr was tethered. Real family. She had given up hope and suddenly Thrand had given her more than she'd ever dreamt. He might not love her, but she couldn't help loving him.

'Shall we let Thrand do it?'

The girl nodded rapidly. 'That would be best. He will think it is another of my games otherwise. We play what will happen when his father comes to claim him. Only I never thought it would be like this. Or that I would get to go as well.'

'And this is what does happen,' Thrand said. 'Is it better than a game?'

Hilde's eyes glowed. 'Much better. It is a dream come true.'

'I have never been anyone's dream before. Nightmare, possibly. It feels good to be a dream.'

The little girl ran out of the pasture.

Later as they waited in farmyard for the farmer to get Aud's things, Cwenneth slipped her arm through Thrand's, breathing in the scent of straw, the final warmth of the evening sunshine and animal. She used to think barns were ugly things, but this one had a certain grace and charm to it.

She closed her eyes and made a memory. She opened her eyes with a snap.

'How will we get to the coast? We can't all ride on Myrkr's back. Aud is far too young to walk any great distance.'

'The farmer has agreed to sell us his cart and a horse to pull it.' Thrand gave a husky laugh. 'Did you think I lacked sense?'

'But the roads…' Cwen attempted to think her way around the problem. 'It took us far longer to reach Acumwick's lands than it should have.'

'The roads may be muddy, but I've a strong back and can get it out of any ruts. I suspect Narfi wanted to go slowly for his own reasons.'

She shook her head in amazement. She

hadn't considered that. 'How long have you have been thinking about this?'

'When something is right, instinct guides you.' He put his hand on the small of her back. 'I'm well skilled at moving armies. Getting you and the children to the coast is little different.'

'A family is very different to an army. You are going to be those children's father, not their commander.'

'We need to go to Jorvik by another route,' Thrand said, changing the subject.

Cwen frowned and allowed it to go. But she silently resolved to make sure he understood his new role. 'Another route?'

'I hardly want to take the two children near to Hagal's holdings. We know they are looking for us and we barely managed to slip through their net. It will take a little longer and we will have to go closer to Lingwold than I would like, but it is either your brother who does not know we are there or facing Hagal who is looking for us.'

'Go past Lingwold, but never stop?'

'Do you trust your brother with the children? With me? We both know he wants my hide nailed to a church door. You send the message just before setting sail for Iceland.'

Cwenneth pursed her lips. Thrand was right.

They couldn't take the risk. Her brother wanted Thrand's head. He'd act and then ask questions. He might even believe the rumours about the kidnapping. 'The last thing I want is Edward making trouble. I'll trust your judgement on this.'

'Spoken like a true wife.'

'They won't take you for Thrand the Destroyer.' She linked her arm with his. 'You will have a wife and two children. Something the Destroyer would never have.'

'Then it is good that I am the man and not the legend.'

His laughter rumbled in the quiet evening. Cwen found it hard to equate this man with the silent stranger who had arrived at the farm only a few hours before. She had to hope his instinct was correct and that they would be safe.

Chapter Twelve

'Please, sir, what is Aud to call you?' Hilde tugged at Thrand's shirt after they had travelled a few miles in the grey early-morning mist.

The cart went little faster than a slow walk, but it allowed the children to rest. They had also been able to take some bedding and a bit of food. Progress was slow but manageable.

'Why are you asking?'

'He is worried and too shy to ask.'

Thrand looked down at the little girl. His experience with females was limited and with girls he had next to none. There had been only him and a few male cousins when he was growing up. He glanced at Cwen to see if she would answer, but she was occupied with readjusting Aud's pack.

The boy had wanted to take all of his treasures and Cwen had managed to get it down to his most precious feathers and stones, but he wanted to carry it rather than storing it in the cart. Both Aud and Hilde had decided at the last stop to walk for a little ways. Thrand hadn't objected as the going was muddy and it took all his concentration to keep the cart going.

'Call me?'

The girl dropped her voice and glanced over her shoulder. 'A special name. People in families have special names for each other. And we're a family now.'

A family. The girl's words caused the enormity of what he'd done on impulse to wash over him. The warrior who had resolutely resisted any complication or entanglement had voluntarily saddled himself with two young children and a woman. These people depended on him for their survival.

He frowned. He just had to approach it as though they were members of his *felag*, rather than his family. He had kept his men safe in the past.

'It all happened so fast that I haven't given it much thought.' He gave Cwen a questioning glance. She nodded encouragingly. He found it impossible to get rid of the impression that she had put Hilde up to this. She wanted to test him.

'Most people call me Thrand. And Cwen answers to Cwen. It is best to keep things simple.'

Hilde's face fell and she let go of his shirt. 'I wanted Aud to have a special name for you. It will make it more like Aud and I are truly brother and sister.'

'We're going to Iceland,' he said, watching Aud struggle slightly with the pack. 'It makes more sense to use the Norse words rather than the Northumbrian words. You are Norse now. Use those.'

'And the proper words are…' Cwen lifted both the protesting Aud and his pack into the cart. 'The children won't know the words and I don't either. Maybe you can teach us all Norse so we can speak the language before we get to Iceland.'

He clenched his fists, feeling his own inadequacy. He should have said the words to begin with. And he should have thought about lifting the boy in the cart. '*Mor* for mother and *Far* for father.'

'Yes, they can use those words,' Cwen said. Her brow puckered. 'It is silly, but…I'm pleased they are not the same in Northumbrian.'

A knife went through Thrand's heart. She still clung to her dead family.

'Can you practise, Hilde?' he asked deliberately turning from Cwen.

'Yes, *Far*.' The girl gave a little curtsy and laughed. Aud laughed as well and took up the chant—*far, far, far*.

'No, you have it wrong. One *far*, not two.'

'Did they go too far with the *fars*?' Cwen asked with an innocent expression on her face.

Her pun sent the children off into fresh peals of laughter.

'Just one *Far*,' Thrand explained, trying to keep a straight face. He knew he should strive to be like his father—dignified and remote so he could instil discipline, but a large part of him wanted the ease that Cwen had. '*Far-far* means something else.'

'What does *Far-far* mean?' Cwen asked. 'Or don't I want to know?'

'Grandfather. My father.'

Thrand paused. His father had been a remote figure and had left most of the child rearing to his mother. Thrand knew in that instant that it was not what he wanted. He didn't want to be the person who always laid down the law and seemed perfect. He knew his imperfections too well. It was one thing to be called *Far* and quite another thing to actually be a father. He remembered vowing that when he had been punished for some minor misdemeanour.

'Is it the same for all grandfathers?' Hilde wondered.

'No, Cwen's father would be *Mor-far*. It means mother's father.' Thrand frowned as the girl continued to look perplexed. 'It is how you tell who belongs to whom. *Far-mor* would be my mother, while *Mor-mor* would be Cwen's mother. It is very simple really. Logical.'

'Shall we play a game, children?' Cwen asked. 'You say a word and then Thrand will give us the Norse word. It can help to pass the time.'

'If we are going to play, I had better have Aud on my shoulders so he can see properly.' Without giving the boy a chance to protest, Thrand swung him up. It felt natural to have the boy grab hold of his hair and cling on.

They continued that way for a little while, but then Aud decided he wanted down and began to kick hard. Thrand stopped and took him down. The boy ran to hold Hilde's hand and they started chatting away.

Cwen quickened her steps until she was level with him. 'Thank you,' she said in an undertone.

'What, for picking Aud up? It is the best solution. He doesn't weigh much and he can see better from up here. Carts used to make my stomach ache when I was little.'

'No, for giving them a special name for me which isn't *mama*. I had been racking my brain, and you came up with the right answer.'

'Cwen, I can't imagine the heartache of losing a child, but I do know that these children are not seeking to replace your son in your heart.'

'How did you become so wise suddenly?'

'I've served under different commanders over the years. Some good, some not so good. There is always a period of adjustment. Our group is like a *felag*.'

'A *felag* rather than a family. Do you see yourself as our commander?'

'I see myself as a father. I know the difference.' Thrand looked straight ahead. 'I wonder if my own father did.'

She put her hand on his sleeve. 'I'm determined to keep my end of the bargain and be a good mother.'

'You will find a way.' He cupped her cheek. 'I believe in you.'

'And I believe in you and finding a way to be a father rather than a commander.'

'Can someone help? *Mor? Far?*' Hilde called out. 'Aud has fallen in a muddy puddle.'

Thrand turned towards where the little boy stood, rubbing his eyes and covered in mud. He rolled his eyes as Cwen gave a long sigh.

'Problem?'

'I had forgotten about this part of parenting,' Cwenneth said and waited for Thrand's explosion. Aefirth had always hated it when Richard was deliberately naughty and if the way Thrand had reacted yesterday when he first met Aud was any indication, she was in for a long day.

Thrand raised an eyebrow. 'Aud seems to attract dirt. He can bathe when we stop. For now take some of the cloth I planned to give Maeri and wipe the worst off.'

She stared at him dumbfounded. 'I thought you would be upset about it.'

'It was hardly Aud's fault. He didn't ask to fall into a puddle.'

'I think the pair were fooling around,' Cwenneth confessed. 'I heard giggling just before it happened.'

Thrand stopped. 'Is that true, Hilde?'

She scraped her toe in the dirt. 'It was an accident, but we were playing.'

Cwenneth watched a variety of emotions cross Thrand's face. Finally, he gave a rich laugh. He stopped suddenly and shook his head a little.

'Before I knew you, I barely laughed. Some questioned if I even could. I see now that I had simply forgotten how to.'

Her heart expanded at the words. She did mean something to him. She put her hand to his cheek and felt the faint rasp of bristles. 'I hope you will laugh often in Iceland, but what are we going to do about this deliberate naughtiness?'

All merriment vanished from his face.

'I can't do this,' he confessed in an undertone. 'If I lose my temper, I'll frighten the children.'

She stared at him and knew what he was asking and how much it must have cost to ask.

'He will have to ride in the cart if he is naughty. If he is good, he can walk or ride on your shoulders.' Cwen patted Myrkr's neck and tried to keep her voice sounding practical. But her stomach churned. It was wrong that she wanted more of him than he was willing to give.

The faint stench of smoke hung in the air. Cwenneth wrinkled her nose. It was far more than chimney smoke from a farm or village.

She glanced towards Thrand. His easy-going stance of a few moments ago had vanished.

'Can you take Myrkr's bridle?'

'What is going on?' Cwen asked, keeping her voice low. The last thing she wanted to do was to frighten the children.

'Impossible to say.' Thrand nodded. 'We keep going forward but be prepared to go into the woods on your left.'

Cwen nodded. They went around a bend and saw the remains of what had been a farmhouse. The small plume of smoke rose in the air. Cwenneth's stomach clenched. Someone had burnt the entire farm including the barns to the ground, and there was the distinct smell of cooked meat. Whoever had done it had not bothered to take the livestock.

'Was it raiders?' Hilde asked, sitting bolt upright.

'Why would there be raids here, honey?' Cwen said. 'We are near the borders of Lingwold and the lord signed a peace treaty with the Norsemen.'

'Not all raiders are Norse,' Thrand commented. 'Even if the Northumbrians would like to think they are.'

'Well, what do you think?'

Thrand shrugged. 'Wrong season.'

'A tragic accident, then?' Cwenneth put her hand to her throat.

'Stay here with the children.' Thrand unsheathed his sword. 'I will check and see if there are any clues. If there are raiders about, it is better we know about them and plan for it.'

'And if anyone needs help...'

'If you hear me shout, get the children away from here. Leave the cart.'

'Off to the left.'

'Correct. I will find you.'

'Will you?'

'I'll always find you, Cwen.'

He went towards the farm. Cwenneth lifted the children down from the cart and stood with her arms about them. Aud stuck his thumb in his mouth and stood watching with big eyes as Thrand cautiously made his way over to the smouldering remains. Silently she prayed that he would come back and say that it was just a fire, probably started by a cooking pot.

'What is *Far* going to do?' Hilde asked, leaning into her.

'He is going to make sure that everyone is all right. And that we can travel on past without a problem.' Cwenneth silently willed Thrand to return.

'Who did this?' Hilde whispered. 'Bad men?'

Every instinct in Cwenneth's body told her that it was Hagal's work, but it made no sense. He should be well to the southwest of here. Edward would never do such a thing. He would not burn people's houses and claim it was the Norse.

'Everyone has left.' Thrand returned far quicker than she had thought he would.

'No...no bodies...'

'A fresh grave in a little graveyard. I reckon the attack happened about two days ago.' His deep-blue gaze met hers. 'And it was an attack, Cwen. I found the marks of a double axe on the door and several arrows. Whoever lived here didn't stand a chance.'

'We were supposed to be at peace.' Cwenneth shook her head in disbelief. 'Things like this were not supposed to happen any more. We wanted time to recover from the war.'

'We don't know who did this.'

'The Norse warriors are the only ones who use double axes. It is supposed to be the hallmark of Thrand the Destroyer.'

A faint dimple shone in the corner of his mouth. 'Funny that. I believe he was otherwise occupied.'

'I know that. You know that, but the villagers around here will not know that. This slaughter will add to the legend of Thrand the Destroyer.'

'We will be keeping away from villages, then.' Thrand gave Hilde and Aud a significant look. Cwenneth knew precisely what he was thinking. It would be very easy for one of the children to blurt out his name. Hilde seemed particularly loyal.

'It would be for the best.'

'The last thing we want is someone recognising me and blaming me. I'm not saying that I am proud of everything that I have done, but I did it in battle against a known enemy. Yes, I have raided, but we were at war. You understand the difference.'

Cwen's stomach knotted, and she gave a small nod. 'You think Hagal did this, but why would he? He signed a treaty with my brother.'

'He broke it when he tried to have you murdered.' Thrand put his sword back in its scabbard. 'I don't pretend to know what is in that man's head. It is none of my concern now. All this…' he gestured about the ruined farmhouse '…all this is someone else's problem. If your brother can't tell honest men from rogues, I pity his people, but I feel no pity for him.'

'I think we had better get going. Put some distance between us and this.'

Aud's stomach gave a loud rumble.

'Aud is hungry,' Hilde announced with great importance.

'As soon as we can we will get you some food.' Cwen placed Aud and Hilde up on Myrkr, glad to have something to do. Concentrating on getting the children fed would keep her mind from worrying about why Hagal had decided to torch that farmhouse.

A hard knot appeared in the pit of her stomach. If Hagal had torched this farmhouse, how many other people had he killed, and worse, had he used her supposed murder as an excuse to do it? Thrand might think they were safe and had no further part to play, but she knew that farmhouse would haunt her.

'The sooner we are in Iceland, the sooner you can stop worrying about this sort of thing,' Thrand remarked.

'But it might still be happening.' Cwenneth picked up Aud. She didn't want to think about the danger to the farm where they had lived.

'It won't be your concern. It is not your concern now. We have chosen a different path. The children will be safe.' He put his hand on her shoulder. 'You can only look after your family, Cwen, not the whole world.'

* * *

Despite the wild flower–strewn glade where they camped, Thrand's nostrils still quivered from the stench of the burnt livestock. He put his cloak over the two sleeping children. Aud and Hilde at least seemed unconcerned by the slaughter they had encountered earlier. Cwen remained a bit pale and subdued.

The children had eagerly eaten the duck he'd caught, which Cwen had cooked with a few herbs and greens she'd gathered, but neither he nor Cwen had eaten much. And the children had waited until Cwen told them they could eat. How Cwen knew these things was beyond him. Looking after children was a whole new world where he had little skill or experience, but he wanted to learn. It surprised him how much he wanted to.

Thrand tore his mind away from the children and attempted to concentrate on the problem at hand, namely who was behind the burnt farmhouse and did it matter to his future? Were they in danger?

Hagal had to be behind it, but it made no sense. But there again, his attempted murder of Cwen made no sense either. At least Cwen lived. He doubted anyone had survived at that farmhouse. It annoyed him that the Northumbrians would say he had done it, but what was the point of worrying about his reputation in a place that he never planned to visit again.

'Do you want any more duck?' he asked, going over to where Cwen sat quietly mending a hole in Aud's trousers. 'You barely touched your food earlier.'

Cwen shook her head. 'I'm not hungry.'

'Can we have a song, *Far*?' Hilde's sleepy voice asked.

'I thought they were asleep,' Thrand said in an undertone.

'Sometimes putting a cloak over a child can wake them.'

'I did it carefully,' he protested.

Her hand stilled. 'Are you going to sing for her? Music used to settle Richard, and she asked for you.'

'The only songs I know are war ballads. You sing, Cwen. You do it. You must know a lullaby or two.'

She pushed the needle in and out of the cloth. 'My voice isn't very good and I haven't sung properly...not since...'

Thrand stilled as the memory of the dream washed over him. 'You do yourself a disservice. You sang once for me.'

She tucked her chin into her neck. 'Special occasions only.'

'Very well. I will try.' He searched his mind and started to sing one of the less violent sagas.

The little girl gave a sigh and turned over. Within a few heartbeats, there was the sound of her soft breathing.

'There, you did it,' Cwen said. 'You sang her to sleep.'

'Why did you sing in the hut?'

'I didn't think you heard me,' she replied. 'A bit of foolishness my nurse Martha told me when I was little. Some people can be brought back from the brink of death if the song is sweet enough. Luckily, as you pointed out, you were never in danger.'

Thrand took the cloth from her hand, put it to one side and laced his fingers through hers. 'You have a lovely voice. Can I hear it again?'

'When we get to Iceland and everyone is safe, then I will sing. It will be a special occasion.' She released his hand and stood up, wrapping her arms about her waist. 'I will be far happier and in better voice when we get there.'

He leant his forehead against hers and put his arms about her. 'Forget about the farmhouse. Forget about everything but these children.'

She laid her head on his chest. 'What if

Hagal did it? What if he did it because of me? I spent my life preparing to run a large house and I know the responsibility a mistress has for her people. I wanted to be a peace-weaver, not a death-bringer.'

Thrand closed his eyes and forced his breathing to be steady. 'What-ifs play no part in our future. Going to Iceland is the best way to protect you and the children. What happens in Northumbria is no longer any of our concern. And you will be bringing peace—peace to my life and the children's.'

'But his reach is long. Knui proved that. How many other people have taken his gold? Who else might be lurking in the shadows?'

'Everyone will be on their guard now that it is known. Bribery only works when people are not looking for it.' He put a finger to her mouth. 'Hush now. I want to enjoy you and this moment. The children are asleep and there is only us. Who knows what tomorrow will bring?

'Make love to me, Thrand. There are no stars to count tonight.'

His head descended. She responded fully, greedily pulling at his mouth.

Afterwards when Cwen lay in his arms, sleeping with her lips softly parted, Thrand watched the faint light of the stars. Only yesterday he would have sworn that vengeance drove him and there was room for nothing more. But now he knew it could contain more. It could be richer than he ever dreamt.

Silently, he prayed, using words he remembered from his childhood, prayers his father used to say—that his sword arm would be strong and not falter. He tightened his arm about Cwen and smoothed her shorn hair. This time, he vowed, he would not fail his family. And he knew who his family was.

He sat up straight. Cwen! There was something he could do for her.

'Tomorrow we go north.'

'North?'

'You need to make your goodbyes…to your son.'

The ice coldness of the crypt hit Cwenneth as soon as she walked in, taking her back to Aefirth's funeral. The lingering scent of incense tugged at her nostrils. She braced her body for tears, but none came.

She walked briskly over to Aefirth's tomb, wanting to get it over with. She hadn't anticipated Thrand would make this gesture. Despite his dismissing the danger, she knew he took a grave risk in coming here.

Thankfully the young priest had not been present when she was last here. Maybe Thrand was correct. Maybe luck was finally on her side.

When she'd imagined coming back here, she'd always anticipated that uncontrollable sorrow would overtake her. Instead, an overwhelming sense of peace filled her as she slowly traced Richard's name on the tomb.

'I'm going to Iceland,' she whispered. 'I will make sure Aud and Hilde learn all the games you used to play. But know my heart is big enough to hold everyone. Loving them won't make me love you any less.

She allowed her hand to linger for a few heartbeats and then turned away. She was no longer the woman who had loved these two so fiercely. She'd always love them, but they belonged to her past. And her future was more important.

'Finished so soon?'

'I'm ready to go.' She touched her chest. 'There is no need to say goodbye as I carry them in my heart. But thank you for bringing me here. It was unexpected, but the risk was far too great.'

He put his hand on her arm. 'The risk was worth it.'

'We need to go now.' Cwenneth glanced over her shoulder. The priest had left them alone. 'Confronting my stepson with you and the children would be less than ideal.'

'The lord is away,' Hilde piped up.

'How do you know?'

'I asked the kitchen boy when he was giving the scraps to the chickens,' the little girl answered.

Thrand beamed. 'If you want to know something, Hilde will find out the answer.'

'Did you find out where he had gone?'

'The kitchen boy said that he was going off to war.'

Cwenneth shook her head as a shiver ran down her spine. Now that she thought about it, the hall seemed devoid of its usual life. 'He will have that wrong. My stepson has a limp. He is no warrior. Kitchen boys the world over like to sound important.'

'Did he say where?' Thrand asked.

Hilde shook her head. 'He wasn't sure. A long way from here. The kichen boy's brother went as well.'

'We need to go to the coast by the quickest way.' Thrand picked Aud up. 'Once we are in

Jorvik, I will let Halfdan know. Your brother may be massing an army.'

Cwenneth swallowed hard. She had to think logically. They only had the kitchen boy's boast to Hilde. Her stepson could be anywhere. The Scots could be massing in the north and then there was Mercia to the west. 'Thrand…it will have nothing to do with us. My stepson would never lift a finger to save me. He believes I cursed his family.'

'I won't leave my king blind. If there are problems in Bernicia, he needs to be aware of them.'

'And Iceland?'

His warm hand curled about hers. 'I'm giving the king information. We will still go to Iceland. War is in my past.'

Cwenneth nodded, choosing to give the appearance of believing him. 'Iceland before autumn.'

Chapter Thirteen

The spring rain pelted down incessantly, soaking and chilling them to the bone. Cwenneth tightened the shawl that the farmer's wife had insisted on giving about her shoulders. They had made good progress after leaving Aefirth's crypt without anyone challenging them.

Without prompting, Thrand had set Aud on Myrkr while Cwenneth and Hilde walked beside him to keep the load light on the cart. Hilde kept up a steady stream of chatter which helped keep her mind from the niggling worry of which war her stepson had gone off to fight. It would not be anything to do with the rumour Hagal had spread. The one thing she knew for certain was that her stepson would never lift a finger to save her.

'You have become awfully quiet, Cwen,' Thrand remarked, lifting a tired Hilde up alongside Aud. 'Do you wish to ride as well? Or should we find shelter?'

Cwenneth's heart turned over. For the thousandth time since they had left the farmhouse she warned her heart not to care or have hope. But her heart had long ago stopped listening to her and it frightened her. She could so easily lose him. And the last thing she wanted was a war between the Norsemen and the Bernicians.

The needle sting of hail attacked Cwenneth.

'We should find shelter. Aud is being very brave, but hail hurts.'

'You must know of somewhere which will take travellers in and not ask too many questions. The children need a hot meal and to thaw out in front of a warm fire.' His brows drew together. 'Like you, I know we are near to Lingwold.'

'There is no point in trying the hall or any of the monasteries or inns. They are sure to inform my brother.' Cwenneth wrapped her arms about her waist. 'The last thing I want is my brother chasing after me, thinking I've been kidnapped as Hagal claimed. Time enough to send a message when we are in Jorvik.'

She took a step and her boot slipped slightly in the pile of hailstones. Thrand put his hand under her elbow, holding her upright. She met his midnight-blue eyes and saw the concern and something more which was instantly masked.

'Are your boots losing their grip?' Thrand asked. 'Go slower and watch where you put your feet. How would we cope if something happened to you?'

'They will last. They are good...' Cwenneth's voice trailed away as her shoulders suddenly became much lighter. There was a place they could stay! Safe with no fear of Edward or Hagal knocking at the door.

'There is somewhere we can stay.' Cwenneth fought to keep the excitement from her voice. 'Someone who would keep our presence a secret until her dying breath.'

'Are you sure of that? Gold and fear can be mighty big inducements. Do you know of any abandoned huts around here? Ones that a shepherd might use?'

'You remember Dain—the boy who had these boots before me. His mother lives near here. On her own. She won't ask too many questions. She was my nurse, my second mother before my marriage and she has no great love for my brother. She rightly blames him for failing to find Dain a place amongst his men. I would like to return the boots.' Cwenneth winced at the sight of the mud-splattered boots. 'Or at least pay for them. She deserves to know her son died bravely.'

When he said nothing, she added, 'The children need shelter from the rain. Somewhere warm where they can dry off in front of a fire. They are far too wet and cold. If one of them gets sick, we'll be forced to delay our journey. And we want to get to Jorvik as soon as possible.'

'I am aware of that. The question is where.'

'I would trust my life to Martha.' Cwenneth paused. 'And I would trust the children's lives to her as well.'

'If you are sure…'

'Very sure. She is my oldest friend.' She put her hand on Thrand's sleeve and felt the comfort of his muscular arm. 'When I was a young girl, she used to hide my misdeeds from my family and most particularly my brother. I would not be standing here if she had told. Edward did threaten bodily harm on more than one occasion.'

'What did you do? I find it hard to credit you were ever naughty. Or behaved foolishly.'

'Once I arranged it so an old bird's nest fell on Edward's head and showered him with spider's webs. Edward had been overly proud of his new ermine cloak. It was ruined beyond repair. And despite Edward offering a reward, Martha kept my secret.'

'This is another matter entirely, Cwen.'

'You did not hear the threats my brother uttered. Or the rewards he offered. I know which side Martha would choose.' Cwenneth concentrated on brushing the hail from Hilde's cloak. 'The children need to have some shelter and hot food, and the area around Lingwold is too built up to risk a fire.'

She waited in silence as Aud began to softly cry as the hail pelted down again, pricking like a thousand needles.

'I trust your judgement on people,' Thrand said, pulling her hood more firmly on her head. 'You took a chance on me, but keep silent about my name unless absolutely necessary.'

Cwenneth threw her arms around his neck and kissed him, drinking from his mouth. 'You won't regret it.'

His arms came about her and pulled her close. 'I plan on making you pay later.'

'Who goes there on a day like today?' an elderly voice asked in answer to Cwenneth's knock. 'I swear it became black as midnight at noon. Does it mean the devil is out on his rounds?'

Cwenneth gave a quick glance at Thrand. She motioned for him to be quiet. If Martha heard a Norseman's voice, she might bolt the door and lock it. The bone-chilling hail and sleet had only increased in the time it had taken to get to the farm.

'Travellers in need of shelter.' Cwenneth hated how her stomach knotted. 'Martha, please open the door and allow us to come in.'

The door creaked open and an eye peered out. 'Lady Cwenneth? By all that is holy, what are you doing here? Do ghosts walk abroad today? Is that why it is so dark out?'

Cwenneth winced. She hadn't realised her voice was that recognisable. 'The very same, but I am no ghost or apparition. I am real. Touch my hand. There are children, Martha. It is bucketing down. May we come in? Please, for the sake of my mother's friendship with you.'

Martha's eyes narrowed and she ignored Cwenneth's outstretched hand. 'We heard you'd been kidnapped. Owen the Plough even went so far as to predict that you were dead. No lady could withstand what happened to you.'

'Owen the Plough always did love to make dire predictions. I've brought Dain's boots back. You can see the mark he made on the back.' Cwenneth lifted up her gown to display the mud-splattered boots. 'You were right. They are excellent boots. Open the door properly and look.'

The door was flung wide open and the elderly woman rushed out. She clasped Cwenneth to her breast before leading them back into the small hut where a fire roared. The smell of warm stew and freshly baked bread perfumed the air. Aud and Hilde instantly went to the fire and started to warm their hands, rather than begging for a taste as she would have done at their age. In the firelight, Cwenneth could see the colour in their cheeks coming back. She breathed easier. Coming here and begging for shelter had been the right thing to do.

'You must tell me all your adventures and how you managed to be here with two children and this…warrior. After you have had something to eat. Those children are too thin by half.' The old woman put out a trembling hand and touched Cwenneth's cheek. 'You are real. You are alive. Did my…?'

Cwenneth shook her head slowly, hating the eager look which had come on to the woman's face.

'Slain before they had a chance to draw their swords. Betrayal of the most cowardly sort. Cold-blooded murder,' Thrand said in a low

voice, 'or otherwise your son would have ac-
quitted himself well.'

Cwenneth rapidly explained what had happened and how Thrand had rescued her. However, she was very careful not to give Thrand
a name as she knew how people in Lingwold
felt about him.

'I would be dead if not for him.' Cwenneth
squeezed Martha's hand as the old woman
wiped away a tear. 'Surely you can see the folly
in saying it is worse than death to be rescued
by a Norseman when the only reason why I am
alive and breathing is him and his sword arm.'

The woman's eyes narrowed. 'And he is? You
are avoiding the question, my lady. What is this
man's name? He must have a name.'

Cwenneth swallowed hard. Lying was out
of the question, but there was no telling how
Martha would react when she knew, particularly after Thrand had been blamed for the
torching of the farms. 'Does it matter who he
is? He saved my life and travels with me. We
will only be staying the one night.'

Martha tapped her foot on the floor. 'I think
it does if I am going to welcome him under my
roof. And I want his real name, my lady. I know
how you try to cozen people.'

'Thrand Ammundson,' Thrand answered,

stepping forward and holding out his hand. 'Thrand the Destroyer in flesh and blood and at your service. I'm grateful you have taken my family in.'

'Then the rumours are true. You did kidnap my lady and seduce her.'

Martha backed up. In another breath she'd run. Cwenneth readied herself to usher the children out. They could get a good few miles on them before Martha had the chance to raise the alarm.

Thrand lowered his hand on Martha's shoulder, keeping her from moving. 'Lady Cwenneth stays with me voluntarily. Initially she wanted to see justice served, but she stays now for the sake of these two children.'

The woman blanched. 'But they said it was all the Destroyer's work. Your bridegroom swore it on a bible.'

'We've been duped for the last few years. And my so-called bridegroom is a pagan. Christian oaths have no meaning to him.' Cwenneth pressed her fingers together. 'I was there. I know who killed your son and who rescued me. And while I don't know who torched those farms, I do know it wasn't Thrand. And I am prepared to swear that oath on any bible.'

Martha sank down on to the bench. 'But they

said…your brother said… I'm only a widow who has lost her only son and whose daughter won't speak to her.'

Cwenneth knelt before Martha, gathering the older woman's cold hands within hers. 'Edward must never know I was here. We only stopped because of the children and the weather. We needed shelter. I will let him know where I am when I reach Jorvik and the children are safe, but right now they need me.'

'My old lady, your mother, would bar me from heaven if she knew I'd refused to shelter her only daughter. Or had betrayed her. Your brother is much altered from the young man he once was.' Martha screwed up her face and appeared to think for a long while. 'For her sake, I will accept you under my roof, Thrand Ammundson, and keep your secret.'

'We accept with gratitude,' Cwenneth said quickly before Thrand exploded. 'We will be gone by morning.'

'Where are you going?' Martha asked.

'We head to Jorvik and then to Iceland,' Thrand replied, a muscle jumping in his jaw. 'Lady Cwenneth is coming with me to look after the children. It is the safest place for her.'

'Iceland! Have you been bewitched, my

lady? It is the end of the earth. Surely your brother will protect you...from Hagal the Red.'

'He failed to before.' Cwenneth could hear the warning note in Thrand's voice. 'If he had heeded the warning signs, your son might be alive today. But instead he allowed himself to be blinded by a legend.'

'This is a bad business,' Martha said, shaking her head.

'Why is it a bad business?' Cwenneth asked.

'So many men dead. Your brother is baying for blood, my lady. He is raising an army to rid this land of Thrand the Destroyer for ever. He wants to free you.'

'How did he learn about my kidnapping?' Cwenneth asked. 'It puzzles me how the news travelled so fast. It took weeks for me to travel there. The roads are nearly impassable with the spring rain. We've had great trouble today with the cart.'

'Hagal the Red arrived a few days ago, swearing vengeance for your kidnapping, but he needed your brother's support.'

Cwenneth froze. Hagal was at Lingwold with her brother. Play-acting. Hagal obviously expected her to make for her old home and would act the contrite bridegroom when she did arrive.

'The best way to avoid a trap is to stay well

clear,' Thrand said in a quiet but firm undertone, putting a heavy hand on her shoulder.
'There are so many reasons why we hold to our
agreed course of action and the two main ones
are sitting across from you right now.'

Cwenneth pressed her hands to her eyes and
tried to will the sick feeling in her stomach to
go. Hagal was here! Not in Jorvik. 'Did I say
anything?'

'We will be on our way tomorrow. First
light,' Thrand said, leaving no room for dis-
sent. He went over to where the children sat
and scooped Aud up. 'Aud is sound asleep in
his stew and Hilde is not far behind. After a
rest they will be ready to continue on. They are
good travellers for ones so small.'

Cwenneth's throat caught as Aud's head
lolled against Thrand's shoulder. Thrand looked
every inch the father. To think he had proclaimed that he could never look after the
children. He was a natural. And he cared for
them. It was the way he carried Aud as if he
was worth more than all the gold in the world
combined.

She pinched the bridge of her nose. Caring
for the children was one thing. Caring for her
was another. She wished she could stop her

heart from longing and from wanting to keep him safe.

Martha pointed to the loft. 'Put the children up there. It'll be warm enough and there is plenty of space for everyone to sleep.'

'I'll do it,' Thrand said. 'You stay here with your friend, Cwen. It will be a long time before you see someone from your birthplace again.'

Hilde went up the ladder first, and Thrand followed with Aud.

'It is quite the family you have there, Lady Cwenneth,' Martha said when the noise from the loft had died down a little.

Cwenneth laced her hand with Martha's. 'I'm glad you agree. I fear my brother would not. He would be beyond all reasoning, but know that I am happier than I have been in a long time. It feels right. I'm needed in a way I never was at Lingwold. Or indeed with Aefirth.'

Martha gave a reluctant nod. 'If you say he is a good man, I'll believe you. And he is the right age. Aefirth was far too old for you. He treated you like a child and never allowed you to make any important decisions.'

'Aefirth was good to me,' Cwenneth protested. 'He sought to protect me.'

'He wanted to play at being young. He should never have gone to war the last time he did. He should have stayed and looked after his estate. When he left you, he never trusted you to make the right decisions.'

Cwenneth pressed her lips together. What Martha said had merit. She had admired Aefirth and had liked being looked after, but he had never encouraged her to think for herself in the way Thrand did. He had left advisors for her. But Aefirth had only wanted her because he felt he needed another heir, one who could be a warrior instead of a cripple, and she was an ornament to his house. 'The woman I was loved him.'

'And the woman you are now? Who do you love?'

Was it wrong of her to keep hoping that Thrand would see her as more than the person who could help him fulfil his promise to his friend? Cwenneth fiddled with her eating knife. Now was not the time to reveal her problems with Thrand.

'There is something more,' she said instead. 'Something you kept from me because Thrand was in the room.'

'Your brother means to march to Jorvik and demand Thrand's head. He has called for all men who hate Thrand Ammundson to flock to his banner. He means to take Jorvik if the king won't listen. Even your stepson has come with men. You could have knocked me over with a feather when I saw his banner fluttering in the breeze the other day.'

'My brother is foolish if he thinks the king will listen. And insane if he thinks he can take Jorvik. Others have tried.' A pain developed in the back of Cwenneth's head. How could her brother be that foolish!

'Hagal has guaranteed safe passage through his lands to Jorvik in time for the Storting. He says that it will be your brother's last chance to get rid of the menace for ever and get you back as his bride.'

'Hagal wants me dead. Aefirth killed his cousin in battle. Unless my stepson is very careful, he too will end up dead.'

'He has never mentioned that. And your stepson is one of the ones yelling the loudest.' Martha tapped a finger on the side of her nose. 'But you always did say that he wanted easy glory.'

'That's because he has never been to war.' Cwenneth clenched her fist. She hated to think about the lives her stepson risked, men she knew and respected. 'Why does Hagal need an army of Bernicians?'

'According to Hagal, the Norse oath of fellowship forbids weapons and private armies during a Storting. My nephew was in the room when he said it. A great cheer went up. Finally a way to defeat the menace.'

A cold prickling went down Cwenneth's back. This was what Hagal had been up to—he was going to use her brother and his men to provide the army so that he could take over Jorvik and become king. And they would not be Norse. He would not be condemned as an oath-breaker.

She leant forward and gathered Martha's hands between hers. 'There is more to tell me.'

'Your brother was not inclined to move as your sister-in-law is pregnant and begged him not to leave her side. But then the burning of the farms started. They all swore it was Thrand the Destroyer. Old John's son watched his father being killed.'

'Thrand was with me.'

'It is better that you are leaving tomorrow. Your brother has a hard lesson to learn. He should listen to his wife and stay put. But since the farms were attacked, there is no reasoning with him. He wants Thrand Ammundson destroyed. Hagal has assured him that Halfdan will listen as he has kidnapped a fellow *jaarl*'s bride and made off with her dowry. And if not, your brother is prepared to take on the entire Norse army.'

Cwenneth closed her eyes and knew she had been living in a dream world. Hagal was not going to stop if they went to Iceland. He was going to take that army south. People would be killed. Other farms would be burnt to the ground. People she cared about. Everything in Lingwold would change. Men would lose their lives, women their husbands and children their fathers. And in Jorvik, there was no saying what would happen if Hagal actually did gain power. Would they even be safe in Iceland? Or able to reach it?

All because she was willing to let people think she was dead.

Hagal had to be faced, shown for the barefaced liar he was, and stopped. Jorvik would be too late. Hagal needed to be stopped before he acquired an army.

'You appear ill, my lady. Shall I fix you a sleeping draught?'

Cwenneth quickly shook her head. She knew what she had to do and there was no point in arguing with Thrand about it. He'd only refuse to let her go alone or insist they wait until Jorvik. If Thrand accompanied her, they'd kill him. And she wanted to spend the rest of her life with him. The children needed him and his sword arm. She, on the other hand, could count on her brother's men to keep her safe. Her brother had no reason to seek her death. Once he knew the truth, his army would turn against Hagal.

'I'm a bit tired, Martha,' she said, a plan beginning to formulate in her brain. She wanted the comfort of Thrand's arms one last time and then she'd do it. Only she could stop this madness before it began.

'You go up and see that man of yours.' The old woman gave a huge smile. 'If I was a few years younger, I would give you a run for your money. Not that he'd notice—anyone with half a brain can see that he is devoted to you.'

'He's not—' Cwenneth responded too quickly and thought better of it. Let Martha believe in the romance. She knew the bitter truth—Thrand was currently interested in sharing her bed and he wanted her for the children. 'What made you change your mind?'

'No monster would take such good care of children. He handles them as if they are made of glass. And they are not even his own. I've misjudged him for years. And no man could ever have conducted as many raids as your brother claimed the Destroyer did.'

'Why do it then?'

'It gave him more power and more men. Your brother could always tell a good tale, particularly if it made him look the better for it. I've known him for a long time.'

Cwenneth reached out and grabbed the woman's gnarled hand. 'I'm glad we came here tonight.'

'Are they asleep?' Cwenneth peered into the moonlit loft. Through the tiny window at the gable end she could see the first stars in a sea of midnight-black.

Typical, she thought. They found shelter because the weather was awful and it had cleared. If only they had continued on, she'd never have known.

'As soon as their heads hit the straw. I was watching them for a little while.' Thrand reached out a hand. 'I was about to come down.'

Cwenneth caught his hand and brought the knuckles to her lips. He had purposefully stayed away so she could have time to talk to Martha. 'I came up instead to see where we would sleep. Aud and Hilde have that side of the loft and we can have this one.'

He tilted his head to one side. 'Did that old woman say something to make you upset?'

Cwenneth gave her head a quick shake. 'Nothing. She approves of you in case you wondered. She thinks you are exactly what I need. Apparently she thought Aefirth too old for me.'

He pulled her into his arms. 'Does she? I'm glad. I'll leave her some gold when we go. Or one of my brooches if you think the gold will offend her.'

'What were you thinking about while you were making yourself scarce?'

'When we are in Iceland, I'll build you a longhouse. It will be little bigger than this house, but I want to have something of Bernicia for you and the children. The configuration is different from the house I grew up in in Viken, but it can be done.' He described it all so vividly that Cwenneth could see it take shape in front of her. The lump grew in her throat.

Iceland was an impossible dream after what she'd learnt from Martha. She could not walk away and allow men to die in her name, trying to rescue her. Making sure Edward understood the truth and acted in his own best interest was imperative. And as Thrand taught her—she made her own luck. She was the only person who could stop this madness before it started, before it did turn into a war.

If things happened how she planned, she'd

be back before Thrand and the children woke.
Then they could continue on to Iceland as if
nothing had happened. As long as Edward
knew the truth, he would not send men after
Thrand. Once he saw that she was alive and
unharmed, he would destroy Hagal rather than
march to his doom in Jorvik.

'Are you cold, Cwen?' Thrand's breath tickled her ear.

'Today took more out of me than I thought
it would.'

He brushed her temple with a featherlike kiss
which sent pulses of heat through her. 'Are you
going to tell me what is wrong, Cwen? What
you intend to do?'

'Nothing is wrong. Everything is right. I
simply have no idea when we shall next have a
soft place to lie. And both children are sound
asleep. We are alone together.' She pressed her
body up to his and felt him harden. 'I want you,
Thrand, and I believe you want me as well.
Here. Now.'

Her hands entangled in his hair and pulled
him closer.

He groaned in the back of his throat.

Slowly she pushed him down the straw. He
fell easily back and pulled her on top of him.

'I'm in charge tonight,' she whispered against his throat. 'And I intend to take my time.'

'A threat or a promise?'

'Both.' She put her fingers to his lips. 'The time for talking has ended and the time for pleasure has begun.'

She slowly lifted his tunic, revealing his warm skin underneath. And then, allowing her hand to trail down his muscular chest, she undid his trousers and took them off.

He lay silver in the pale moonlight, naked and watching her. There was something very powerful about having a warrior such as him at her mercy.

She bent her head and tasted the hollow of his throat. Slowly, she moved her lips down his body, taking her time to taste and sample. So far most of their encounters had been about him taking charge—this time she wanted to be the one.

He groaned in his throat as she lapped at his nipples, enjoying the rough texture.

She cupped his erection and felt how he grew harder and longer in the palm of her hand. Giving in to impulse, she bent her head and tasted the tip of him. Silk smooth, but hard underneath. Ready for her. She moved her mouth lower on him and his body bucked upwards.

His hands gripped the straw as if he was struggling to maintain control. She lifted her head and ran her thumb over the tip of him.

'Too much?' she asked.

'You are too dressed,' he gasped. 'Want you naked.'

He caught the hem of her tattered gown and brought it up over her head. Then his hands cupped her breasts and flicked the nipples, sending rivulets of pleasure throughout her body.

'Now we can both enjoy,' he murmured. He lifted his mouth and his tongue flicked her core. She ground her hips into him with each new sensation as she tried to concentrate on stroking him.

Finally, when she knew she was about ready to explode, she tore away from his pleasure-giving mouth and impaled herself on him, opening her hips to take his whole length in one fluid movement.

She started to rock back and forth, allowing her body to say all the things that she dare not whisper and to offer up promises for the future.

Thrand slowly came back down to earth. Something tonight had been different between Cwen and him. He couldn't put a finger on it, but for the first time in a very long time he felt as if he belonged to other people. She was in truth a part of him. She was the keeper of his heart, the sort of woman his father had told him that he would find one day.

'Cwen,' he rumbled in her ear when they were still joined. 'Thank you.'

She lifted herself up from his chest. Her entire body thrummed. 'I should be the one thanking you. I never knew it could be like that. It is much more pleasant to share.'

Thrand released his breath. He was tempted to tell her how much he loved her, but the last time he had said such words he had ended up fighting for his life. When they were in Iceland, when he had built a house for her, then she'd understand what she meant to him. How she was at the heart of the new family he planned. He could confess his dream then. 'It feels good to be part of a whole again. I had not realised that I missed it.'

'Part of a whole?'

'You, the children and me. They need parents.' Thrand knew his words were weak, but they were all he dared admit. He worried if he said anything more before they reached Iceland, he'd spoil everything. He wanted a family. His family. People he had ties with. He had lost one family and now it would appear he had gained another.

She struggled out of his arms. 'Always the children.'

'Someone has to look after them. You said so yourself.'

'I know, but…'

Thrand put his hands behind his head and looked up at the blackened beams. 'Once we arrive in Jorvik, it should take less than a week to find a boat. Many boats make the passage in the summer. Soon we will have both begun a new life and will be able to give those children the future they deserve. And I will let Halfdan know about Hagal's scheme. He will end it.'

Rather than wrapping her arms about his neck and thanking him, Cwen reached for her gown. 'And if your old life calls you back? If Halfdan needs you to rout Hagal?'

'It won't.' Thrand slammed his fists together. 'My focus is you and the children. I'm through with war, battles and revenge. Let someone else do it. But I'm also no traitor. I'll not allow Hagal to use the Bernicians to seize power.'

'Why do you think this?'

'Hagal is here and plotting something with your brother. Your brother can command an army, but it would be suicide to move against the Norse. Once Halfdan knows of Hagal's plotting, he will act. There is no need for either of us to do anything yet. When we are in Jorvik, I will set things in motion, but then we go to Iceland. Trust me.'

He hoped she understood what he was saying and how much she meant to him and how scared he was of voicing his feelings out loud.

With a sigh she laid her head back on his chest. 'It is good to know.'

He tightened his arms about her and bid the feeling that somehow he was about to lose her to go.

Chapter Fourteen

Gwenneth waited, wrapped in Thrand's arms until she was certain he was sound asleep. She pressed a gentle kiss on his mouth and slipped out from his arms.

In the moonlight she swiftly dressed. And then she kissed each of the children. Their little faces looked like angels. Tears welled up in her eyes. She wiped them away with fierce fingers. She was going to see them again. All of them. They wouldn't even know she had gone.

'I will return,' she said. 'I refuse to allow Hagal to destroy any more families. I refuse to allow Hagal to destroy you. I'll be back before you wake.'

She stole away downstairs.

'So you are truly leaving?' Martha said from the shadows.

Cwenneth stopped. 'You waited up. You should have gone to bed hours ago.'

'I wondered if your man had talked some sense into you. I hoped he had.' Martha came forward. 'I know what you are like, my lady. Meddling will get you nowhere.'

'Meddling? My brother is about to be tricked into a war which he will lose. And while he may deserve to lose his life for being a fool, the men of Lingwold deserve to live. One of the reasons I agreed to marry Hagal in the first place was because I wanted peace for my people. I don't want to be the cause of destroying lives. I am the only one who can stop this madness. How could I live with myself knowing people died to avenge my supposed kidnap?'

'Your man agrees?'

Cwenneth covered Martha's hands with her own. There was little point in telling of Thrand's decree. Jorvik would be far too late. 'I kept it from him. What can he do except get killed? My brother wants his head. It is why he agreed to an alliance with Hagal the Red in the first place. It is why he will march south—to put an end to Thrand the Destroyer.' She tightened her grip on Martha's fingers and willed her to understand the future. 'None of those men will make it back to the north. Hagal then will really be able to pillage this land. I'm the only person who can stop this.'

'You might want to believe that, but your man will have other ideas once he learns where you have gone. You belong to him now.'

'I don't belong to anyone,' Cwenneth said quickly. 'I have worked it out in my head. I will go in by the side entrance and through the kitchens. Once I'm there, I will send one of the servants to quietly fetch my brother. We will have a brief conversation and I'll leave a free woman. I will be back before anyone awakes.'

Martha's face turned mulish. 'You should discuss it with your man first. He is supposed to be a great warrior, which means he understands strategy far better than you. Even I can see your brother could have you followed.'

'I want to spend the rest of my life with him and the children, Martha.' Cwenneth pressed her hands together to keep them from trembling. Always people treated her like a child, rather than recognising that she did have a mind. 'Hagal needs to be exposed for the lying murderer that he is before he can ruin all of Lingwold. I'm the only one who can do it. Once Edward knows I'm alive, this nonsense will stop. And he won't keep me. Even if he tries, I know all the ways out of the hall. I grew up there. Remember how I used to escape to visit you on baking days?'

Martha squeezed Cwenneth's hands. 'Your mother despaired.'

'There, you see. You should have some faith in me.' She patted Martha's shoulder. 'If I could escape my mother, I can escape from the hall.'

'And what shall I tell him if he wakes and you have failed to return? Confronting an angry Norseman is a fate I wish to avoid.'

Cwenneth stared at the dying embers of the fire. Martha's question was something she preferred not to think about. Thrand would be furious with her when he found out what she had done. She had to hope that he'd listen.

'Before the cock crows, I'll be back. Edward will listen to me and heed my advice. He has in the past.' Cwenneth straightened her shoulders and refused to think how long in the past it had been since Edward had listened. She would make him listen if she had to tie him down and beat him about the head. 'Failure is not an option.'

'If you haven't returned by mid-morning, I will tell him where you have gone, and if he is half the man I think he is, I won't be able to hold him.' Martha waggled her finger. 'Think on that, my lady. Think on that.'

* * *

A few stars faintly twinkled in the sky. Cwenneth raised her hood and stepped into the darkness.

A black shape stepped in front of her. 'Where do you think you are going?'

She missed a step and nearly fell. 'Thrand? You are supposed to be asleep.'

'Once Martha told her tale, it was obvious what you were going to do.' He lifted a brow. 'I asked you to stay with me and to confide in me. You refused.'

She dipped her head. He was making her out to be in the wrong, but it wasn't that way at all. 'I wanted to save your life.'

'How? By running away?'

'By going to my brother and telling him the truth?' She held out her hands and willed him to understand what she was doing was for him. 'It is the only way to stop this madness. If he knows the truth, my brother will stop Hagal. His interest is in saving his people rather than having a vendetta against you.'

'And what do you think he will do? Just let you go? Allow you to return to me? The kidnapped bride?'

She glared at him. 'Once my brother knows the truth and sees how he was duped, he will understand he owes you a life debt. Do you really think Hagal will be planning on keeping him alive?'

She waited for him to agree.

He ran his hand through his hair. 'You should always say goodbye when you go, even when you think you will only be gone for a short while. One of the things I always regret is that I never said goodbye to either of my parents. I slipped away to meet Ingrid. I was supposed to be working in the barn, mending a byre as punishment for disobedience.'

'I'm sure they knew you meant to,' Cwenneth said quietly.

He clenched his fists. 'My mother's body was in the barn. She'd left her hiding place and had gone searching for me. If she had stayed hidden, she would have survived. If I had said goodbye, she would have lived.'

Cwen went cold. His quest for vengeance made more sense now. Why he blamed himself. All the self-loathing and naked longing to change the past was written bare on his face. 'She should have trusted you were old enough. You were hardly a baby. You knew what to do in case of attack.'

His mouth twisted. 'You didn't know my mother. She was always fussing. I was her one chick. She knew my father's rules. She would have stayed hidden if she thought I was safe. But she didn't. She came to get me and I wasn't there. She died because of my lust for a faithless woman. I have regretted it every day of my life.'

Cwenneth breathed deeply. She had to get it right. Her instinct told her that Thrand had carried his guilt close to his heart and had never confided it before. 'We all make mistakes. You were barely more than a boy. How could you have foretold the future?'

His mouth twisted. 'It is nothing I am proud of, knowing that my actions caused my parents' death. But the children should know where you are going. Think about them and stop. They need a mother. They have bonded with you.'

'And if I do nothing, if I continue on to Iceland, what am I guilty of?' She held out her hands and willed him to understand that her decision had not been an easy one. 'People will die. Other boys will be left without their parents. Hagal needs to be stopped and I am the only one who can stop him. Here. Now. Before he has a chance to murder more innocent people.'

'And you think going to Lingwold will make a difference?'

'Doing nothing will allow Hagal to get stronger. If he leaves Lingwold with an army, he might succeed. Are you prepared to take that risk?'

Thrand looked down at her. His brow creased. 'Hagal wants you dead.'

She put her hand to his cheek. 'I can stop this madness before it starts, Thrand. I can expose Hagal's lies.'

'Then go to Jorvik and tell the king. Halfdan will listen, particularly as we know the true extent of Hagal's treachery. We will get there before any army.'

'I want to avoid more death, not destroy a generation of Bernician men.' Cwenneth wrapped her hands about her waist. 'One of the main reasons I was willing to marry Hagal was that I didn't want another woman to go through what I did when I lost Aefirth.'

'I...I...care about you, Cwen, and want to save your life. Throwing it away like this is madness.'

Her heart soared. Thrand cared about her. But then she forced herself to think and Cwenneth's heart shattered. Too little too late. She had settled for Aefirth caring for her. She had settled for a lot of things, but no longer. She wanted Thrand's love. She deserved more than lukewarm caring. She deserved his whole-hearted love.

'Part of you remains that boy who found his parents murdered.' She raised her chin. 'We need to stop Hagal while we can…unless you are afraid?'

'I've lived my life, hoping for the opportunity to destroy Hagal.'

Thrand waited in the silence. Inside he felt a great hollow open as if his heart was being ripped from his chest. He was a liar. Cwen was his life. Without her, he was nothing. And she did not love him enough to put him first. He might have confessed that he cared for her, but she didn't care for him. Her loyalty remained with her old family.

'Fine. I'm glad we have that settled. Now if you will let me go so I can return to *my* home…'

He gasped her upper arm. She might have rejected his love, but he couldn't allow her to stumble blindly into whatever trap Hagal had laid for her. 'You are not going alone, Cwen. I forbid it.'

Cwen took his fingers from her sleeve. 'You forbid it? You forbid nothing.'

Thrand clenched his fists. He ought to turn his back on her, but he couldn't. She might not believe in his love for her, but he knew it was fierce and strong. The reason he lived now was to protect his family— his new family.

'I will go with you. In the background as insurance in case your brother does not behave how you'd expect.'

She arched her brow. 'What shall we do with the children?'

'Take them with us, of course. We are a family. We stay together. If it is safe enough for you, it is safe enough for them.' He glared at her, daring her to say differently. 'And who would think Thrand the Destroyer would be travelling in the company of two children? How many people have actually seen me? I will wear a cloak to cover my hair and will keep silent unless you actually need my help.'

'You are willing to do that? To let me speak first? To keep silent if necessary?'

Thrand put his hand on his sword. What he was about to do was the hardest thing he had ever done—allow the woman he loved to go into danger. But he knew she was right, not because he needed vengeance for his long-dead family but because he needed to protect the family he had acquired. Looking over his shoulder and worrying was doomed to failure.

Hagal had to be stopped now before he had an army on his side.

'Shall we put your theory to the test?' He raised her hand to his lips.

She bowed her head. 'I didn't expect you to agree.'

'So you could go off all indignant and lose your life?' Thrand put his hand on her shoulder. The faint stain of colour told him everything he needed to know. 'If you are going to face Hagal, then I'll be there, ready with my sword.'

'Thank you.' She laid her head on his chest. Thrand enfolded her in his arms and knew he'd protect her with his dying breath.

Cwenneth stared up at the grey stone walls of her old home. They had made good time from Martha's and had arrived before the main gate opened. Once she had dreamt of this moment, but now, instead of the welcome comfort, she knew it was potentially her prison and a death trap for Thrand. However, she could not turn her back and walk away. She had to stop Hagal, for good. And this was the only way she knew how to do it.

It meant a lot to her that Thrand walked at her side, carrying a sleepy Aud as Hilde held her hand. Each step she took, she was reminded of why she was doing this. These children deserved to grow up free from the menace which was Hagal.

Cwenneth hoped the children along with the cloak they had borrowed from Martha would provide enough of a disguise for Thrand. They had discussed the plan several times on the way over. Thrand reluctantly agreed that he needed to stay in the background until her brother learnt the truth.

'I will go through this back passage. You will go through the main gate and stay in the main hall. Once I have spoken to my brother, I will join you and we can walk out together. Slowly and carefully. If I am not there by the time it is noon, you must go back to Martha's and I will get there as soon as possible.'

Thrand's eyes glittered. 'I hope you are right, but if there is any trouble, I will be there. I will protect you.'

Cwen gave Aud a kiss and then knelt beside Hilde, rather than answering Thrand.

'I wish I had something…' She stopped and remembered the rings she had hidden in the hem of her skirt way back when this adventure first began. She rapidly extracted them. 'If anything happens to *Far*, you are to take these to the Lady of Lingwold and tell her what has gone on. Show no one but her.' Cwen looked over Hilde's head at Thrand. 'My sister-in-law may be many things, but she has a soft heart for children. She knows my rings. She will find a place for them...if the worst should happen.'

'Hilde, if there is trouble, we discussed what you do.'

Hilde nodded. '*Far* told me that I was to go to Martha. He showed me where he has hidden some gold for us. But it won't come to that, *Mor*. *Far* trusts you and your judgement.'

At Cwen's sceptical look, Thrand nodded. 'I have trained her well.'

She stood awkwardly, not sure what she should say to Thrand. There was far too much she wanted to say. 'I will see you soon.'

His hand curled about hers. 'I am counting on it.'

He turned with the children and didn't look back.

Keeping to the shadows, Cwenneth crept over to where the hidden passage ended and pulled the covering open. It smelt danker than she recalled, and she wished she had a light. The woman she had been when she'd left this place would never have dared to do this. Thrand believed in her and moreover had taught her that she was capable of far more than she dreamt.

Everything had seemed clear back at Martha's and indeed on the path here. But standing in front of the walls, it seemed a much harder proposition. Edward hated being duped. He always reacted badly. She had to hope that he turned on Hagal quickly and never discovered his most hated enemy was on his lands. She'd slip away quietly.

'There is no hope for it.' She spat on her hands and felt for the knife Thrand had insisted on her wearing. It remained securely strapped to her calf. 'I have to begin before I can be finished.'

She crouched down and began to crawl. Spiders' webs entangled in her hair, and she bumped her knee against a particularly hard rock. When she had nearly given up hope, she saw a faint crack of light. She pushed against the door, and it gave way.

She tumbled out on to the hard stone with a clatter which seemed to echo.

She froze, waiting, but there was no sound of anyone stirring.

A wild excitement filled her. She might just do it. She started towards the kitchen. Someone there would know where her brother slept. It would be safer. Edward would understand, she told herself for the thousandth time. He would let her go when she asked.

A hard hand descended on her shoulder. 'Who goes there?'

'I am Lady Cwenneth of Lingwold,' Cwenneth said with as much dignity as she could muster. 'Unhand me and take me to Lord Edward. There is much I want to say to him. There is much he needs to know before he makes the biggest mistake of his misbegotten life.'

'Not so fast, my lady,' the man replied with a thick Northman accent. 'Hagal the Red has business with you first.'

Chapter Fifteen

'Unhand me.' Cwenneth struggled against the restraining paw of Hagal's henchman as he dragged her to where Hagal was holding court in a small room at the back of Lingwold. Hagal gave her a look which was pure evil. 'I am perfectly able to walk. I demand to see my brother. He is the lord here, not you.'

Hagal gave a nod. 'Release her. You will have your time later with the lady. You wish to see your brother, do you, wife?'

Cwenneth hated how her scalp crawled. She tore her arm away from the great hulk and silently vowed that he was never going to have any time with her. Thankfully, she still had the knife and she would not hesitate to use it.

'If you will take my arm, my lady.' Hagal held out his arm in a parody of a gentleman's pose.

'Where are we going?'

'Where else but to see your brother?' Insincerity dripped from every feature. 'We have all been worried sick about you, my lady. Thrand Ammundson has a fearsome reputation. Your brother will rejoice to see you unharmed.'

'I am sure he will.' Cwenneth forced her feet to keep moving. All of her muscles tensed. Somehow she had to find a way to escape and warn Thrand. Hagal was not acting as though he suspected that Thrand was in the hall. She breathed a little easier and tried to hang on to that.

'Look who has returned, Edward!' Hagal crashed open the main door to the hall and propelled her forward into the tapestry-lined hall. She could remember how she used to play a game of echoes when she was little. If she stood in the right spot, just about where Edward now stood, her voice would bounce off the walls. In the wrong spot, it was as quiet as the grave.

The force of the blow made Cwenneth drop to her knees. She gritted her teeth and slowly rose to her feet, concentrating on the red and gold of the tapestries. The stench of sour wine intermingled with ale hung in the air. Her father would be spinning in his grave. She did not dare look around to see where Thrand and the children stood. If they had made it this far…

She lifted her chin. 'Brother, it is good that you have given me such a warm and heartfelt reception.'

'Cwenneth!' her brother said, rising from where he sat discussing something with several of his followers. Her sister-in-law was nowhere to be seen, but her former stepson sat beside him.

Edward's face was puffy and his nose red. He had the air of a man who preferred to drink and carouse rather than to lead an attack of any sort. In any fight with Hagal, he'd lose. Cwenneth's heart sank. Edward was blundering about like a fly unaware that he was caught in a web.

'You are alive.' He held out his arms. 'Thank God, you are alive. That monster let you live. And you've returned unharmed to us. Hagal is willing to overlook everything. We can still have the wedding.'

'I survived the attack, yes,' she said cautiously and remained where she stood.

Cwenneth looked at each of the men at the high table, including her former stepson. Her heart sank. There was not one she could fully trust to believe her story, not with Hagal and his men camped inside the gate.

'My sister is more resourceful than you predicted, Hagal the Red,' Edward remarked.

'A great relief to us all,' Hagal said with a bow. 'Thrand Ammundson does have a certain reputation with women. Back in Norway, he caused the death of my beloved Ingrid.'

'Still, my sister has returned to us after her ordeal. And she will give witness to what happened. Your king will have to listen to her. A delegation can be sent, rather than an army.'

Hagal's face turned crimson. 'One hopes that she is not a traitor.'

Cwenneth kept her gaze trained on her brother and willed him to believe her. 'Thrand Ammundson rescued me after Hagal's men slaughtered everyone else. Edward, you above all people should know my love for Lingwold is without question.'

'Why would Hagal want you dead?' her stepson asked.

She directed her gaze to him. 'Because your father, my late husband, killed his close kinsman. And Hagal made a battlefield vow. Narfi took great pleasure in informing me of it before he challenged Thrand Ammundson.'

Her stepson blanched.

'Where is Thrand Ammundson now?' Hagal asked, muscling forward. 'How did your ladyship escape?'

Cwenneth's stomach clenched. If she lied,

her brother would know. He had always had the uncanny knack of knowing when she lied. She had to keep to the truth as much as she could. There remained a possibility that Thrand would not be required to rescue her, that she could walk away from this unscathed and Thrand undetected.

'Where I left him, I presume.' She batted her eyelashes and hoped. 'He was badly injured in the fight with Narfi. Luckily I found the right track and made my way here.'

'And you are asking me to believe that you made it across country on your own? Cwenneth, you can barely make it across the castle yard.'

Various people laughed. She raised her chin and glared at her brother. 'I stand before you. Surely your eyes tell the truth.'

'Where did you get those clothes?'

'From Martha. Dain's mother. I stopped there to return Dain's boots. My slippers would not have held up on the long march home.'

Hagal snapped his fingers. 'She lies. Tell me where this Martha creature lives. Ammundson will be there. Let me send my men. Let me prove this to you. Your sister will be in league with your enemy. He has seduced her. She is damaged goods.'

'Do you take orders from a Norseman now?' Cwenneth poured all the scorn she possibly could into her voice. 'Why should you doubt my word?'

Her brother looked from one to another. 'What am I going to do with you, Cwenneth?'

'Allow me to live my life in peace. I've no wish to be married to him.' Cwenneth pointed a finger at Hagal. 'Nor do I wish to enter a convent. And I want my dowry returned to Lingwold's coffers, the dowry that his men stole from the baggage cart. It is all I ask.'

'We have an agreement, Lingwold. Honour it.' Hagal slammed his fist down. 'Or it will go the worse for you.'

'And what was that agreement?' Cwenneth argued. 'To call your followers and march to Jorvik, demanding Thrand's head? Did you truly think Halfdan would give it? Thrand is his man.'

'Thrand Ammundson has ravaged our lands!' her stepson shouted and the rest of the high table beat their hands against the wood in agreement.

'He has been in the south for the last two years,' Cwenneth retorted, meeting his gaze straight on. 'Thrand has been in the south these past two years. Hagal and his men used Thrand's name to extract the gold.'

'Who told you this? Ammundson?'

'Narfi. He was determined that I should understand and despair before I died.'

Her brother frowned. 'You know little of politics, sister, but you speak very boldly.'

'I tell you that if you leave Lingwold, you will never see it again. Hagal will ensure it. All of you.' Cwenneth walked over to the table and dumped her brother's wine goblet out on to the rushes. 'Our father would be disgusted with you.'

'Hey, what are you doing?'

'Hagal will claim you were a drunken sot, brother, and that is why you ended up with a knife in your back. And there would be some truth to this assertion. Start acting like the lord of these lands instead of some Norseman's lapdog.'

'You need to put your tale to Halfdan. He is the only one who is able to tame that mad dog Ammundson.' Hagal pounded his fist on the table, making the goblets jump.

'And you wish to go to war with the Norsemen? The entire Norse army? The Storting is amassing and they will defend their own. You only have Hagal's word that they will leave their weapons. You and I know what happened in the second siege of Jorvik,' Cwenneth said softly, training her eyes on her brother. 'Surely we have had too many years of war recently. You first considered this marriage contract because you wanted to plant crops and see your children grow up to honourable manhood. It can still happen, Edward, but not if you blindly follow Hagal the Red, Hagal the False.'

Her brother swayed where he stood and he looked at her. For the first time in a long time, she saw his eyes soften and the brother she had once known return. 'My sister has returned, unharmed. There is no need for me to go to war with the Norsemen. I will send a message of protest at the kidnapping.'

'You will do what?'

'My sister's claims must be properly investigated before I take further action. And once the truth is known, then I will move against the culprit.'

The high table stamped their feet in agreement.

Cwenneth pressed her hands to her eyes. It was over. Edward had seen sense. Hagal had nowhere left to turn. Edward had the greater army.

'Of all the weak-livered, mealy-mouthed responses!' Hagal strode over to her brother and jabbed him in the chest. 'You can't do that!'

'Can't I?' Her brother reached for another jug of wine. 'I believe I have done it.'

'Then you're surplus to requirements.' Hagal withdrew a knife and stabbed her brother in the side and twisted.

Before Cwenneth had a chance to scream, her brother collapsed to the floor, clutching his side. Hard hands captured her and dragged her to where the triumphant Hagal stood.

The reality of the situation slammed into her. Her only brother lay bleeding on the floor, possibly dying. Whatever wrongs he'd done her in the past, he'd cared enough to muster an army and, when confronted with the truth, he'd believed her. She'd never been more proud of her brother than when he stood up to Hagal. Somehow she'd find a way to get him help.

Cwenneth clenched her fist. The old woman's curse had no power. She made her own luck.

'Next!' Hagal called, stepping over her brother's body and giving it a contemptuous kick as he stared directly at her former stepson. 'I claim the right to lead as Lord Edward is incapacitated. I'm his anointed successor, his brother-in-law and I say we march to Jorvik. Does anyone dispute me?'

'I do!' Cwenneth cried. 'You cannot murder in cold blood and get away with it. A marriage contract does not a marriage make. I repudiate it! Get out, Hagal! Go!'

She regarded each of her brother's loyal followers, but they remained seated, pale-faced and immobile. Fear. They feared Hagal more than they wanted to avenge Edward's stabbing.

'You are a monster!' Cwenneth tore her arms from the restraining hands. She fumbled for her knife and lunged towards him.

'Shut up and learn your place, woman!' Hagal's hand hit her face with a crack. 'Be grateful that you still live. You will tell me where Thrand Ammundson truly is.'

The blow would have once set her reeling, but Cwenneth stood her ground and lifted the knife. A great calm settled over her. Panic and running away were not the answer. 'Never ever raise a hand to me again! You don't frighten me, Hagal the Red! I know you for what you are—a coward and a bully.'

With a hard blow to her wrist, he sent the knife spinning through the air. She stared at him in dismay. Her only chance gone. He captured her face. 'There will be payment, Lady

Cwenneth. You will die slowly and painfully. Who will lift a finger to save you?'

'I will!' A large man stepped from the crowd and threw back his hood.

Cwenneth's heart gave a leap. Thrand! She wasn't going to die without seeing his face again. She gulped hard. But it meant he was in danger. The children were in danger.

'Thrand Ammundson. An unexpected pleasure.' Hagal made a slight bow, keeping hold of Cwenneth's face. 'You will see I have no need of your assistance, Old comrade.'

'Unhand my woman.'

'Your woman?' Hagal shook his head. 'My wife! To do with what I will!'

'The marriage has never been consummated!' Cwenneth yelled, tearing her face from his fingers. 'I will never be your wife. But I am proud to say that I'm Thrand Ammundson's woman!'

The entire hall gasped. Edward struggled to sit up. 'Ammundson is here?' he rasped out, holding his side. 'Seize him!'

'No, keep your places! I'll deal with him on my terms,' Hagal said.

No one moved except for Aud, who toddled out towards her. Cwenneth gave a cry and picked him up, holding him close.

'Bad man,' he said, touching her face and pointing towards Hagal. 'Bad.'

'Stay here with me,' she whispered. 'Your *Far* will beat the bad man.'

'Will you fight, Hagal the Red?' Thrand banged his sword against his thigh. 'For the possession of this woman? And the right to command these lands?'

'You will fight a fellow member of the *felag*?' Hagal gave a pitying smile. 'I can get you safe passage back to Jorvik or wherever you want to go. Leave now. This is none of your concern. You and I share a fellowship. I'm merely seeking to subdue the north.'

'My oath permits me to fight for a woman. And even if it didn't, I would still fight. Some things are beyond codes. Some things strike at the heart of a man's existence.' Thrand's face showed no emotion. 'It is time, Hagal, that we tested our strength. Man to man. Sword to sword.'

'You won't get out of here alive, Ammundson.' Hagal drew his sword. 'You know that. They will fall on you when I am gone. Lord Edward, you may die, knowing that I do keep my promises.'

'Neither will you. I guarantee it.'

They circled each other, testing and probing. Hagal was a worthy opponent who seemed to have studied Thrand's strengths and weaknesses.

Cwenneth put her hand over her mouth. Thrand couldn't lose. Could he? He had said that Hagal was better than good. She started to inch over towards where the knife had fallen.

Thrand went on his back foot and stumbled to one knee.

'This is the best the great Thrand Ammundson can do?' Hagal raised his sword over his head, preparing to deliver the death blow.

Cwenneth's hand closed about the knife. What was the first law of sword fighting? Never be distracted. Had Hagal learnt that lesson as well as Thrand? She had to try. She was in the right spot.

'Justice! I want justice for all who died in the wood!' she shouted.

'Justice! Justice! Justice!' the walls echoed back.

Hagal half-turned his head towards the noise. His sword checked. That heartbeat was all Thrand needed. He drove upwards with his sword and connected with Hagal's throat.

Hagal gurgled as he fell backwards.

'First rule of sword fighting—never allow anyone or anything to distract you.' Thrand stepped over the body. 'Do you understand what I was trying to teach you now, Cwen, back at the hut?'

'Completely,' she answered, going towards him. 'And we have nothing to fear from Hagal any longer.'

'Yes, you are a free woman.'

His arms encircled her and held her tight. For a long moment, neither spoke.

'Where is Hilde?' she asked, looking about her for the young girl.

'She will be here,' Thrand said. 'As soon as I suspected all was not going to go as you planned, I sent Hilde to fetch your sister-in-law. Let's hope she succeeded.'

'What is going on here?' her sister-in-law's voice resounded in the hall. 'Edward, this girl brought me Cwenneth's—' Her sister-in-law rushed towards where Edward had propped himself up against the table. 'What happened here? Cwenneth has returned…unharmed?'

'I made a mistake and believed the wrong man,' her brother gasped out, clutching his side. 'Hagal the Red was the problem, not Thrand Ammundson. I made a mistake because Ammundson had bested me in battle and now I owe him my life. My sister saved us. She saved Lingwold.'

'Hush. You have been stabbed. You need a healer.'

'My *mor* is a good healer,' Hilde said, tugging on the woman's skirt with her free hand. 'She healed my *far*. He told me. Aud will tell you that as well.'

'Where is she?'

Hilde pointed to Cwenneth and with a doubtful frown her sister-in-law beckoned to Cwenneth. 'Cwenneth, I can see you have returned a changed woman. You have acquired two brave children. Can you help my husband?'

Thrand gave her a little push. 'Go on. Show them what you can do. Show them that you are not cursed.'

Cwenneth went over to her brother. The wound was less serious than she first feared. Rather than hitting his middle, the knife had glanced off his side and the cut was less deep than the wound Narfi had given Thrand. Yes, there was blood, but her brother should live once he sobered up.

'Can you do anything?' Her sister-in-law wrung her hands. 'I don't know how long it will take a monk to get here.'

'I can try. I make no promises, but I suspect it is his destiny to live.'

Her sister-in-law narrowed her eyes. 'You've

changed, Cwenneth. I can hear it in your voice. The woman who left here would not have been able to stand up to Hagal the Red, nor would she put herself forward to try to heal anyone. You used to believe you were cursed. What happened?'

'There came a time for me to take charge of my destiny, and I have. You make your own luck, sister dear. Thrand Ammundson taught me that.'

Edward grabbed Cwenneth's hand. 'Will you forgive me, sister, before I die?'

Cwenneth resisted the urge to roll her eyes. She had forgotten that her brother hated any sort of pain. 'If I dress it, it will be fine until the monks arrive. Goodness knows you have enough wine to pickle yourself, Edward. Some of this mess is from your spilled wine.'

'What…what are you saying?'

'I suspect you will live a long time, but hopefully less foolishly. And Hagal the Red is to blame for what happened here, not you.'

Her brother closed his eyes and his words slurred. 'It is good to have you home, Cwenneth. It is where you belong, with your proper family. I have felt so guilty about sending you away. It was wrong of me. Do you forgive me?'

'Of course I forgive you. Hagal fooled us all.'

* * *

Cwenneth worked quickly and bound up the wound. When she had finished, her brother gave a soft snore.

'Cwen, will he live?' Thrand asked, coming to kneel beside her.

'That wound won't kill him, but I say nothing about the alcohol.'

Two monks arrived. The elder one praised the neatness of her bandaging, making Cwenneth absurdly happy. But with the monk's arrival, Cwenneth became aware the mood in the hall had altered. The faces of the men and women showed little relief or friendship. In the time she had been treating Edward's wound, they had closed ranks, sealing off not only Hagal's men's retreat, but Thrand's way out as well.

'May I have a moment with Lady Cwenneth in private?' Thrand asked before Cwenneth could mention the danger he faced. 'I have no wish to outstay my welcome.'

Her brother nodded, his face creased with pain, and whispered something to her sister-in-law, who nodded.

'You may use my husband's private chamber. You may take as long as you wish to say goodbye.' Her sister-in-law laid a hand on Cwenneth's sleeve as she went past. 'Take care. We are family and we're delighted to have you with us again.'

'I make my own decisions, sister.'

'Yes, yes, but I don't want you to feel obligated to a man like that. He is reputed to have a stone for a heart.'

'You needn't worry. Obligation is the last thing I feel towards him.'

Cwenneth followed Thrand with a sinking heart into her brother's private chamber. Thrand was going to leave. He could see she and the children would be looked after. She felt the walls of the room press down on her. Hagal was dead and there was no longer any pressing need for her to go to Iceland. She should be rejoicing, but all she wanted to do was find a way to keep him with her and hold fast to the dream they once had.

He closed the heavy door with a loud bang and crossed the floor to her. 'Your sister-in-law lies. I do have a heart and I do care. I care passionately about what happens to you. I used the wrong words earlier. Can you forgive me?'

'Forgive you for what? You saved my life. You were right. I needed your help.'

His arms came around her. 'We defeated

Hagal together. Together we are far stronger. It was right to act as you suggested. Waiting until Jorvik would have been wrong.'

'My sister-in-law has offered me a home. The children as well,' she said moving out of his embrace. There had to be a way of getting him out of here alive. Later, she'd find a way to join him, if it was what he truly desired. 'We will be safe here…in case you were worried. You can go in peace.'

'Hagal has ceased to threaten you. You can live here in safety and without fear of reprisal.' His face began to look like it was sculpted from granite. 'I will ensure that. Lingwold will be safe from Norse raids.'

Cwenneth put her hand to her mouth and tried to hold the sob back. Thrand's dream of a farmer's life in Iceland seemed to have vanished like the mist on a spring morning. She raised her chin and refused to beg. 'Then I must wish you a good life. You will be able to go back to doing what you love best.'

He put his hands on her shoulders, preventing her from moving. 'Without you, I have no life. I wanted to say that before you started on about you staying here so I can get free or some such nonsense. It is not going to happen. We are a family now and families stay together. The children, you and me. Together.'

She completely stilled. A lump rose in her throat. 'Together because of the children?'

'No, because of you. You are the heart and soul of my existence. Until I met you, I was so preoccupied with my need to revenge my family that I forgot to live. You showed that there is more to life than vengeance and war. You made me want to live.'

Cwenneth's heart began to thump so loudly she thought he must hear it. 'I made your family? You fought today to fulfil your vow.'

'Earlier I got the words wrong and I am making a mess of it again.' He gathered her hands in his and held them tight. 'The next time you even think about throwing your life away to save mine, think about this—without you, I am nothing. Before you, I only had hate in my heart and with you, my life has begun again. I was able to fight today not because I wanted vengeance for my parents, but because I wanted to protect my family. And the heart of my family is you and always will be. You're my everything.'

'Always?' She stared at him.

'I tried to show it to you, but I will say the words, if you need to hear them. Believe me, please.' He went down on one knee. 'I love you, Cwen, and I won't leave here without you.' His eyes softened, and she wondered that she ever thought them dead or full of ice. They were warm; they were eyes she could drown in. 'With you I have discovered what it is like to live again. I had become one of the walking dead, and my parents never wanted that for me. They wanted me to have a life as full as theirs was.'

Her breath caught in her throat. Thrand loved her. Truly loved her. 'I love you as well, Thrand. Very much.'

He gave a half-smile. 'You love me? How could you?'

Cwenneth's heart opened. 'Very easily. I want to go with you, to be your woman, to follow you about even though I will have no dowry, nothing to recommend me. I want to be a part of your family. Our family.'

'No, not my woman, my wife,' Thrand corrected. 'We will marry, Cwen. Come with me to Iceland, sit by the fire and grow old with me. I need you beside me for the rest of my life.'

'I would like that that very much.' She leant her head against his chest, breathing in his familiar scent. 'I have loved you for a long time. I believe I fell first when you healed my blisters. I had thought my heart was buried along-side Aefirth and Richard, but I see now that I was wrong. A small part of me will always love them, but hearts expand and grow. You and the children have become my family, the people I want to spend the rest of my days with.'

'The first time I saw you when you were caught in the thorn bush, you made me feel something beside the deadened dull emotion which had been my fate for so many years. I thought I had banished all feelings years ago and you taught me to love again.' He put a gentle hand to her cheek. 'You taught me to believe.'

She laced her fingers with his. 'Shall we go out and let them know our decision?'

'Together.'

'Yes, together.'

Cwenneth walked out of the room, holding Thrand's hand. Her sister-in-law raised her brow in surprise as the entire hall fell silent. Even the monks tending to her brother stopped.

'We are leaving. You may try to stop us if you wish, but I hope you don't. I am going to Iceland to be with the man I love. I have made my choice.' She held out her hands and both children ran to her. Thrand picked up Aud and put him on his shoulders. 'I have chosen my family, my true family of the heart.'

As the crowd parted they walked out of Lingwold together without a backward glance.

Epilogue

A farm in the east of Iceland a year later

The late-evening sun shone down on the newly
constructed longhouse. Although it was mainly
in the style of Norse longhouses, there were
a few Northumbrian touches here and there.
It had taken several months of hard work for
Thrand and his men to build it once they arrived in Iceland, but Cwenneth thought it well
worth the wait.

Cwenneth drew a deep breath, enjoying
the rare moment of calm. Aud and Hilde were
tucked up in bed. The household chores were
done.

Thrand had allowed her to select the spot for
the house and had been surprised at her choice.
When she asked why, he said that the situation reminded him of something he'd seen in

a dream once and then he confessed about the dream he had had in the hut when he had lain injured the previous year.

'Here you are,' Thrand said, coming out of the house, carrying a bundle. 'There is someone who wants to see you and show what she can do.'

She smiled and reached for their daughter Sinriod, who had been born a month ago. They had named her after Thrand's mother. If she had had any lingering anxieties about the curse, it had been laid to rest the first time she felt Sinriod kick in her womb. But Cwenneth knew even if she had never had Sinriod, she would still have felt blessed. She had her husband and her two children of her heart. Sinriod simply added to her happiness and contentment.

The baby opened her eyes, blinked and gave a huge smile at both her parents.

'She's smiling. Properly smiling. What a very clever girl. How long do you think she has been doing that?'

Thrand put an arm about her waist and pulled her and Sinroid close. 'After I finished my chores, I went in to check that our children were all asleep and this little one smiled at me. She wanted to come out and see her mother.'

'If she had smiled at Aud or Hilde, you

would have heard the excited shouts from here to Reykjavik and possibly even to Bernicia.'

Thrand laughed, sending a warm tingle down her spine. 'They are both very proud of their baby sister.'

Cwenneth leant back into his embrace and looked up into his summer-blue eyes. Over the past year, the shadows had slowly faded from his expression. 'And why shouldn't they be?'

'You were looking pensive earlier this evening. Is there some reason why?'

'It has been a year since my caravan was attacked.'

'Only a year? It seems like a lifetime ago.' His arm tightened about her shoulders. 'It is hard to believe that I once thought my life should consist solely of war and vengeance. Through you, I learnt the best revenge is a life well lived with people who love you.'

'My thoughts exactly.'

They stood there, watching their baby daughter smile up at them, and knew that all was right in the world because they had each other and their growing family.

* * * * *

MILLS & BOON®

Want to get more from Mills & Boon?

Here's what's available to you if you join the exclusive **Mills & Boon eBook Club** today:

✦ *Convenience – choose your books each month*
✦ *Exclusive – receive your books a month before anywhere else*
✦ *Flexibility – change your subscription at any time*
✦ *Variety – gain access to eBook-only series*
✦ *Value – subscriptions from just £1.99 a month*

So visit **www.millsandboon.co.uk/esubs** today to be a part of this exclusive eBook Club!

MILLS & BOON®

Maybe This Christmas

0914_ST_1

MILLS & BOON®

Why shop at millsandboon.co.uk?

Each year, thousands of romance readers find their perfect read at millsandboon.co.uk. That's because we're passionate about bringing you the very best romantic fiction. Here are some of the advantages of shopping at www.millsandboon.co.uk:

* **Get new books first**—you'll be able to buy your favourite books one month before they hit the shops

* **Get exclusive discounts**—you'll also be able to buy our specially created monthly collections, with up to 50% off the RRP

* **Find your favourite authors**—latest news, interviews and new releases for all your favourite authors and series on our website, plus ideas for what to try next

* **Join in**—once you've bought your favourite books, don't forget to register with us to rate, review and join in the discussions

Visit **www.millsandboon.co.uk**
for all this and more today!